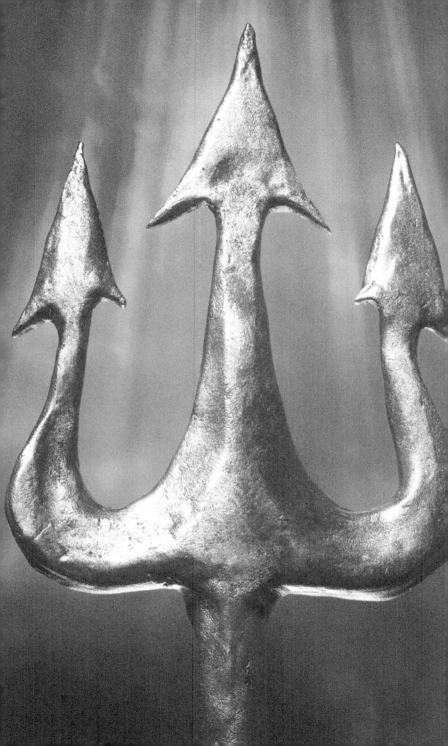

LEATHER & LACE

Trident Security Book 1

Samantha Cole

Leather & Lace
Copyright © 2015 Samantha A. Cole
All Rights Reserved.
Suspenseful Seduction, Inc.

Leather & Lace is a work of fiction. Names, characters, businesses, organizations, places, events, and incidents either are the product of the author's imagination or are used fictitiously. Any resemblance to actual persons, living or dead, events, or locales is entirely coincidental.

Cover designed by Samantha A. Cole
Editing by Eve Arroyo—www.evearroyo.com

AI RESTRICTION: The author expressly prohibits any entity from using any part of this publication, including text and graphics, for purposes of training artificial intelligence (AI) technologies to generate text or graphics, including without limitation technologies that are capable of generating works in the same style or genre as this publication.

The author reserves all rights to license uses of this work for generative AI training and the development of machine learning language models.

No part of this book may be reproduced, scanned or distributed in any printed or electronic form without permission. Please do not participate in or encourage piracy of copyrighted materials in violation of the author's rights. Purchase only authorized editions.

ACKNOWLEDGMENTS

Thanks to my beta-readers—Abby, Angie, Charla, Nicole and Stephanie. Without you, this book would never have been ready for publication.

Thanks to my editor, Eve, for all your help it fixing what was wrong.

WHO'S WHO AND THE HISTORY OF TRIDENT SECURITY & THE COVENANT

***While not every character is in every book, these are the ones with the most mentions throughout the series. This guide will help keep readers straight about who's who.

Trident Security (TS) is a private investigative and military agency co-owned by Ian and Devon Sawyer. With governmental and civilian contracts, the company started when the brothers and a few of their teammates from SEAL Team Four retired to the private sector. The company is located on a guarded compound, which was a former import/export company cover for a drug trafficking operation in Tampa, Florida. Three warehouses on the property were converted into large apartments, the TS offices, a gym, and bunkrooms.

In addition to the security business, there is a fourth warehouse that now houses an elite BDSM club, co-owned by Devon, Ian, and their cousin, Mitch Sawyer, who is the manager. Much time and money have made The Covenant the most sought-after membership in the Tampa/St. Petersburg area and beyond. Members are thoroughly vetted before being granted access to the elegant club.

There are currently over twenty Doms who have been appointed Dungeon Masters (DMs), and they rotate two or three shifts each throughout the month. At least four DMs are on duty at all times at various posts in the pit and playrooms, with an additional one roaming around. Their job is to ensure the safety of all the submissives in the club. They step in if a sub uses their safeword and the Dom in the scene doesn't hear or heed it, and ensure the equipment used in scenes isn't harming the subs.

The Covenant's security team takes care of everything else that isn't scene-related and provides safety for all members and are essentially the bouncers. The current total membership is just over 350. The fire marshal had approved them for 500 when the warehouse-turned-kink club first opened, but the cousins had intentionally kept that number down to maintain an elite status.

Between Trident Security and The Covenant, there's plenty of romance, suspense, and steamy encounters. Come meet the Sexy Six-Pack, their friends, family, and teammates.

The Sexy Six-Pack (Alpha Team) and Their Significant Others

- Ian "Boss-man" Sawyer: Devon and Nick's brother; retired Navy SEAL; co-owner of Trident Security and The Covenant; Dom.
- Devon "Devil Dog" Sawyer: Ian and Nick's brother; retired Navy SEAL; co-owner of Trident Security and The Covenant; Dom.
- Ben "Boomer" Michaelson: retired Navy SEAL; explosives and ordnance specialist; son of Rick and Eileen.

- Jake "Reverend" Donovan: retired Navy SEAL; Dom and Whip Master at The Covenant.
- Brody "Egghead" Evans: retired Navy SEAL; computer specialist; Dom.
- Marco "Polo" DeAngelis: retired Navy SEAL; communications specialist and back up helicopter pilot; Dom.
- Nick Sawyer: Ian and Devon's brother; current Navy SEAL.
- Kristen "Ninja-girl" Sawyer: author of romance/suspense novels.

Extended Family, Friends, and Associates of the Sexy Six-Pack

- Mitch Sawyer: Cousin of Ian, Devon, and Nick; co-owner/manager of The Covenant, Dom.
- T. Carter: US spy and assassin; works for covert agency Deimos; Dom.
- Shelby Christiansen: human resources clerk; two-time cancer survivor; submissive.
- Curt Bannerman: retired Navy SEAL; owner of Halo Customs, a motorcycle repair and detail shop.
- Jenn "Baby-girl" Mullins: college student; goddaughter of Ian; "niece" of Devon, Brody, Jake, Boomer, and Marco; father was a Navy SEAL; parents murdered.
- Mike Donovan: owner of the Irish pub, Donovan's; brother of Jake.
- Charlotte "Mistress China" Roth: Parole officer; Domme and Whip Master at The Covenant.
- Travis "Tiny" Daultry: former professional football player; head of security at The Covenant and

Trident compound; occasional bodyguard for TS.
- Rick and Eileen Michaelson: Boomer's parents. Rick is a retired Navy SEAL.
- Charles "Chuck" and Marie Sawyer: Ian, Devon, and Nick's parents. Charles is a self-made real estate billionaire. Marie is a plastic surgeon involved with Operation Smile.
- Will Anders: Assistant Curator of the Tampa Museum of Art; Kristen Anders's cousin.
- Dr. Roxanne London: pediatrician; Domme/wife (Mistress Roxy) of Kayla.
- Kayla London: social worker; submissive/wife of Roxanne.
- Chase Dixon: retired Marine Raider; owner of Blackhawk Security; associate of TS.
- Reggie Helm: lawyer for TS and The Covenant; Dom/boyfriend of Colleen.
- Colleen McKinley-Helm: girlfriend/submissive of Reggie.
- Carl Talbot: college professor; Dom and Whip Master at The Covenant.

Members of Law Enforcement

- Larry Keon: Assistant Director of the FBI.
- Frank Stonewall: Special Agent in Charge of the Tampa FBI.

The K9s of Trident

- Beau: An orphaned Lab/Pit mix, rescued by Ian. Now a trained K9 who has more than earned his spot on the Alpha Team.

To my parents, who always encouraged me to follow my dreams.

AUTHOR'S NOTE

The story within these pages is completely fictional but the concepts of BDSM are real. If you do choose to participate in the BDSM lifestyle, please research it carefully and take all precautions to protect yourself. Fiction is based on real life but real life is *not* based on fiction. Remember—Safe, Sane and Consensual!

Any information regarding persons or places has been used with creative literary license so there may be discrepancies between fiction and reality. The Navy SEALs missions and personal qualities within have been created to enhance the story and, again, may be exaggerated and not coincide with reality.

The author has full respect for the members of the United States military and the varied members of law enforcement and thanks them for their continuing service to making this country as safe and free as possible.

CHAPTER ONE

"Damn it!"

Kristen Anders slammed her laptop shut, removed her glasses, and shoved her fingers through her long, brown hair in exasperation. Glancing at the digital clock on her cable box, she couldn't believe it was one in the afternoon. Three hours wasted. If she didn't develop a workable storyline soon, she would go insane. Now that her move to Tampa was complete, her things were unpacked in the rented two-bedroom apartment, and the empty moving boxes were in the recycle bin, she had no more excuses not to get back to her latest novel. No excuse except her damn writer's block.

On the desk, her phone rang, and she rolled her eyes when she spotted the name on the screen. Just what she needed . . . Jillian Tang. Her editor had given her three weeks to deal with everything involved in the move before she began demanding to see a new plot outline. And, according to the *Playgirl* calendar her cousin had given her as a happy divorce present, those three weeks had come and gone four days ago, and all Kristen had was a working title.

Hitting the answer button, she brought the phone to her ear. "Hey, Jillian."

"Don't 'hey, Jillian' me unless you have something more than a working title by now."

Leather and Lace would be the follow-up to her first oh-so-non-vanilla romance novel, *Satin and Sin,* which her readers had gone crazy for. "Not yet, and before you yell at me, do you want it fast, or do you want it good?"

Jillian's laugh came over the line, and Kristen had to smile. They spoke simultaneously, "Sounds like something my ex-husband would say."

Both knew what it was like to divorce a cheating husband.

After her laughter died away, Jillian jumped back to the original topic. "You know your readers are dying to get their hands on your next BDSM novel. I'm still floored you went that route after nine 'vanilla' romances, but with how your sales soared, I'm not complaining."

Kristen's first two books had been self-published e-books. After they'd been downloaded in large numbers and received glowing reviews from her readers, Jillian had contacted her with a proposal to become a Red Rose Books-endorsed author. She'd been thrilled since being sought out by the large publishing company, which specialized in the romance genre, was an honor most self-published writers could only dream of. The deal benefited both parties. Red Rose Books signed a new and popular writer with an established fan base waiting on pins and needles for her next book, and Kristen's books were now available in print, audio, and digital. She no longer had to contend with editing, uploading, book cover designs, and promotions.

"I'm not complaining either, but I can't even decide which sub-character should become my new hero."

"Shit, I gotta run to a meeting." Kristen could hear the rustle of papers on Jillian's end. "Listen. Go into that fantasy world in your head and picture each one of those hunky guys. One of them will stand out. I'll call you tomorrow, and you better have an answer for me. Love ya. Bye."

Dropping her cell next to her laptop, Kristen sighed. She got up and headed to the master bedroom, pulling her shirt off over her head. She hoped a hot shower, followed by a change of scenery, would help get her creative juices flowing. Plus, she was hungry. Maybe it was time to check out the Irish pub a few blocks over. She'd passed by Donovan's several times over the past few weeks and noticed it was a popular place. It didn't appear too crowded at lunchtime, but it was usually packed by happy hour and stayed that way into the night.

Walking through her bedroom, she thought of calling Will to join her for a bite to eat, but the idea left her mind as fast as it came. As much as she loved her cousin's company because he could always make her laugh and relax, Kristen knew she wouldn't get any work done with him around.

Not long after her arrival in Florida, Will had taken it upon himself to show her around Tampa and introduce her to all his friends since he was the only person she knew in the area. Unfortunately for her, most people he hung out with were gay, not that anything was wrong with being gay. She'd become comfortable with her cousin's homosexuality a long time ago, and even though she had a good time with Will's crowd, she was tired of turning down date requests from his lesbian friends. Kristen had no sexual interest in women, and none of the men in her cousin's circle were interested in her as anything more than a friend. They were a great bunch of people, but since her divorce was finalized, she wanted to get back into the dating game. She wasn't looking for a steady relationship, her failed marriage had soured her on anything permanent, but maybe a friends-with-benefits thing would be something she could get into. However, the benefits portion of that might be a problem.

She wasn't very good at sex, and, if she was honest, it bored her. She found she could finally admit it to herself even though her ex-husband, Tom, had used it as an excuse for cheating. Although she could orgasm while masturbating, she had never been able to come during sex. At the beginning of her marriage, Tom said it was because she didn't relax enough to enjoy it, which Kristen might agree with. She was so nervous at first, wanting to please him but not knowing how. But after more than six months of disappointing sex, her husband began to tell her she was frigid and unresponsive. Maybe she was. But having nothing else to compare it to, she wasn't sure if it was true. She'd been a twenty-four-year-old virgin on her wedding night, and Tom was the only man she had ever slept with.

She stopped at her dresser and picked up the large envelope holding her divorce papers. A few weeks after their first anniversary, she found out Tom had cheated on her with several women before and after their wedding. She'd kicked him out the same day, but she couldn't bring herself to even think about having sex with anyone else until the ink was dry on said papers. Whether her ex had or not, she took her marriage vows to heart and couldn't move on until everything was final. Although the documents in her hand were signed two weeks before her move to Tampa, she hadn't found an opportunity to spread her wings—or legs, as Will had so eloquently put it.

Putting the envelope back where it was, she sat on the edge of her bed and hugged one of her decorative pillows.

When it came to sex, Kristen believed she could take it or leave it, but she missed the intimacy of sex. She squeezed the pillow tighter and realized what she missed the most. It was the cuddling and pillow talk which occurred after sex. She could live without the act itself, but it felt like forever since she'd snuggled up to a warm body and felt content.

Content. *Huh?* What a boring word.

Her readers would be shocked to learn that the author of a best-selling BDSM book was only content with her sex life. Too bad life wasn't a steamy romance novel, with a hot and hunky hero knocking on her door, primed and ready to sweep her off her feet, throw her on the bed, tie her down, and do naughty, sensual things to her.

Right, like that would ever happen.

But that was what made great fiction. Fantasies. Fantasies of delicious and dirty sex.

Even though her own sex life was lacking, Kristen had read many erotic novels over the years and decided to spice up her last book by basing it around a private sex club for the rich and famous. To her shock and delight, it'd become a bigger success than her first four of nine vanilla books put together. Now she was supposed to write an even more exciting follow-up that her fans were clamoring for, and she couldn't even decide which sub-character from the first book she wanted to write a story about.

Should she use Master Zach, the sexy movie star who liked to flog his submissives to orgasm, as her new hero? Or Master Wayne, the blond billionaire who preferred to share his women with his best friend, Jonah. Or maybe she should pick Master Xavier, who owned the sex club, Leathers, they all belonged to. He was the strong, brooding type women were always attracted to in romance books.

Kristen tossed the pillow back on the bed and stood to remove her sweatpants. She dropped them and her shirt into the hamper as she walked into the bathroom. Reaching in, she turned on the shower, letting it heat up as she peeled off her underwear. When she stepped into the tub, the warm water surrounded her as she thought about Master Xavier. He hadn't been a main character in *Satin and Sin*, but the fictitious man had grown on her somewhere during her writing sessions.

In her head, she brought up a picture of the strong alpha male as she had described him in her book—the same alpha male who had somehow ended up starring in a few of her own fantasies. Six-foot-two, jet black hair, startling blue eyes, a chiseled jaw with a hint of a five o'clock shadow, and a body that would make any heterosexual adult female drop her panties instantly. She imagined his deep Dom voice resonating in her mind as he told her to touch herself while he stood there and watched. Grabbing a bottle of her favorite body soap, she squirted a small amount into her palms before putting it back on the tub's shelf. She closed her eyes and roamed her hands over her heated skin with light sensual strokes.

"Touch your breasts," he'd say. *"Play with your nipples. Pinch them and pull them."*

Kristen did what her fantasy Dom told her to, her hands caressing her heavy orbs. As she played with the sensitive peaks between her thumbs and forefingers, the growing sensations of pleasure shot straight to her clit, making it throb. Making her want to be touched there.

"Spread your legs wider, my love. Let me see your bare pussy. It belongs to me, and I want to see what's mine. I want to watch you finger yourself for me."

Her breathing increased as she eased one hand down her

torso. She wanted to move faster but knew Master Xavier would never allow it. He would punish her if she sped things up without his permission. Maybe he'd spank her ass with his strong, calloused hands or perhaps bring her to the brink of orgasm repeatedly, yet continue to deny her the ultimate ecstasy.

"That's it, love, touch your pussy. Rub your pearly clit for me. Imagine it's my fingers touching you, loving you. Nice and slow. Such a good girl. Picture my tongue between your legs, licking your sweet cream."

Kristen moaned as her fingers followed her Master's demands as if they had a mind of their own.

"You like that, don't you, love." He wouldn't ask but state it as fact, and she wouldn't deny it. She couldn't.

"You please me, love. You make me want to bend you over and take you from behind, fucking your wet pussy, slow at first. So very slow until you're begging me to go faster. Harder. Beg me, love, beg me."

"Please," Kristen whispered aloud as she felt the pressure build, threatening to send her over the edge into a vast abyss.

"Faster, love. Faster. Come for me, love. Now!"

And then she flew. Screaming her release, her body shook with the force of the orgasm, which tore through her as she tried and failed to stay standing. Somehow she ended up on her knees on the tub floor without hurting herself. Gasping for air as if she had run a mile at top speed, she slowed the hand between her legs as the last shudders quaking through her body faded.

Holy crap! That'd been the most explosive orgasm of her entire life, and it'd been at her own hand while a fantasy man she'd dreamed up told her what to do. It was crazy—crazy but amazing!

As she drifted back to reality, she noticed the water

pelting her back had started to cool. Getting to her feet on shaky legs, she grabbed the shampoo and rushed to wash and rinse her hair before it was too late. As she turned off the water and reached for a fresh towel, Kristen knew she had made her decision. Master Xavier was definitely going to be the hero of *Leather and Lace*.

CHAPTER TWO

A half-hour later, carrying her laptop case, Kristen wandered into Donovan's Bar & Grill and fell in love with the place. A combination of high tables and chairs in dark wood and emerald green walls gave the pub a comfortable atmosphere. Enlarged photos of Irish landscapes and points of interest hung in various groupings on three of the four walls. The fourth wall on her right was the setting for a beautiful cherrywood bar with brass accents. It ran the length of the long room with seating for at least twenty-five people with additional space between the bar and tables for those who preferred to stand. Behind the bartender and rows of liquor bottles was a large mirror framed with the same cherrywood. The Celtic carvings in the frame made it a work of art, and Kristen wondered how long it had taken to make such a majestic piece of furniture. Above the mirror, several flat-screen TVs hung from the ceiling, and they were all tuned to sports channels, except one showing a news report. The TVs were muted while classic rock played through unseen speakers throughout the room, loud enough to be heard but still low enough to allow patrons to talk without raising their voices.

After she took in the décor of the pub, she found herself checking out its current occupants. A few tables were taken with groups of two to four people, and a couple of old-timers, arguing good-naturedly over some sporting event, had settled in for the afternoon at the near end of the bar. Taking a step further into the room, Kristen glanced down to the far end of the pub and almost stumbled, certain she had tripped over her own tongue. *Holy crap!* Standing and sitting at the other end of the bar, talking to the bartender, were six men who were almost as majestic as the bar itself. Talk about a *Playgirl* calendar fantasy come true.

"Who needs twelve hotties when these six are available?" she muttered to herself. Each could take up two months, and Kristen would be more than happy.

"Hi, can I help you?"

Kristen's head whipped around to face the pretty young woman who had appeared next to her. She was dressed in a black polo shirt with Donovan's Bar & Grill embroidered on the left side and a pair of jeans. Her long strawberry blond hair was pulled up in a ponytail, and her overall look was neat yet complemented the laid-back feel of the pub.

"Oh, hi . . . I mean, yes," Kristen stammered, then paused, forgetting where she was and why she was there. *Okay, get your girlie parts and brain cells under control*, she told herself. It's not as if she had never seen a bunch of good-looking men before, but damn, the testosterone rolling off the group had her almost melting on the spot.

Taking a deep breath, she regained her composure and told the waitress she was there to get something to eat, and no, she wasn't waiting for anyone else. She was eating alone. *Yup*, she thought. *All alone. Table for one.* Oh well—at least between the eye candy at the bar and her earlier fantasy in the shower, she should have more than enough inspiration to start on Master Xavier's story.

The young woman grabbed a menu from the nearby hostess stand and gestured toward the rest of the room. "Would you like a table or a booth?"

"A booth, please." Kristen lifted her laptop case for the woman to see. "It'll be easier to get some work done."

"Gotcha. No problem. We have a few regulars who work through their lunch breaks. They tell me the booths are more comfortable than the pub tables."

Kristen followed the friendly waitress and realized she was being led closer and closer to the Sexy Six-Pack. The only unoccupied booths were at the back left side of the pub, directly across from them.

"Here you go." The woman placed the menu down at the booth she was giving her. It was the second to last one before the kitchen door. "Can I get you something to drink?"

Kristen put down her laptop and took the seat facing the front of the pub. "Do you have any iced tea?"

"Yes, we do. Sweetened or unsweetened?"

"Sweetened, please."

"Sure. I'll be back in a second. Oh, and the specials are on the back of the menu."

She smiled as the young woman approached the bar and placed her order. *Cheerful little thing.* Since it was a school day, it was obvious the waitress was out of high school, maybe by a year or two. And if Kristen had to guess, she was only eighteen or nineteen years old. As she stood at the bar waiting for Kristen's iced tea, one of the Sexy Six-Pack leaned over and said something to the girl, which made her giggle and blush. Kristen frowned. *Seriously?* The guy had to be in his mid-thirties, and here he was, hitting on a girl who was just over the jail-bait age. Well, no one said perverts had to be ugly. Kristen had the sudden urge to say something, but she didn't know these people, and the girl appeared to be enjoying the attention.

She was about to turn back to take her laptop out of its case when movement from the other end of the Sexy Six-Pack caught her attention. Her breath hitched as her gaze met a pair of ice-blue eyes. *Master Xavier.*

Oh. My. God! Kristen couldn't believe it. If Master Xavier were a real, live person, this would be him. He had jet black hair, a little long at the neck, a firm jaw showing the start of a five o'clock shadow, and a body that almost had her glancing around to see if any of the few women in the pub had lost their panties. But it was those amazing blue eyes looking right at her as if they could see her soul, which had her spellbound. She was probably drooling, but, Lord have mercy, she couldn't look away.

When the man's right eyebrow arched in obvious acknowledgment of her stare, her mouth went dry, and she shifted her gaze to the floor before looking up again. Despite his intense look, she thought she noticed the corner of his mouth twitch as if he was holding back a smile. Oh God, she would love to see him smile and wondered how it would transform his face. If it was anything like the rest of him, she knew his smile would be devastatingly gorgeous.

Neither moved, and her eyes worked their way back up to his, her pulse pounding in her veins. Just when Kristen thought she would drown without a drop of water in sight, those eyes disappeared as her waitress returned, her body blocking Kristen's view of the rear half of the bar.

"Here you go." The girl placed a glass of tea in front of her and took out a pad and pen from the small black apron tied at her waist. "Did you decide what you wanted?"

Shaking her head, Kristen tried to regain control of her senses and concentrate on the question. "Um . . . no. Can you . . ." She cleared her throat. "Can you give me a few minutes? I didn't look at the menu yet."

"Sure, take your time."

Anxious to see those eyes again, Kristen held her breath as the young woman moved away, only to see her Master Xavier look-alike was once again facing the bartender. Disappointment ran through her as she took a sip of iced tea to quench her parched throat and picked up the menu. Without a sound, she tried to will the man to turn around again as her gaze flicked back and forth from the menu to the bar area. This time she refused to observe him blatantly and kept her head bent forward. Anyone watching her would assume she was scanning the menu, but her eyes kept shifting to view him out of the corner of her eye.

A few minutes later, her lunch order was placed, and Kristen resigned herself to the fact that the man would not turn back around. She removed her laptop from its case, booted it up, and got to work.

DEVON "DEVIL DOG" SAWYER COULDN'T HELP HIMSELF. HE was used to being a voyeur at the club, but at his friend's brother's bar, he almost felt like a creepy stalker. Despite the feeling, he still spent the better part of the last hour staring at the brunette's reflection in the mirror. Well, it was only fair since she had stared at him first. And yes, now he'd gone from creepy stalker to a childish grade-schooler.

He and his teammates were taking advantage of a slow day to eat lunch and catch a Tampa Bay Rays baseball game when he first spotted her watching his friend, Brody, talk to

Jennifer. For some reason, she frowned at them, and Devon wondered what she was thinking. The guys were always joking around with Jenn, otherwise known as Baby-girl, and there was nothing wrong with it. If it wasn't for them, Devon didn't think their niece would've adjusted to living in Tampa as fast as she had. The past six months had been rough on her, but it was obvious having her surrogate uncles around had helped her transition through the worst of it. Between them and the counselor Jenn was seeing, she was coming out of her depression and moving forward with her life. He was happy to notice she was smiling and joking more as time passed. She may have lost her parents without warning and had her world turned upside down, but her uncles were determined never to let her forget they considered her family. She would always be loved and protected by them.

Devon studied the five men who were like brothers to him—although his older brother Ian, on his immediate left, was the only one to whom he was related by blood. The others were brothers of his heart. They had gone through hell and back together and, by some miracle, survived with only a few battle scars. They always had each others' backs, and it was rare if a day or two went by without seeing each other working at Trident, hanging out here at Donovan's, or playing at The Covenant—unless they were away on an assignment.

Brody "Egghead" Evans, standing at the end of the bar where Jenn picked up her bar orders, was the joker and flirt of the group, as well as their resident tech-geek. The man could put most computer hackers to shame, and despite the FBI's best efforts over the years to recruit him, Brody preferred to stay with his team—first with the SEALs and now with Trident Security.

Marco "Polo" DeAngelis, their helicopter pilot and

communications specialist, sat beside Brody while talking trash about his buddy's beloved Dallas Cowboys. Marco had been born and raised in Staten Island, New York, and was a lifelong Giants fan. As he told it, no self-respecting Giants fan would pass on a chance to rank on a Cowboys fan. That was the only bad blood between the two men—otherwise, they were best friends, having known each other from basic training through SEAL training to being on the same team. Hell, they tended to be so joined at the hip, they'd even left the Navy at the same time to join Trident. So, to their friends, it came as no surprise when they shared their women on occasion. The duo was pretty popular with the submissives at the club.

He watched as Brody glanced over at the brunette and nudged Polo while tilting his head in her direction. The other man looked over his shoulder, then grinned at his ménage partner. "Sorry, Egghead, but I've got plans with my sister tonight. Some other time."

Devon was surprised when his tense body relaxed. He hadn't realized his muscles had gone rigid at the thought of the two men hooking up with the woman he'd been eyeing for the last hour or so.

Next in line of his teammates was Tampa native Jake "Reverend" Donovan, their sniper and younger brother of Mike, the owner of Donovan's, who was tending bar for the afternoon. While Mike had learned about the bar-restaurant business from their father and took over the pub upon the old man's death a few years ago, Jake had signed up for the Navy the afternoon he graduated from high school. From what Devon understood, the relationship between Jake and his father had been destroyed during the last semester of Jake's senior year following an argument. Foregoing the football scholarship to Rutgers that everyone expected him to accept, Jake ended up going to basic training. Devon didn't know for sure what caused the deep rift between the two, but he had a feeling it was over Jake's sexual orientation. It didn't bother Devon, or any of the other guys, that Jake was gay, but with the "don't ask-don't tell" policy, which had been in effect for years in the military, it wasn't something they'd discussed while in the Navy. After the military, Jake was more comfortable keeping his personal life to himself, and the rest of them respected his decisions while still letting him know they supported him. Hell, Devon suspected his younger brother, Nick, was gay, and it didn't bother him at all. Ian, Devon, and their friends all had their individual kinks and perversions, so who were they to judge anyone else?

Jake was talking to Boomer, sitting on his other side, and they seemed to be arguing over something trivial. Boomer's head whipped around to stare at Ian with a look of disbelief on his face, and Devon smirked at his question. "You topped Savannah McCall? What the fuck? How come I didn't know this?"

Ian shrugged his shoulders, but the smile on his face told their explosives and demolition expert the rumor was true. The Boss-man had had a D/s relationship, brief as it was, with the thirty-year-old supermodel, who was still hot enough to grace the current cover of *Sports Illustrated's* annual swimsuit edition. "Before your time, Baby Boomer. She was still a struggling model when I met her many years ago."

"Holy shit, and damn! As usual, I bow to your greatness."

Although they had all served on the same team for several years, Ben "Boomer" Michaelson ended up staying in the Navy for another two after the others retired. He'd only rejoined them a few months ago following a close call with an RPG, which almost cost him his left leg and landed him in the hospital for three months. Even though he now sported an artificial knee, the doctors had been fortunate to be able to save the limb, but it'd been touch and go there for a while. After recovering, he was ready to switch to a career that had a lower percentage of people trying to kill him with projectiles.

Boomer was the youngest of the group at thirty, so, sometimes, to bust his ass, they called him "Baby Boomer." But they only resorted to that when they wanted to rile him up since you didn't want to piss off the guy carrying the explosives too often. Boomer came from a long family line of military men, and his father had been a SEAL before him.

Devon looked up as his brother stood from his stool. "Going somewhere, Boss-man?" Even though they co-owned their businesses fifty-fifty, Devon referred to his older brother as the head of the company since Ian had outranked him in the Navy and been their team leader.

Ian gave one of his usual grunts as he threw some money on the bar. "Yeah, I want to run back to the office and handle a few things before heading to the club. Are you going later?"

Devon glanced at the brunette's reflection in the mirror again before answering. "Not sure yet."

Ian took a quick look over his shoulder toward the booths behind him and then turned back to Devon with a knowing smirk on his face. "Uh-huh."

Devon chuckled as his brother clapped him on the shoulder. Telling the others he would see them later, Ian headed to the door, giving Jenn a peck on the cheek as he passed her. Through the mirror, Devon noticed the current object of his lust was frowning again as she watched Ian kiss his niece on his way out. He groaned to himself as he realized she was most likely thinking they were a bunch of perverts, hitting on a pretty teenager who was young enough to have been fathered by any one of them. Well, maybe not Boomer since the guy would have been around ten or eleven at the time of conception, but without asking him, Devon couldn't be sure.

Yes, a lot of people would call him a deviant—*huh?* Devon the deviant . . . now that was pretty funny—if they knew about the kinks he and his friends enjoyed. And yes, in the past, Devon had been with a lot of nineteen-year-old girls, but he had been in his teens and early twenties back then. That pretty much ended when twenty-seven-year-old Ian introduced him to the BDSM lifestyle at the age of twenty-four.

For the first few years of Devon's Navy career, he was stationed on the west coast, while Ian was based in Virginia. They only ended up in the same place after Devon graduated from Basic Underwater Demolition/SEAL training, otherwise known as BUD/s, and was assigned to Ian's SEAL Team Four. A few weeks after their reunion, his brother brought him to a private sex club for the first time. The club was about thirty minutes from the base, and a few of the guys were frequent visitors whenever the team was on U.S. soil and off duty. Ian had been in the lifestyle for a few years and recognized his brother could benefit from the control which came with being a Dom. Despite the five-and-a-half years since their eighteen-year-old brother, John, had died, Devon had still been struggling with his grief.

He took to the lifestyle like a SEAL to water and spent his first few years learning from Ian and other Doms, as well as several experienced submissives who took pleasure in teaching a new Dom to be . . . well, a Dom. Ian always stressed it was the best way to become a good, responsible Dominant. In fact, the motto of the BDSM community was "safe, sane, and consensual." An inexperienced Dom playing with an inexperienced submissive was a recipe for disaster, and the chances of the submissive being hurt, physically or psychologically, increased dramatically. The last thing Devon or any respectable Dom wanted was to hurt an innocent submissive beyond what they needed.

As he got older, he continued to lean toward experienced subs, which meant he didn't often play with women under the age of twenty-five. It didn't mean there weren't older newbies, but it was more likely the submissives had done some experimenting by that age and were familiar with the dynamics of BDSM. The more experienced subs were aware not to confuse playtime with being something more than what it was. He'd seen it happen over the years to other Doms with subs new to BDSM. No matter how many times it was explained to them that just because a Dom played with a sub a few times, it didn't mean they were in a traditional "boyfriend-girlfriend" relationship, and he'd witnessed many a new, young sub get their heart broken as a result.

That all said and done, it didn't mean Devon didn't like to educate a newer sub from time to time, but he made sure he observed the woman at the club over several weeks before approaching her to negotiate a scene. He could make sure she wasn't the type to cling and get too attached to him. Attachments were not his thing. One or two scenes were all he would do with a sub before moving on to the next one. He did have a few favorites, who he hooked up with more than others, but he was careful to wait several weeks or months between scenes with the same sub. Lucky for him, there were plenty of unattached subs at The Covenant for him to choose from.

The Covenant was an elite and private BDSM club Devon owned with Ian and their cousin, Mitch. After Devon and his brother left the SEALs a little over three years ago, they settled in Tampa and started their private security and protection business, Trident Security. When Mitch approached them about starting the club, they found a large piece of property with four warehouses. The government had seized it after they discovered it was being used to run an illegal drug operation disguised as an import-export company. It was on the outskirts of Tampa, far enough from any neighbors, and was perfect for their plans, so when the place went to auction, they bought it for much less than the property was worth.

The fenced-in property, complete with an armed guard at the gate, was surrounded by wooded areas and afforded them the privacy needed for the club as well as for Trident. With the government connections they'd made over the years, Devon and Ian's team did some contracted work for various alphabet agencies. They needed an office where no one would pay attention to their comings and goings, as well as the occasional visit from federal agents. The first building on the lot housed The Covenant. From the outside, it was a blue metal and cement warehouse. On the inside, however, it was a fetish lover's dream.

The other three buildings, identical to the first on the outside, were separated from the club by a second fence. The first contained the offices and war-room where Trident was run from. Toward the back of the building was a garage, along with weapons, ammunition, and equipment vaults. On the second floor, there were six spare bedrooms and bathrooms in addition to a rec room where the team could crash and watch the big screen TV or play darts and a game of pool. A small kitchenette completed the amenities.

The next structure contained storage areas on the second floor, and on the first, an indoor shooting range, a gym and training room, and a panic-security room in case of an emergency. The room was similar to an old nuclear bomb shelter, except it was above ground with reinforced concrete and steel walls and had been an unexpected find after they purchased the property. The last building housed Ian and Devon's apartments, although, like the other buildings, the outer façade gave no indication of what was inside. When the renovations were completed, both had been more than pleased with the results.

Taking another sip of his cola, Devon returned to studying the brunette. Having been with many attractive women over the years—more than he dared to count—he wouldn't characterize her as a gorgeous woman but more of a pretty girl next door. She was undeniably a woman who would get a second and third glance from most men. He wasn't a hundred percent sure due to the distance between them, but he thought her eyes were hazel. Her silky brown hair was pulled up in a ponytail, and he wondered what she would do if he walked over and removed the band holding it in place, allowing the soft strands to fall around her face. His fingers itched to find out.

She hadn't been wearing glasses when she'd first sat down but had put them on before she began typing away on her computer. The glasses gave her a naughty librarian look he loved to see on a woman, and he felt the semi-erection he'd been sporting since he first noticed her swell a little more. Letting his eyes roam, he took in the heart shape of her face, her high cheekbones, and those plump, pink lips which would look fantastic wrapped around his cock.

Shit! If he kept this up, he'd be hard as granite, and he hadn't even moved his gaze past her neck. Well, at least he hadn't in the last minute or two, and yup, now that the thought came to mind, he was staring at her chest. She was wearing a V-neck, short-sleeved T-shirt, which gave him a tiny hint of her cleavage, and from his vast experience with the female body, he would guess she was a 36-C cup. Not too large or too small, just the way he liked them. He wondered if her bra was the same fire-engine red color as her shirt, and the thought made his mouth water. Swallowing hard, he watched as she leaned back and stretched her arms over her head in an obvious attempt to work out the knots which had to be in her back and shoulders after typing so long. The movement thrust her chest out a bit, and . . . okay, it was official. He was now painfully erect. He shifted to ease the pressure and knew if he had any hope of walking out of there sometime this afternoon without his dick leading the way, he had to stop staring at her.

He may not have met her yet, but he'd bet his prized 1966 Mustang convertible she was a submissive. The question was, did she know it? He doubted it. After catching her eye earlier, he'd waited a few seconds before raising his eyebrow in a look that would've had most submissives questioning whether their words or actions were about to get them in trouble. He was delighted to see how fast her gaze had fallen to the floor before it crept back up to his face as if she couldn't resist the urge to look at him. If Jenn hadn't interrupted his view of the woman, he would've given into the temptation to go over and introduce himself, something he hadn't done outside of the club in a long time.

Over the years, he learned most of the women he'd met outside of the BDSM community were either turned off by his kinks or only thought they understood what was involved with pleasure-pain before attempting to experience it for themselves. Devon had a few brief encounters in the past when the woman he was with began to panic when faced with his demands and attempts to push her out of her comfort zone. At that point, he would halt the scene without complaint and wait to see if she wanted to continue. If she didn't, he would ensure the woman was all right and back in the right frame of mind before he wished her well and walked out the door. He would never force his lifestyle on anyone—again, *safe, sane, and consensual.*

Most people didn't realize that a certain amount of pain could be morphed into intense pleasure with the right mix of trust and arousal. Without the proper mix, though, any D/s encounter was doomed to fail. That was why he found it so much easier to leave his hook-ups to the submissives at the club. But, damn, he wished he met his little librarian at the club because he could definitely get into her, no pun intended . . . or maybe it was.

"Oh, my God! Really?"

Devon turned around at his niece's sudden loud exclamation. Jenn was standing next to the brunette, and her voice lowered again, but it was still obvious she was enthusiastic about something. He strained to hear what she was saying without success and wondered what all the excitement was about. Whatever it was, both women were now smiling and chatting as Jenn took the empty seat in the booth.

Damn, he wished he was Jenn right now.

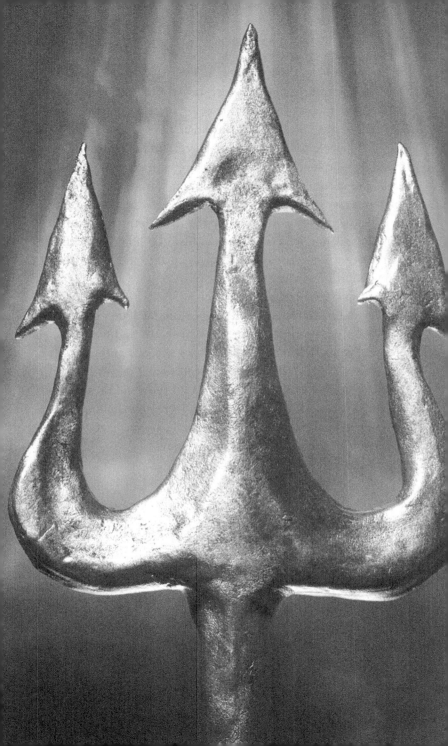

CHAPTER THREE

An hour passed before Kristen leaned back in the booth, happy with the rough draft of the first two chapters. Inspiration had struck, and she managed to provide an interesting background for the story. By the end of chapter two, Master Xavier had just laid eyes on the future love of his life, Rebecca, for the first time. Kristen sighed as she stretched her arms over her head and looked around. Most of the tables were now empty, and the waitress was wiping one down with a damp rag. Glancing at the bar, Kristen noticed the Sexy Six-Pack—she needed to stop calling them that—was now minus one, the man who kissed the waitress on his way out. The stool to the left of the man she had been drooling over earlier was empty, and it appeared he had no intention of moving closer to his buddies, content to stay in his original spot.

"So, you decided to come up for air."

She turned her head to see the waitress standing beside her and smiled. "Yeah, I guess I did. Sometimes I get so into my writing the rest of the world ceases to exist."

The young woman laughed. "I can see that. I checked on

you a few times, and you were oblivious, so I kept refilling your iced tea."

Kristen eyed the tall glass and saw it was indeed full again. Since there was a plate next to it with a few french fries and crumbs, it was a safe bet she'd eaten her chicken salad sandwich but didn't remember doing so. Yeah, she must've checked out of there for a while. "Thanks," she told the woman. "I appreciate it."

"No problem. What are you writing anyway? You were pretty much nonstop, but, every once in a while, you would look up at the ceiling for a few minutes, then say 'a-ha' and start typing again."

Kristen blushed in embarrassment. "Oh jeez, tell me I wasn't doing that too loud."

The waitress giggled, and it made her appear even younger. "No, not at all. As a matter of fact, I think I was the only one who noticed."

"Thank God," she responded with an exaggerated sigh of relief. "I'm writing a book, and sometimes I get carried away."

"Really? What kind of book? Fiction?"

"Yes." Kristen nodded. "A suspense romance. I've written a few which have been published, and I'm starting a new one now."

"Oh, wow, that's so cool. I have tons of romance books on my e-reader." She indicated the small tablet sticking out of the pocket of her apron. "I wonder if I've read any of yours."

"It's possible. I'm Kristen Anders."

The waitress let out a loud squeal. "Oh, my God! Really?" Covering her mouth with her hand for a second, she continued at a lower decibel. "I'm reading one of yours now. I think it's your second one. I read so many books, and I'm terrible at remembering the titles, but the characters are Jeb and Amy."

Kristen nodded. It always pleased her when she met one of her readers out of the blue. Her ex-husband had been condescending about her books, saying they were the result of her little hobby, and he was always shocked to hear people had bought them, read them, and, indeed, loved them. "Yes, that's my second one, *Wildfire*. The first was *Hearts Ablaze* with Keith and Shannon."

"Yes! That's the first one I read. I loved it so much that I looked to see if you had written anything else and downloaded the next two in the series."

Kristen smiled when the woman took the seat across from her, probably not even realizing she was sitting down with a customer, but Kristen didn't mind. "I'm so glad you liked it. I love when I run into one of my readers, and they tell me they enjoy my books."

"Oh, I do. I really do. You have a great mix of suspense and romance, which makes me not want to put it down. When I was finishing *Hearts Ablaze*, I was up until about three a.m. because I couldn't wait to see how it ended. I mean, it's a romance, so there's always a happy ending, but I couldn't figure out who the murderer was. And I hate when I figure it out way before the author wants you to know who it is." The waitress extended her hand out over the table. "By the way, I'm Jenn . . . Jennifer Mullins."

Kristen shook the proffered hand. "It's nice to meet you, Jenn."

"Oh, it's so nice to meet you too. I've never met anyone famous before."

She couldn't help but chuckle at the girl's enthusiasm. "Well, I don't know if I'm exactly famous."

"Well, to me, you are. Now I really can't wait to read the rest of your books."

"I'm glad, but don't buy them." She knew what it was like to work her way through college. Her parents had paid for her tuition and books, but Kristen had earned money for any extras and fun by working at a bagel shop near campus and then as a proofreader for anyone who wanted her services. She was sure the waitress needed her money for more important things than a few romance books, and if Kristen could save her a few dollars, then that's what she would do. "I have a few print copies at my apartment you can have. I'll drop them off to you the next time I come in for lunch."

Jennifer squealed again, but not as loud as the first time, to Kristen's relief.

"Seriously? That's so nice of you, but you don't have to."

"I know I don't, but I want to. My publisher always gives me a bunch of hard copies to hand out to whomever I please, so it's no big deal," Kristen assured her.

"Jennifer."

At the sound of the male voice, both women looked over to the bar, where the bartender pointed to the front of the restaurant. Turning their heads, they saw a few people standing at the hostess station. Kristen was glad to see the bartender, who she assumed was the boss, wasn't mad Jennifer was chatting with a customer. Instead, he kindly let the girl know people were waiting. She didn't want the girl to get into trouble for being sociable, which made for repeat business from the customers, in Kristen's opinion.

Jennifer jumped up. "Oops, gotta get back to work. And thanks for offering to bring me the books. I'm here every afternoon except Wednesdays when I have a class."

Nodding her head, Kristen confirmed, "Any day except Wednesday. Got it."

"I'll be back with your check in a second."

"Take your time," Kristen reassured her with a wave as the other woman turned to hurry toward the front.

What a sweet girl, Kristen thought as she focused her attention on her laptop once again. Touching the mousepad, she brought it back out of sleep mode, and her heart stopped. The screen was blank.

"Oh, no," she whispered as her stomach dropped. She couldn't remember if she'd hit the save button after she stopped typing, but the program was supposed to do an "auto-save" every few minutes. "Please, please, tell me it's saved."

Damn it! She knew she should've gotten a new laptop before she started writing again. This one had been giving her trouble as of late, freezing and rebooting itself without warning, but this was the first time a manuscript had disappeared. She remembered creating a new file when she first started typing, but now she couldn't even get into the program to find it. She began hitting different keys as her panic began to rise. "No, no, no! This can't be happening."

"What's wrong?"

She looked up to see Jenn had returned and was placing her check on the table with a look of concern on her face.

"I don't know." She continued to try and get the computer to respond. "It freaked out on me, and I think I lost my first two chapters. Damn it—I hate friggin' computers!"

Jenn put her hand on Kristen's forearm. "Wait, stop! Don't do anything else. My uncle is a computer genius. If it's there, he can find it."

"Your uncle?" she asked, but it was too late since Jennifer had turned around to face the bar and waved.

"Uncle Brody? Can you come here for a sec? We need your super-duper technical powers."

Kristen watched as the guy Jenn had been laughing with earlier raised his eyebrow in a silent question and put his beer down before walking toward them. Well, he wasn't exactly walking. It was more like sauntering.

He smiled and chuckled as he approached. "No need to boost my ego with compliments, Baby-girl. You know I'll do anything for you." Putting his arm around the young woman's shoulders, he looked down at Kristen. "What seems to be the problem, darlin'?"

Oh Lord, did he really just pour on the charm with a sexy drawl?

"Uncle Brody," as Jenn had called him, stood about six-two and didn't seem to have an ounce of fat on his chiseled body. His short blond hair was neat except for a small section that fell over his brow, and his chocolate-brown eyes twinkled as he flirted with her without shame. Wearing a tight black T-shirt with jeans, a silver belt buckle, and western boots, all he needed was a cowboy hat, and she could picture him on a ranch, roping a few bulls. The man was sin on two legs and knew it.

Kristen mentally shook her mushy brain and looked back at her laptop. "I don't know what happened. I was in the word processor and, now, poof! It's gone. I think I lost the file I was working on."

"Poof, huh?" Brody teased and then gestured toward the empty booth seat across the table from her. "May I?"

Her head bounced like a bobblehead doll. "Oh, please. I'd appreciate your help. I know nothing about computers."

Sitting down, Jenn's uncle turned the laptop to face him and started hitting the keys. The difference between what she'd been doing earlier and his actions was he appeared to have a clue what he was doing, while Kristen had none. She twisted her hands in her lap and prayed he could find the file.

She'd been pleased with all she had written thus far and wasn't sure if she could remember the precise wording she'd used.

"Everything all right?"

She shivered at the sound of a deep male voice, which penetrated and reverberated throughout her body, making all her girlie parts stand up and take notice. Looking up, she saw Jennifer had stepped away, and the man with those beautiful blue eyes was now standing in her place, staring at Kristen.

"Nothing I can't handle, Devil Dog."

Kristen was so glad the man named Brody answered his friend as he continued to type away on her keyboard because her mind had become a complete blank except for the thought that she wanted to hear "Devil Dog" speak again. He was about the same height as Brody but not as broad. Although his frame was a little leaner, he was just as sinewy, and her hands yearned to touch his chest and abs to see if they were as hard as they looked. Dressed in a navy-blue T-shirt, jeans, and sneakers, he could be any guy walking down the street, but no, this was not any guy. This man made women forget their own names. This man was strong, virile, and commanded attention with his mere presence, yet she could imagine him being gentle when he needed to be. She continued to gawk at him until she noticed his mouth was turned up in an amused smile. He cocked his head toward Brody, and it was at that moment she realized the other man had said something to her.

Swallowing her embarrassment, she looked across the table to see he also wore a grin.

"I'm sorry. What did you say?"

Brody chuckled at her. "I asked what the file name you were looking for was."

She felt her cheeks grow warmer and burn bright red. Seriously? He needed to know the name of the file? *Well, of course, he did, you idiot . . . how else would he be able to find it?*

"Leather and lace," she mumbled, looking at the dark surface of the table and wishing it was a black hole she could fall into.

"What was that?"

Still looking downward, Kristen cleared her throat and repeated louder and clearer, "Leather and Lace."

When neither man spoke nor did she hear any typing, she glanced up and saw both were staring at her. Oh, Lord help her, this was so mortifying.

Brody's grin became even wider, and when she looked into his eyes, she swore she saw the laughter he was trying to hold back. She didn't even want to know what she would see if she peered up into the blue eyes of the man still standing next to the table.

"Well, okay then." Brody gave her a flirty wink before he started typing again. "Here it is. Leather and Lace."

Kristen's eyes rolled at how the man drew out those last three words with his sexy drawl before she realized what he'd said and sat up straighter in her seat. "Oh, my God, you found it? Seriously?"

"Of course, darlin'. Piece of cake."

"Thank you so much," she gushed. "You saved my life."

He laughed at her exaggeration. "Well, maybe not your life, but at least an hour's worth of work, right?"

"Right. Yes. I don't know how to thank you."

Her cheeks flamed again when he responded, "Well, now, I'm sure we can come up with some way you can thank me that we'll both enjoy."

Jeez, there was the adorable charm again, and, *wait* . . . did "Devil Dog" growl?

"Did you find it?" Jenn asked as she rejoined them.

Brody stood and winked at her. "Was there any doubt?"

"Not at all, Uncle Brody," she said teasingly. "I would never doubt your superior geek skills."

"Brat." Brody tweaked the young woman's nose as an obvious sign of affection before looking at Kristen. "Check to see if everything you were working on was saved. If you give me a minute to grab my laptop from my truck, I can clean up your hard drive a bit so this doesn't happen again."

She nodded and spun the laptop back to face her. "That would be so great. I'd appreciate it."

As he strode toward the exit, Kristen felt the stare of the man next to her. Trying to swallow the sudden lump in her throat, she looked up and saw he was no longer smiling. The fact would've disappointed her if she hadn't seen the heat smoldering in his eyes as he studied her. Another shiver shot through her spine, and her panties became soaked with a sudden rush of arousal.

"So." His voice had a low timber she felt from her head to her toes. "Leather and Lace?"

"Is that the title of your new book?"

Kristen hadn't realized the young waitress was still with them until she heard her question. Somehow she managed to pull her gaze away from those eyes, which seemed determined to devour her, and looked at Jenn. "Um, yes . . . yes it is."

"You're writing a book called *Leather and Lace*?"

And there went her blush again at the sound of his deep, sexy voice, and her eyes flickered to him again. She was grateful Jenn answered the question for her because Kristen couldn't think of a single response to save her life.

"Yup, Uncle Devon. She's a romance writer. I've even read one of her books and started another yesterday."

"Really?" he murmured as if trying to figure out a complex puzzle. The man may have asked a question, but it didn't appear he expected an answer.

Wait . . . what? *Uncle* Devon?

"You're her uncle, too?" she asked.

"Mm-hm. They're all my uncles." Jenn gestured over to the remaining group of men, unaware the question had been directed at Devon. "We're not blood-related, but I call them my uncles. I've known them all my life, and, well . . . they're my family."

Devon broke eye contact with Kristen and beamed at Jenn with love in his eyes for the girl he considered his niece. He put his arm around her and pulled her into a hug. "Damn right, we're family, Baby-girl."

For a brief second, Kristen was jealous of the younger woman tucked up against his hard, yummy body as his strong arms enveloped her small frame. Jennifer hugged him back and kissed him quickly on the cheek before letting go and heading toward the kitchen door. "Gotta check on my orders."

After she disappeared, Kristen verbalized her earlier thought, "She's a sweet girl."

Devon nodded in agreement. "Yes, she is."

When he didn't say anything more, she opened her mouth to ask him a question, any question that would keep him there talking to her. But her words died in her mouth when Brody returned to the table and sat down again, oblivious to the mounting sexual tension between the other two. He pulled his laptop from its protective case and set it beside hers. Taking a cable, he connected the two computers and glanced at her. "It will only take a few minutes to download the program, and then I'll show you how to run it when you get home. A full scan will take about an hour or two to clean up your hard drive depending on how many programs and files it has to search through."

"What's it searching for?" She didn't know much about computers beyond the bare basics.

He started to type as he answered her. "Excess files, temporary downloads, and malware, among other things. Stuff like that can drag down your hard drive and cause problems like the one you had earlier. This program will also help protect you from any viruses."

"I already have an anti-virus program."

He winked at her. "That may be, darlin', but my program will stop those files from building up."

"Your program?" She smiled at his playfulness. When she was younger, if a man like Brody had flirted with her, she would've been too shy to respond. But since she began writing sexy dialogue for her characters, she'd gained confidence with talking to the opposite sex. She would never be a shameless flirt like some women were, but now she felt she could hold up her end of a conversation with a Casanova like him. His intense friend was a different story. Devon made her want to drop to her knees and let him do things to her. Things she'd never experienced before. And she didn't know how the thought made her feel.

"Well, considering I wrote it, yup, it's my program," Brody responded to her question, sounding like a little boy who was showing off his project at a science fair.

Kristen let out a little laugh. The man was a charmer. "Wow, now I totally feel computer illiterate. I won't lose anything important, will I? My life is on it."

"Nope." His fingers were still typing away. "Your files will be safe. But if you don't have a flash drive to back up your files, you may want to invest in one."

"I have one at home, but I don't like to bring it with me

because it's so small, I'm afraid I'll lose it." She had a bad habit of misplacing things. If it was smaller than a bread basket, Kristen had lost it at one time or another.

"Go anywhere that sells them, and you can find one to put on your keychain."

"That's a good idea as long as I don't lose my keys, which happens at least once a week."

While Brody continued talking about her computer, once every few seconds, Kristen's eyes drifted toward Devon, who still stood beside the table. He hadn't taken his speculative gaze off of her, and she tried not to squirm. She gave him a small smile and wondered what he was thinking of.

Devon's mouth ticked upward when she flashed him a shy smile as he considered her with interest. Although she was engrossed in the conversation, he didn't feel like he was being ignored since she kept glancing up at him as if confirming he was still there. Interesting. And what was even more interesting, he wanted to rip Brody's head off every time the geek turned on his Southern charm. It was apparent his buddy found her attractive—what heterosexual male past the age of puberty wouldn't—and it was only a matter of time before Egghead asked her out. The man didn't have the same reservations as Devon about hooking up with a woman outside the club.

The more he observed her, the more he wanted to learn about her. She smelled like wildflowers and fresh air, almost as if she had walked through a meadow on a spring day, subtle and enticing. He detected a northern accent in her speech—his first guess had been New York, but now he wasn't sure. And her laugh . . . damn, her laugh went straight to his groin. Thank God his shirt was untucked to hide the semi-automatic sitting at the small of his back. The shirt was now doing an excellent job of hiding other things, like his erection, from her view.

What was it about this woman, whose name he didn't even know, who called to him like a mystic siren? Damned if he knew, but he was looking forward to finding out. He was about to extend his hand and introduce himself when he noticed Brody giving her a scrap of paper with his name and phone number on it. The bastard beat him to it. Well, Devon deserved it for dragging his feet for over an hour when he could have found some inane reason to approach her and strike up a conversation. As much as he wanted to pound his buddy to a pulp and claim the woman for himself, he would never cock-block a good friend.

Devon stepped back and pivoted toward the bar as the two climbed out of the booth. Through the reflection in the mirror, he saw her thanking Brody, and then his stomach sank as she wrapped her arms around the grinning geek and hugged him. There was nothing sexual about the contact, but it still sent bolts of jealousy through Devon. He could imagine his buddy's response if he knew Devon wanted to deck him. *You snooze, you lose, Devil Dog!* And yes, he was back in grade school again.

Moments later, he watched as his little librarian gathered her things, said goodbye to Brody and Jenn, then made her way to the exit. With a hesitant backward glance in his direction, she walked out the door.

At times like this, he almost regretted not drinking alcohol because he could use the distraction.

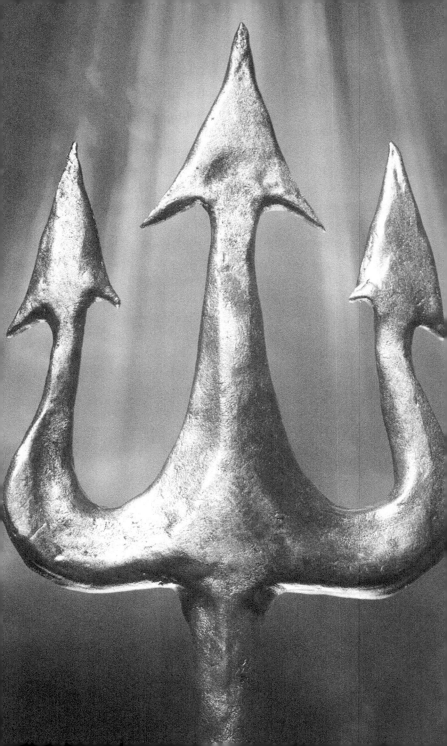

CHAPTER FOUR

Devon spent the rest of the week alternating between being in a shitty mood and dreaming about his little librarian. No, make that *Brody's* little librarian. The bastard.

He'd acted like a petulant child and avoided Brody, whenever possible, since that afternoon six days ago. He didn't want to hear how his buddy had hooked up with the brunette, whose name he now knew was Kristen Anders. She'd dropped off copies of her books for Jennifer at the pub, and his niece was now reading the next paperback in an ongoing series of vanilla romances after finishing one on her e-reader. And yes, he knew the stories were vanilla because when no one was looking, he'd skimmed through Jenn's book, *Passions Uncaged,* after she left it on the bar for a few minutes while working.

Although he didn't read more than a few passages, the story was well written, and Ms. Anders had evident talent. He was surprised that her sex scenes were pretty hot—vanilla but hot. Knowing his niece was reading those same scenes was also a little embarrassing. He thought back to when Ian and he had an awkward conversation with Jenn about what type of club The Covenant was. They had to tell her since she'd be driving past it and living three buildings down from it in Ian's apartment when she moved to Tampa. After much blushing and stuttering on their part, Jenn let them off the hook and told them she understood and it wasn't a big deal to her. It wasn't her thing, and she wasn't one to judge. They were thankful she expressed no desire to see the inside of the club. She probably didn't want to think of her uncles having sex of any kind, just like they didn't want to think about her having sex with some horny little bastard someday. They'd both been a little shocked yet relieved when she blew it off with a nonchalant explanation of how she'd read many books with similar clubs in them. Granted, those clubs were fictional, while theirs was a reality, but she got the gist.

Flipping through the book, he'd found Kristen was descriptive about what her characters were doing up in the barn loft, down by the creek, and, of course, in the bedroom. And even though the writing was steamy and sexy, he doubted the author would be into his type of sex and play. But, unlike Devon, Brody Evans didn't mind the occasional vanilla sex. Brody was willing to go with the flow for a few dates if he was attracted to a woman. The only problem for the women was, after those few dates and some romps in the sack, the man became bored, and they would be history. There was a long line of women with broken hearts trailing behind Evans. He didn't do long-term relationships, either. And it had never been a concern for Devon until now—the thought of Brody dumping Kristen after using her to scratch his current itch angered Devon almost as much as the thought of them dating in the first place.

Forcing the aggravating thoughts from his mind, Devon climbed out of his Mustang before shutting the door and locking it. He'd left the top up on the drive over to Donovan's due to passing rain showers forecasted throughout the day. The gray skies matched his mood as he strode toward the entrance to the pub where he was joining Jake for lunch. His teammate wanted to review some observations he'd made on a runaway case he had worked on for the past week. The teenage girl's father hired them after she allegedly ran away when he grounded her for missing her curfew on a regular basis. Jake had yet to locate the teen but was starting to suspect the reason she took off was more sinister than anyone realized. Since it was after twelve, and Jake had mentioned he was hungry, the two men agreed to meet for a bite to eat.

Entering the familiar hangout, Devon looked around to find his buddy hadn't arrived yet. All but a few tables were taken, but they usually didn't sit at one, and he headed to the far end of the bar out of habit. He gave Jenn a quick wave as she hurried out of the kitchen with a food tray. She gave him a huge smile as she passed him and successfully put one on his own face. Jenn could brighten up his foulest mood just by being herself. Her dad had been Devon's Lieutenant on SEAL Team Four for several years before taking a non-fieldwork promotion due to medical reasons. The man had also served with Ian for many years before that. Ian and Jeff Mullins became close friends as eighteen-year-olds, suffering through basic training together. When Jeff's wife, Lisa, gave birth to a baby girl two years later, following a shotgun wedding, Ian became a godfather.

The Mullins had lived less than fifteen minutes from the Navy base, and the team spent many a relaxing afternoon or evening being entertained and smitten with little Jenn. Over the years, team members came and went, but Jenn considered them all her uncles. Most of the men kept in contact with her through emails and phone calls after they'd left the team for whatever reason—retirement, transfer, or promotion. No matter what, though, her uncles were always guaranteed a card from Jenn for their birthdays, Valentine's Day, Veterans Day, and Christmas. There wasn't a team member, past or present, who wouldn't drop everything and come running if Jennifer Mullins needed them. And with a great amount of pain, she discovered those words to be true in the worst way possible.

A little over six months ago, Ian received a phone call from a hysterical Jennifer. Before he could calm her down, a police detective took her phone and, in a grave voice, informed Ian that Jeff and Lisa Mullins had been murdered in their home during a suspected burglary gone wrong. The two were found shot to death in their living room by a neighbor who noticed the front door ajar while walking his dog at six in the morning. Knowing Jeff, and thinking it odd, the neighbor knocked on the door and saw the carnage from the foyer. The couple had both been shot several times late the night before, and detectives later found several rooms ransacked, with jewelry, wallets, and computers missing from the home. It had been fortuitous Jennifer was spared from harm or finding her parents' bloody bodies because she'd slept at a friend's house following a night out at the movies.

Within an hour of the phone call, Devon and Ian were on a plane heading to Virginia and never left Jenn's side over the ensuing ordeal. As soon as former team members were notified, they arrived in droves. Jenn never had to do a thing except mourn her loss. Her "uncles" took care of everything from the funerals and burials, life insurance, and veteran death notifications to selling and packing up the house when Jenn moved to Tampa to live with Ian three months later.

Jenn's sole remaining family members were on her dad's side, but they weren't close, and the Mullins had long ago named Ian as her guardian if anything ever happened to them.

After the funeral, while Devon returned to Florida to keep their businesses running, Ian stayed in Virginia until Jenn completed high school. It'd been difficult for her to get through, but with her teachers, friends, and Ian's help and support, she was able to complete the requirements for her diploma. On a sunny day in June, over forty retired and current Navy SEALs filled the local high school football field stands to watch their little girl graduate. Devon didn't think there'd been a dry eye among them.

Now settled into a dorm for her freshman year at the University of Tampa on the other side of the city, Jenn was doing well. Although she still had moments of depression and sudden bouts of tears, and who could blame her, she continued to see a trauma psychologist to deal with her loss. Devon believed, however, that the love she received every day from her uncles was the most helpful in healing her devastated heart.

"Hey, are you okay?"

Devon was startled out of his thoughts at the soft voice beside him and swiveled his stool to see Kristen looking at him with concern. He hadn't thought she could get any prettier, but today she was stunning. She wore a little bit of makeup, not that she needed it, and it was enough to highlight her eyes and lips. Her soft brown hair was down, framing her face and falling below her shoulders, the tips resting at the swells of her breasts. Today's cotton V-neck was a soft purple which complemented her pale skin tone and brought out the green of her hazel eyes. It was also a little deeper than the one she wore the other day, giving him a generous view of her cleavage. And just like that, his jeans became snug.

He didn't respond immediately, which seemed to fluster her. "Sorry, I didn't mean to bother you, but you seemed a little . . . well . . . I don't know, sad about something."

He shook his head. "No, no, I'm fine, and you're not bothering me at all. I was just thinking about . . . never mind, it was no big deal." No matter how much he wanted an excuse to talk to her, there was no point dredging up the past to a stranger. He forced his mouth into what he hoped was a convincing smile, and it turned into a real one at her sigh of relief as the corners of her own mouth tilted upward.

"Good, I'm glad. I'm Kristen Anders, by the way."

He shook her outstretched hand, marveling at how soft it was and wondering if she felt the same jolt of awareness that rocked him to his core. "Devon Sawyer."

"It's nice to meet you." She paused, and he waited to see what she would say next, wanting to hear her lyrical voice again as much as he wanted his next breath. But a wave of disappointment hit him as she shook her head a little, pulled her hand from his, and began to turn away. He opened his mouth to stop her from leaving when she spun back around, and her words came out in a rush. "Look, I'm usually not this forward—actually I'm never this forward—but . . . but would you like to go out sometime?"

Devon couldn't have been more surprised if she had pulled a gun and shot him between the eyes. *She* was asking *him* out?

He must have hesitated too long because she held up her hand. "You know what, forget I asked. You don't have to answer the question."

He reached for her arm before she had a chance to run away. As much as he wanted to say yes, he would love to go out with her, he found himself uttering, "I'm flattered, I am. But Brody's my friend and, well . . ." He left the sentence hanging instead of telling her he would never poach his friend's woman.

Kristen frowned. "I don't understand. What does Brody have to do with anything?"

Really? She had to ask?

Maybe he was wrong about her being sweet and innocent. Maybe she bounced from guy to guy. He gazed into her eyes. No, he didn't think he was wrong. Not about this. "Didn't he give you his phone number the other day?"

Kristen's smile returned, along with a look of understanding. "He gave me his number in case I had any problems with the program he gave me."

Devon couldn't hide his shock. "You mean he didn't ask you out?"

"Well, he did. But I didn't say yes."

Was she for real? He'd never heard a woman turn Brody down before. Egghead had women of all ages throwing themselves at him left and right. "Why?"

"Why didn't I say yes?"

He nodded.

"Well, he was nice and all, and don't get me wrong, he's good-looking, but," she shrugged one shoulder, "I wasn't attracted to him."

His mouth curled up in a sexy smirk, and he lowered his voice. "*Huh.* So, does this mean you're attracted to me?"

Kristen blushed. "I wouldn't have asked you out if I wasn't. So, I guess the big question is . . . are you attracted to me?"

Devon knew he should deny it and send her on her way, a little embarrassed maybe, but with her gentle heart intact. And then she'd blushed. At that moment, he knew there were a million and one reasons why he should say "no," but he couldn't remember what they were. His mind became completely blank at her hopeful expression, and he found himself saying, "Yes. Yes, I am very attracted to you."

God, he was a selfish ass. Here was a beautiful young woman, and she was most likely looking for her Prince Charming and a "happily ever after," which she would never find in him. She would want a long-term commitment, and he was Mister One-Weekend-Only. Well, to be accurate, he was *Master* One-Weekend-Only. And there was another reason he should have said no. After reading the romantic scenes she'd written, he figured his vanilla librarian would run away screaming when he told her how he wanted to tie her up and flog her luscious ass until she begged him to fuck her into oblivion. He ached for her to kneel at his feet while he dragged his cock across her tongue. An image came to mind of what it would be like to pump in and out of her sweet mouth until he came, and she swallowed every drop. He wanted to own her, possess her, and then, when he had his fill, he would walk away as he always did.

Instead of doing what he knew was right, he found himself making plans with her for the following evening. When Jake arrived a few minutes later, Devon had a dinner date scheduled with her for seven o'clock at a little Italian restaurant around the corner from Donovan's. And she gave him a sexy smile when she bid him goodbye.

After Jake and he ordered a couple of burgers, his teammate let him know he'd caught at least part of Devon's conversation with Kristen. Keeping his eyes on one of the TV's over the bar, Jake let out an amused snort. "So, hell must have frozen over, huh?"

Devon frowned at the other man. "What the fuck does that mean?"

"It means, Devil Dog, in all the years I've known you, I can't recall you ever having a vanilla date with a woman, complete with dinner at a fancy little restaurant. The most effort I've seen you put into seducing a woman was buying her a drink while you negotiated a scene and found out her soft and hard limits."

"Fuck you, jackass," he retorted without any real heat, considering everything the man had said was true. Instead of admitting it, though, he lied. "I've been on plenty of dates before."

Jake didn't respond but gave Devon a look, saying he knew his friend was blowing smoke out of his ass.

"Besides, you're not one to talk, Reverend. When was the last time you went out on a date, huh?"

Devon was astonished as his buddy grinned and turned beet red simultaneously.

"You're dating someone?" He couldn't believe it. His eyes went wide with shock. "How did I not know this? It's not anyone from the club, is it?" Jake Donovan didn't do relationships any more than the rest of them did, maybe even less.

Jake shrugged and then sighed. "Yes, I'm dating someone. No one knew until now because it's only been a few dates. And no, it's not anyone from the club, and before you ask, no, you don't know him."

As curious as Devon was, he knew he wouldn't get anything more out of his buddy. He was surprised the man revealed as much as he did. So instead of asking more questions, he raised his soda glass in a gesture of good luck. "Well, here's to you, my friend. I hope it works out for you. And if it does, there may be hope for the rest of us."

Jake touched his glass to Devon's and chuckled. "I wouldn't go that far, brother, because if that happened, hell *would* definitely freeze over."

CHAPTER FIVE

Kristen couldn't believe she was there. She could imagine her ex-husband's expression if he knew she was standing outside a private BDSM club with the intention of going inside. She'd found out about The Covenant from one of her beta-readers who helped proofread her novels. Although they had never met, she chatted with Shelby Whitman, a member of the club, through Facebook and email. When Kristen had mentioned wanting to see the inside of a sex club for research, the woman put her in touch with the owner, Master Mitch. After several phone conversations and a background check, the man finally agreed to let Kristen tour the facility while it was closed.

When they'd scheduled the appointment, the Dom had been adamant that she come alone and leave her phone in her car. She'd balked at being in a strange place with a strange man with no way to call for help, and he'd relented but asked her to keep the phone off while in the club. His clientele valued the club's privacy, and he would not put that at risk for anyone. Kristen was fine with his reasoning but also told the man she would let her cousin know who she was meeting and where for her own safety. She didn't want to be one of those women she saw on the news every once in a while, who disappeared without a trace. It was the same thing she would do for her date tonight with Devon.

She was still shocked she'd asked him out on a date. Ever since puberty, she'd been shy around men, and the more attractive she found them, the shyer she became. But that was the "old Kristen." The "new Kristen" was starting over after a failed marriage. She was no longer a virgin, but she knew she was still inexperienced. The only position she'd ever had sex in was the missionary one. Maybe it hadn't been her fault she was cold in bed, maybe it'd been Tom's.

She wanted to be a woman who wasn't afraid to try new things, a woman men found attractive, to have flirty conversations with them, filled with sexual innuendos. She wanted to find what she wrote about, what other women bragged about—a man who gave her incredible orgasms which made her scream and beg for more. Was Devon the right man? She wouldn't know unless she went to bed with him, and she didn't think she could have a one-night stand, so she had to get to know him better.

Glancing through her windshield again, she shook her head in disbelief. When she'd arrived a few minutes ago, she thought she'd gotten the directions wrong. After exiting the highway where Master Mitch told her to, she followed the side road past a small forest of trees. The area then opened up, and she found herself looking at a large piece of property surrounded by a security fence topped with barbed wire. Behind the fence, there was a row of four warehouses reminding her of an industrial park. Another portion of fencing separated the first two buildings. Once Kristen pulled her car up to the security shack next to the gate to find out where she'd made a mistake in the directions, she discovered she was indeed in the right place. The cordial but armed guard had checked her driver's license and taken a digital picture of her before he opened the gate and pointed to where she should park. He indicated she should take an awning-covered staircase at the near end of the first building to the second-floor main entrance.

Parking next to the building, she'd stared at the blue metal and cement monstrosity and had a difficult time imagining this was the outside of an elite and private club catering to people's individual sexual fetishes. Now, Kristen climbed out of the car and locked the door before shutting it. She took one step then she froze at the sound of a dog barking. Looking around, ready to jump on the hood of her car if she had to, she spotted a large black lab-mix running back and forth and was thankful it was on the other side of the second fence. Despite his loud greeting, he appeared friendly, but she wasn't taking any chances by approaching the barrier between them.

"Hi, boy, good doggie. Stay on your side of the fence, okay? Good boy," she cooed in what she hoped was a soothing tone as she dashed to the stairs.

When she reached the doors, she found them locked but located a doorbell and pressed it. As she waited, she took in her surroundings again and realized there was no signage indicating a place of business on any of the buildings and fences. She also couldn't remember seeing any signs at the highway exit or on the side road leading to the complex other than a street sign which read Fairwood Drive. Curious, she wondered what was in the other three buildings. There were a few cars parked next to the second one, but she didn't see anyone other than the one guard. She also noticed several security cameras, some on the buildings, including the one above the door she stood in front of, and others atop some of the nine-foot fence posts. It was a little overkill to her, but what did she know?

The door opened, and she was greeted by a handsome man whom she guessed to be in his early thirties. "Hi, Ms. Anders? I'm Master Mitch. It's nice to meet you."

She would be embarrassed to admit he wasn't what she expected, which was an older, brooding, vampire-like-looking man, dressed head to toe in leather. Instead, he reminded her of her high-school math teacher, who all the female students had crushes on. About six-foot-one, he had black/brown hair with gentle, blue eyes. His easy smile was framed by a trim goatee and mustache, which might be adding a few years to his age. Instead of being dressed in black, he was wearing a navy blue golf shirt, blue jeans, and sneakers. It was obvious he kept himself in shape, maybe by running and playing sports, because he didn't have the bulked-up look weightlifters did. Despite his pleasant demeanor, she could imagine him transforming into a commanding Dom with submissives dropping to their knees to please him.

"It's nice to meet you, too."

He stepped aside so she could enter, and she was amazed at how the outside of the building belied its interior. They were standing in a lobby that was decorated in a Victorian-era style. It was just large enough to contain a hotel-style check-in desk and a comfortable sitting area. The walls were painted a deep red while the carpet was a complementary gray. On several walls were paintings that some might call pornographic, but Kristen thought they were sensual and erotic. The space was separated from the main club by a set of large wooden doors which she swore once graced an old European castle somewhere. The dark wood was beautiful with intricate carvings and round wrought-iron pulls.

Before Master Mitch allowed her through the doors, he took a moment to convince himself she was not taking any pictures or recordings of his business. He then gave her a privacy contract to sign, stating it protected his business and clients and it was legal and binding, having been drawn up by the club's lawyers. After she read and signed the paper, he took it from her and handed her several others.

"I thought these would help you with your research. The top two pages are general contracts that some members use when negotiating a temporary relationship between Dominant and submissive that's going to last more than one or two nights. Usually, the contract indicates both parties agree to play for a certain amount of time, such as a week or a month, and what the play will consist of. At the end of the agreed upon time, both parties go their separate ways."

"Isn't a contract a little cold?" There was little she could do to hide the cynical tone in her voice or her shocked expression.

He tilted his head as if he was thinking about her question—a contract could seem cold to someone not familiar with the lifestyle. "You have to understand something. Although there are couples here who are married or in long-term relationships, there are many others who aren't looking for anything other than something temporary. This way, there's an end date and there is no awkward quote-unquote breaking up at the end of the relationship."

Kristen nodded, writing a few notes in the notebook she brought with her. She understood what he was saying but wasn't sure if she could ever sign a contract to have sex with a man that included a deadline stating when they would stop seeing each other.

"The other papers are the club's rules, a list of protocols that submissives are expected to follow, and a long list of

BDSM activities. Submissives fill out the checklist with their hard and soft limits, or red and yellow limits as some people call them. Do you know what those are?"

Before she wrote *Satin and Sin*, she did a lot of internet searches on every aspect of BDSM she could find. She was far from an expert on the subject, but she knew the basics. "If my research was correct, hard limits are something a submissive has no desire to try, things which are a total turn-off for them. Soft limits are things they're curious about and might be willing to try, but they've never done them before, or if they have, they haven't made up their mind on whether they want to do it again."

"Correct. And after they try one of their yellow soft limits, they tend to move it to the green, okay activity column, or the red, hard limit column. There are some activities that only appeal to a select few, while there are others that pretty much everyone is into. Submissives' hard and soft limit lists are available here at the front desk for the Doms to look at, so they know who would be receptive to a certain activity. On the checklist, the starred activities are not allowed in the club at all."

Kristen cocked her head. "Such as?"

"Such as fire-play and anything involving blood, urine, or feces, among a few other extreme activities."

"*Eewww.*" Kristen winced. She had read about body-fluid play on the internet and the thought of it still grossed her out.

He smiled and laughed at her reaction. If she had met him anywhere else, she would have a hard time believing he was a Dom. Despite his age, the man had a boyish charm to him.

"Exactly! I'm with you. Body-fluid play does not appeal to me at all, but believe it or not, there are some people who get into it. Along the same subject line, every client must have a physical and blood work with one of our doctors every six months in order to keep their play privileges, and vaginal and anal sex without condoms is forbidden in the building, even between long-time partners.

"Let's see, what else can I tell you? Um . . . oh, we have a bar, and alcohol is restricted to two drinks if members are planning to play. The bartenders have a computer program to track how many drinks have been served to a member. The same program is used to bill the members each month, so they don't need to carry any cash, just a key card. It's similar to what's used on cruise ships. The waitresses and security have handheld computers which track the same information, and it's checked before a member is allowed to enter any play area, public or private. The same program is used to flag a member who is overdue for a physical."

Master Mitch continued to talk as Kristen scribbled in her notepad as fast as she could. "Every once in a while a client will ask to bring a guest. It's only allowed after a background check of the guest, and they're not allowed to play at all while on the premises unless they have been cleared by one of our staff doctors. It takes a few weeks before a guest is cleared, so it's not something that can be done on the spur of the moment. The client who invited the guest is held responsible for them and cannot leave them on their own. Guests are given a yellow wristband, so the Dungeon Masters and security know who they are. All clients have gone through extensive background checks, and every few months their names are checked for any arrests or dealings with the police which may concern us, such as a domestic violence call at their house."

She looked up from her notes. "Wow. Isn't it a lot of work for you?"

"Well, we have a security company that does it for us, but it's necessary to keep our clients safe."

"Any other rules?" she inquired, finding the information he was giving her fascinating. There was plenty of data on the internet, but sometimes it took a live person to help you understand a subject to the fullest.

"Well, it's obvious you've done some research on the topic, right? So you know what a safeword is, correct?"

She nodded. "If a submissive uses their safeword all play comes to an immediate halt."

"Right. We use color safewords here so there are no misunderstandings between our members, the Dungeon Masters, and security. If a sub uses a different safeword and a Dom doesn't heed it, a Dungeon Master may not know there's a problem. Red means stop. Yellow means to slow down or pause to clarify an issue. And green means they're good to go. Failure to heed a safeword is an automatic three-month suspension of play privileges, and a second offense results in termination of membership. But we've never had to terminate anyone for that reason."

Satisfied she would adhere to the privacy contract she signed, he finally opened the left wooden door and gestured for her to walk in ahead of him. Three steps past the threshold, she stopped short in complete awe of the fantasy land before her. The second floor where they stood consisted of an extra wide balcony in the shape of a horseshoe overlooking the main floor below. To her left, there was a large curved bar following the lines of the horseshoe bottom. The two long, opposite sides of the balcony contained many sitting areas similar to the one in the lobby.

High above the sitting areas were horizontal tinted windows that let light in during the day, and he told her the inside of the club couldn't be seen from outside at any time.

Along the brass railings, there were stools and pub tables where people could sit and observe what was happening below them. About twenty feet in front of the bar was a grand staircase with brass banisters leading downstairs and reminding Kristen of the one her wedding party had taken pictures on at the hotel where her reception was held.

At the opposite end of the building, where the horseshoe ended was a wall with two doors, one glass and the other wood. Master Mitch explained the glass door belonged to a small store where they sold a variety of sex toys and fetish wear. The other door was to a hallway leading to the business offices and an emergency exit. The locker rooms were located right below the bar. There was an entrance next to the double exit doors with a short hallway and two sets of stairs leading to the women's and men's locker rooms. Members could also enter the rooms from the first floor.

As they walked further into the club, his cell phone rang. Taking it from the holster at his hip, he looked at the screen. "I apologize, but I have to take this. Please have a seat at the bar, and I'll be with you in a moment." He placed the phone to his ear and stepped a few feet away from her. "Hey, Ian, what's up?"

She did as he asked and took a seat while skimming through the paperwork he gave her. She never realized how involved the lifestyle was—contracts, lists, protocols, and rules. It was a wonder anyone had time for sex. Although he'd said a negotiation between Dom and sub was a common part of BDSM, she couldn't help but think it was all so clinical, like going to her GYN for her annual physical.

She was disappointed it was the middle of the afternoon and the club was empty except for her and Master Mitch. She would love to take in the sights and sounds of the club when it was in full swing. It would have been a tremendous help with the descriptions she wrote of her fictional club "Leathers," but it hadn't been an option offered to her.

Several minutes later, Mitch hung up the phone and gestured for her to join him at the top of the grand staircase. She listened as he began to explain the different areas and pieces of equipment while he led her down the stairs to the "pit."

"The pit?" she asked with curiosity.

He laughed and shook his head. "Yeah, in the beginning, we called this the dungeon . . . a little cliché, but it's basically what it is. Somewhere along the line, the observers upstairs began calling it the pit and it sort of stuck."

"I like it . . . it fits," she told him. "It makes me think of the Coliseum in Rome."

"*Hmmm*, maybe we should schedule some gladiator games. The subs would love it."

Kristen chuckled, as she made a quick note on her pad. "I might steal that idea and put it in my book."

"Only if you give me partial creative credit," he teased.

Kristen laughed harder. "It's a deal."

When they reached the first floor, she took a few more steps, then rotated in a three-hundred-and-sixty-degree turn, taking in as much as she could. The red-and-gray color combination continued throughout this part of the club and was the perfect complement to the different pieces of equipment located in individual areas. Each was sectioned off by red velvet ropes hanging from brass hooks, while the wrought iron sconces and chandeliers completed the look.

"So, is it what you imagined it would be?"

Kristen turned back toward Master Mitch. "It's better than I ever imagined," she told him honestly. "I didn't think I would say this, but it's beautiful."

"Expected something more along the lines of a damp,

dark dungeon in some castle somewhere?" He laughed. People new to his lifestyle always seemed amazed at how elegant his club was.

"Sort of, I guess. I'm not sure what I expected, but I know it wasn't this."

He began to show her the different sections and stopped in the center of the huge oval room, next to a two-foot-high stage. On it sat a seven-foot tall, wooden St. Andrew's Cross with black leather padding covering part of its surface, and it could be seen from every angle of the room. At the top and bottom ends of the cross were leather wrist and ankle restraints. Although it brought to mind medieval torture, Kristen knew it was common apparatus used in the lifestyle she was researching. An erotic shiver went through her as she imagined herself, naked and restrained on it, for everyone to see.

Shaking off the thought, she began to go through a list of questions she had written down before she came. She found his answers valuable to her research as she took several more pages of notes. "How many members do you have?"

"Over three hundred and fifty, but some of them live in the area part-time so they only come a few times a year. The waiting list is over two hundred people and that's only for this club. There are four other clubs in the Tampa area, but only two of those are private. The others are open to the public, which isn't safe, in my opinion. They don't keep track of their members and anyone could walk in off the street and start to play. Anyway, The Covenant has an elite clientele and the reputation of being *the* club to belong to. And that's not my ego talking. We've worked hard to become the best in the area."

"Holy cow!" Over three-hundred-and-fifty members,

with more than half of that trying to get in? She'd expected him to say less than a hundred members.

"Didn't think so many people were into kink, did you?"

Kristen shook her head in amazement as he continued. "We have a capacity for five hundred people in here, as approved by the fire inspector, but I doubt we'll ever let the numbers get that high."

"Hey, Mitch, did you talk to Ian yet?" A male voice boomed and echoed in the empty club. As they both turned toward the grand staircase, where someone was descending, Kristen heard, "What the hell are you doing here?"

She froze and searched her mind for an answer as a very sexy, and very pissed-off, Devon strode up to her and stopped inches from her face. *Uh-oh*. This wasn't good.

Wait a minute . . . what the hell are you doing here? What the hell was *he* doing here?

Mitch glanced from Devon to Kristen and back again. It was evident he was both amused and curious. "Um, last time I checked Dev, I run the place. That's what the hell I'm doing here."

Devon never took his eyes off her, and she suddenly wished she was anywhere but here when he growled. "Shove it, Mitch. I asked you a question, Kristen. Don't make me ask you again."

Kristen's back straightened. Who did he think he was? "Not that it's any business of yours, but Master Mitch was nice enough to give me a tour of his club for some research I'm doing for my book."

"Research?" His brows furrowed in confusion. "In case you hadn't noticed, this is a BDSM sex club, Kristen."

Seriously? "Of course I noticed, and it's obvious that little fact didn't get past you, now did it? Now, please leave and let me finish my tour."

Devon's lethal glare cut off Mitch's laughter, and he stepped back, clearly trying to hold back his amusement.

"What were you thinking, Mitch? A tour? What are we, fucking Disney World?"

"I had Marco do a background check on her. Brody was busy. After I confirmed she wrote fiction and wasn't some reporter trying to check the place out, I figured it was fine. She has no cameras or recorders."

"How the hell did you find out about the club in the first place?" He was back to questioning her again.

She raised her chin in defiance. There was no way she would let this man intimidate her no matter how much she was attracted to him—and damn it, was it getting hot in here? "One of my beta-readers is a member, and she contacted Master Mitch for me."

Devon's eyes flicked toward his cousin with an unspoken question. "Shelby" was the response he received.

Kristen huffed. She'd answered his questions, but now she was becoming infuriated with him sticking his nose where it didn't belong. "This is really none of your business, Devon."

Devon stared back at her and growled again. "None of my business? See, that's where you're wrong, Pet. This *is* my business. I own this club."

Her mouth dropped open as she looked back and forth between the two men. "Y-you own the club? I thought Master Mitch owned it."

"He's my cousin. We're co-owners, along with my brother. So, allow me to re-introduce myself to you, Pet. I'm Master Devon."

Kristen's mouth went dry. *Shit!* There was no way this could be happening. Of all the things which could go wrong today, she hadn't expected this. He was a Dom? She knew she was in so much trouble but didn't know why or what to say, so she just stared at him, her chin almost hitting the floor.

* * *

"What kind of research are you doing? Your books are pretty vanilla when it comes to sex, so why the hell do you need to research a BDSM club?" Devon realized his mistake as soon as the words were out of his mouth, but there was no way to take them back.

"You read my books?"

She sounded as shocked as Mitch looked. *Great, just great.* It would be a long time before his cousin forgot this conversation. Devon crossed his arms, forcing her to back up a step. Since Marco had done her background check, the name hadn't been familiar to him. Brody, who usually did the checks, would have recognized it immediately and mentioned it to him, saving him from this little surprise meeting. "I didn't read any of them. Jenn left one of the books you gave her on the bar. I was curious about you and flipped through it. Now stop dancing around my questions."

Mitch cleared his throat. "I have a question. How do you two know each other?"

Refusing to give his cousin any ammunition for future jokes, Devon rolled his eyes. "Shut it, Mitch."

But to his dismay, Kristen spoke at the same time. "We have a date tonight."

Mitch's eyes widened as if he hadn't heard her right. Devon could almost guess what his cousin was thinking. *Devil Dog? On a date? Like a date date? Damn, the end of the world must be near.*

With a flair for the dramatic, the asshole stuck his finger in his ear to clear any blockage. "I'm not sure I heard you right—can you repeat that? It sounded like you said you two had a date."

Before she could answer him, Devon growled—which he seemed to do a lot in her presence. "Mitch, if you know what's good for you, you'll go upstairs and do some inventory or something. I'll finish taking Ms. Anders on her . . . tour."

* * *

To Kristen's shock, Master Mitch sighed and headed toward the staircase. "Don't forget—she's not allowed to play."

"I know. I was there when we wrote the club rules."

The man didn't stop walking up the stairs but raised his voice so she could still hear him. "Ms. Anders, don't worry. You're in good hands. Oh, don't forget, the club safeword is 'red.' I'll be at the bar if you need to use it."

Her eyes widened. There was no way he was leaving her alone with Devon, right? The man looked like he wanted to spank her ass for the next three days straight, and, good Lord, why did the thought make her wet?

Devon took a step toward her. Kristen's response was instantaneous, and she took two steps back, looking for a way to get around him. He arched his brow and took another step. She tried not to react again, but before she knew it, he'd backed her up to the wall and stopped right in front of her, blocking her escape. Without saying a word, he reached out and took her pad and papers, tossing them on a small table behind him before doing the same with her pen and purse.

He then took hold of her wrists and brought her arms above her head. There were only a few inches between their bodies, and she could feel his heat. She wished he would take half a step toward her, and then she would know what it felt like to be in contact with his hard chest, sculpted abs, and trim hips. Oh, and don't forget the massive erection he was sporting.

"Eyes up, Pet."

Heaven help her. She lifted her chin to find a perceptive grin on his face, and she turned red, knowing she'd been caught staring at his crotch. He leaned forward, his mouth almost touching her ear, and whispered, "You still haven't answered my question."

The words may have been simple, something you could hear in an everyday conversation, but somehow, he made them sound erotic, and the heated feel of his breath on her ear didn't help. She swallowed hard, her legs trembling. Not in fear—he wouldn't physically hurt her. She didn't know how she knew it, but she did. But no, it was the sexual electricity between them which had her unable to control her quivering muscles. "What . . . what was the question again?"

"Why are you researching BDSM when you write vanilla sex?"

Couldn't he back up a little? "Um . . . well, my first nine books are . . . are vanilla, but my last book was based on a BDSM club and . . . and now I'm writing the second one in a series."

"You gave my niece a kinky romance to read?" He didn't sound happy about it at all.

"Act . . . actually, I didn't give that one to her, only the others. It felt a little weird giving a nineteen-year-old a BDSM book."

She drew in a deep breath, relieved when he took a step backward. But her relief didn't last long when she realized her arms were stuck. Tilting her head up, she tugged on her arms to find he'd shackled her wrists with Velcro restraints dangling from the balcony overhang. How did she not know he was doing that? Oh God, she was trapped.

She gaped at him and was annoyed to see him laughing at her with a sinister smirk and his arms crossed over his muscular chest again. Damn, the man was gorgeous . . . and dangerous. Not in a bad way, but also not in a good one. And here she was with no way to escape. She wouldn't panic. Master Mitch was right upstairs. She was safe, wasn't she?

"Let me go." She hoped the demand would sound confident, but instead, it sounded breathy.

He shook his head. "Not until your tour is complete."

Damn, how had she not noticed how arrogant the man was? "I didn't know class participation was part of the tour."

Devon let out a full-blown laugh. "Oh, how I love bratty submissives. They give me plenty of reasons to spank their asses beet red. And I'll tell you, at the moment, my hand is itching to get at your sweet ass."

"I'm not submissive."

The look he gave her said he didn't believe her for a second before he turned around and took three steps to the table where he'd put her things. Turning a wooden chair around, he straddled it and sat down facing her. Without saying a word, he picked up her pad and the papers Mitch had given her and began to look through them.

"Hey, that's my stuff. I didn't give you permission to look through my notes."

"Quiet."

He never looked up as he issued the deep-voiced command, and it sent a shiver through her body. She glanced around, trying to figure out how to get out of the restraints. She should have been scared out of her wits, but, for some reason, she wasn't. Instead, she was turned on, which freaked her out a little . . . well, actually, a lot. Yes, she'd fantasized about this stuff and she wrote about it, but it didn't appeal to her in real life, did it? Apparently, it did because during her entire marriage, she had never once been this aroused, and Devon had only touched her wrists. What would happen if he touched her in other places? Did she want him to? Her body screamed at her—hell, yeah!

She looked back at him and realized he was now reading the papers Mitch had given her. *Shit!* While Mitch had been talking on his phone, she'd skimmed through the soft and hard limit checklist. She didn't fill out the entire form but had checked off what she considered to be hard limits for her. Everything else she skipped over, planning to go through the list again later to figure out what she thought she would like and what she wasn't sure about. "Hey, stop! That's private!"

Devon rolled his eyes and sighed, then got up from his seat. Without looking at her, he strode over to open a cabinet she hadn't noticed, which was built into the wall a few feet away from her. He grabbed something and shut the door again before returning to his seat. Pivoting to face her, he held up an object. "Do you know what this is, Pet?"

She had a feeling she did, but she bit her bottom lip and shook her head.

"It's a ball gag. Usually, I only give an order once and expect it to be obeyed, but since this is new to you, here is your second and final warning. Stay quiet unless I ask you a question. Your only responses should be 'yes, Sir' or 'no, Sir' unless I ask you for a detailed answer. Anything else from your mouth will result in me using the ball gag. Understood?"

As her girlie parts began to throb, Kristen nodded her head, and he frowned at her. "Y-yes, Sir."

"Do you wish to use your safeword? If you do, I'll let you loose and escort you out . . . without your research, of course."

What?! Crap, he was serious. "No, Sir."

* * *

Devon placed the gag on the table, where she was sure to see it every time she looked at him. He was pleased to see a shudder run through her body and a nervous but heated look in her eyes. He loved to play the psychological games involved in BDSM, and, damn it, he wanted to play the physical games with her, too, but now was not the time. Instead, he sat back down and looked over her checklist again. Having seen hundreds of them in the past, it didn't take long for him to read her partial list, but he pretended to take his time.

He waited . . . and waited. And yes, there it was. She began to squirm, her hips and feet moving ever so slightly but enough for him to notice. She rubbed her thighs together, and he knew without a doubt her pussy was wet. "I'm pleased to see most of your hard limits are similar to mine, but I'd love to see where you place the activities you haven't checked off yet. I'm also curious why nipple clamps are a hard limit for you. I don't think I've ever seen that on a submissive's hard-limit list before."

Kristen swallowed hard, and her pink cheeks turned a deeper shade. "M-my nipples are too sensitive, Sir. The thought of clamps freaks me out."

Confused, he stared at her and tried to figure out what she wasn't telling him. Something about her statement felt off to him. "Out of all the hard limits you checked off, if you had to move one to a soft limit, which one would you choose?"

She paused in evident thought. "The bullwhip, Sir."

What the hell? "You would choose a whip over nipple clamps?"

"Yes, Sir."

With a surprised expression, Devon stood again and stalked toward her. "I think there's something more to it than just sensitive nipples, but I'll leave it alone for now. Have you ever been tied up or spanked before?"

"No!"

"But the thought of doing those things turns you on." He stopped in front of her. His words may not have come out as a question, but he still waited for an answer.

She opened her mouth with what he knew was denial but slammed it shut again when his eyes narrowed. "Don't lie to me, Pet." She was wise enough to remain silent, and he stared at her for a minute before speaking again. "I think I'm going to change our plans for this evening."

* * *

Kristen's stomach dropped. "You're canceling our date?"

Taking the index finger of his right hand, he reached up and set it on her left forearm. His touch was light as he trailed his finger down her arm toward her elbow, then further, touching her ear and neck. His eyes tracked the movement. He followed the scoop-neck edge of her shirt from her collarbone, down to her chest, over the swells of her breasts, and back up to her right ear. Her breathing increased, and her nipples had a mind of their own, pebbling into hard little nubs, begging for him to touch them.

"Oh, no, Pet, not at all. I'm just going to add to it. We'll still go to dinner." He paused, and her tongue shot out to moisten her dry lips. Heat flared in his eyes in response. "*Mmmm*. But afterward, we'll come here, and I'll give you the full tour as my guest. Since Marco ran a security check on you, it won't be a problem. I do have a few requirements, though, since our plans have changed. I want you to wear the sexiest dress or skirt you own and no underwear. And I mean no panties *or* bra, Pet. You will go to dinner like that. If you disobey me on this, I'll take you into the women's restroom and remove them myself. Understood?"

Kristen was salivating. Her panties were soaked. Was it possible to come, while she was fully dressed, from a feather-light touch and his words alone? Her voice came out raspy. "Y-yes, Sir."

"And wear your hair down." He gave her ponytail a gentle tug. "I want you to read and understand the club protocols. You'll be expected to follow them, although I'll give you some leeway since this is new to you. If you have any questions, you may ask them at dinner. Last but not least, I want you to finish filling out your limit list."

Her eyes widened because he couldn't be serious. "But I thought guests weren't allowed to play without a physical and . . . and stuff." At his raised eyebrow, she added, "Sir."

His finger retraced its earlier path, down her neck, across her breasts, and then back up again. "Correct. But by having you complete the list, I know what scenes I should let you observe. Now, before I let you go home to get ready for our . . . date, do you have any questions?"

She had more than she could count in the next hour or so. However, she found herself saying, "No, Sir."

"Do you want to cancel our date?"

Did she? Absolutely not! "No, Sir."

"Good." He reached up and removed the restraints from her wrists. "I'll walk you to your car."

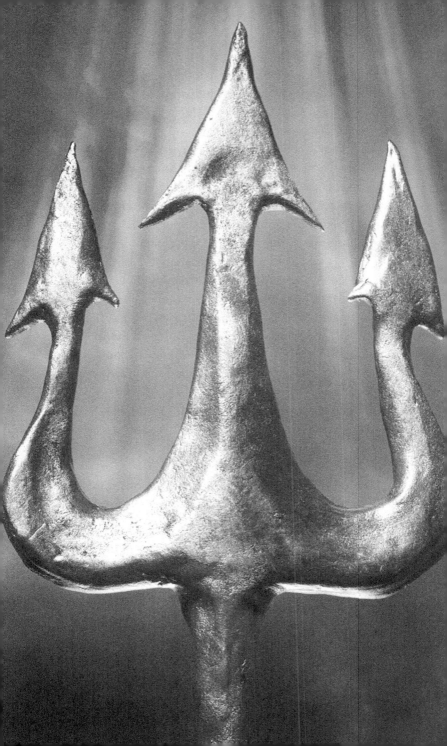

CHAPTER SIX

"Try this one on. I think it will be perfect."

Kayla London took the little black dress from Kristen's closet and handed it to her as Will reclined on her bed, propped up on a few pillows. On the way home from the club, Kristen had called him in a semi-panic. He, in turn, had called Kayla. The woman was one of Will's closest friends, and Kristen had clicked with her the first time they'd met. Will had introduced the two of them a few months earlier when Kristen had traveled to Tampa to find an apartment before moving. Kayla and her wife, Roxy, had become her fast friends, and although they teased her about it, they never tried to hook her up with one of their female friends.

After Kristen explained about her dinner date and where they were going after, the fashion-forward duo came running to her rescue. She had no idea what to wear. It had to be something appropriate for dinner and hide the fact she was not allowed to wear underwear, yet sexy enough for the club.

She was so nervous. Her stomach still had butterflies fluttering around, which started when she realized Devon had shackled her wrists. He'd worn such a wicked grin as he watched her struggle with the restraints for a moment before giving up. She had a feeling if she'd panicked, he would have released her without question, but she surprised herself by only asking him to let her go the one time. Then she'd become so focused on him and the tingling throughout her body that she'd pretty much forgotten she was being held hostage.

While he read through her notes, she'd studied him a little more. When she first met him, she'd thought he was walking perfection, but today, she'd noticed his nose was a tad crooked as if it had been broken once. He also had a faint two-inch scar along his jawline, slightly below his right ear, and she wondered what'd caused it. Those minor imperfections only enhanced his good looks and made him seem even sexier, if possible.

As she walked into the bathroom and shut the door to change for the third time, Kayla told her, "I'm so jealous you're going to The Covenant tonight. Roxy and I put in a membership application six months ago, and from what I understand, the waiting list to get in is almost a year unless a Dom sponsors you. And even then, it takes a while."

Kristen pulled the cotton-spandex dress over her head and dragged it down her body, smoothing the fabric as she went. "I didn't know you two were . . . in the lifestyle."

"We don't advertise because most people don't understand BDSM and tend to be negative about it. Roxy got me into it when we first met years ago. She became a Domme in college but didn't have much time to play when she hit med school. At the moment, we belong to another private club called Heat but don't go as much as we would like. We'd prefer the guarded privacy and exclusiveness The Covenant is known for. Some parents of

Roxy's kids would flip if they found out she likes to flog my ass."

Kayla was a social worker, and Dr. Roxanne London had a thriving pediatric practice. They were also the complete opposites of each other. Where Kayla was five foot two, a "size twelve on a good day and a fourteen on a bad one"—her words—and a blue-eyed blonde, Roxy was seven inches taller and a size six, with auburn hair and hazel eyes. Kayla was disorganized and loved sci-fi movies, while Roxy was a neat freak who went to at least one indie or foreign film a month, either alone or with a friend because her wife tended to fall asleep during them. But, despite their differences, or maybe it was due to them, the two made the perfect couple.

"I can see why you would want to keep it private." She zippered the side of the dress and looked at her reflection from the waist up in the mirror above the sink. *Not bad.*

"Most members of the BDSM community do. If we run into other members outside of the club, we either act like we know them from someplace else or don't know them at all."

Kristen opened the door and stepped out for them to see. She'd only worn the dress once before, to a gala on New Year's Eve after she first got married. Her ex hadn't liked the revealing one-shoulder design, complaining she had too many men staring at her. But she loved how the ruching at the waist gave her size-twelve body an hourglass figure. The hem stopped mid-thigh, and she tugged it down a little, trying to hide the fact she had no underwear on.

"Bow-chicka-wow-wow." Leave it to Will to say something to make her laugh and forget how nervous she was.

Kayla whistled. "Damn, girl, I'll have to borrow that someday. You look hot."

Kristen looked at her reflection in the mirror attached to her closet door, turning from side to side to see the dress from all angles. She may never be skinny by today's standards, but some of Will's friends had told her, with her generous curves, if she added a blond wig, she would've given Marilyn Monroe some serious competition. "You sure I look okay? It's not too slutty looking?"

"Slutty? No. High-class call-girl? Yes. And it's the way you want to look. Trust me on this. Now, let's see what we can do with your hair and makeup. Will, can you find her a pair of shoes to wear?" Kayla led her back into the bathroom, and Kristen tried to imagine Devon's reaction when he saw her. Would he like her dress, or would he complain about it like her ex-husband had? She prayed it was the former.

* * *

Devon glanced at his watch for the fourth time in under two minutes as he paced back and forth in front of Tuscany, the restaurant they were meeting at. She was ten minutes late. He'd wanted to pick her up at her home but decided not to suggest it, figuring she would be more comfortable this way, given the fact he was still a relative stranger to her—a fact he intended to rectify as soon as possible.

As much as he wanted to use her lateness as an excuse to spank her delicious backside, he was more worried she'd changed her mind and chickened out. He'd been shocked when he first saw her standing in the middle of the pit. However, the shock had morphed into anger and jealousy at the fact she was in his club with Mitch and not with him. The two of them hadn't been doing anything other than talking, but, damn it, he wanted to be the one to introduce her to BDSM . . . especially since he now knew she was researching the lifestyle he loved.

Behind him, he heard the sound of heels clicking fast down the sidewalk. Turning, he froze as Kristen hurried toward him. She was beautiful. Her brown hair fell around her face in soft curls, and he longed to run his fingers through them. Her styled hair and the subtle makeup which lit up her face made him realize she put in extra effort while preparing for their date, and the thought made his heart race. He watched as she approached him, and he got a peek at her black dress under the lightweight raincoat she wore. Although the temperature was cooler than normal for a late September evening, it wasn't cold or rainy, and he assumed the coat was for modesty. He hoped it meant her dress was a little out of her comfort zone.

"Sorry, I'm late." She tried to catch her breath. "I couldn't find my car keys, and then I couldn't find a parking spot." Unlike Donovan's, Tuscany didn't have a lot, and customers had to find on-street parking.

"It's all right, Pet. I'll just take it out on your backside later."

Kristen gaped at him. "You want to spank me because I'm ten minutes late?"

"Yup." He looked at his watch. "And you're thirteen minutes late, which calls for thirteen smacks. It's a decent amount for your first spanking."

He took her arm and escorted her into the restaurant without giving her a chance to respond. While they waited for the hostess, he helped her out of her coat and tried to keep from swallowing his tongue. Damn. When he told her to wear the sexiest dress she had, he didn't expect her to have one, which made her look like a seductive siren. The woman would give him a heart attack between the dress, her mile-long legs, and those three-inch black stilettos. He would have to fuck her in nothing but those heels at some point, real soon.

He folded her coat over his arm, using it to hide the swelling in his pants, and leaned over to whisper in her ear.

"You look gorgeous, Pet. I wish I could bend you over a table and fuck you right here in front of everyone. But since I can't, tell me—did you obey my orders? Did you leave your underwear at home? Because if you didn't, we're heading straight to the ladies' room, and I don't care who sees us."

* * *

A pink blush rose to her cheeks, and Kristen almost wished she'd disobeyed him because she could feel a rush of arousal coating her pussy. If he kept talking to her like that, it would soon be dripping down her legs.

"Yes." She whispered the word, afraid someone would overhear her and know how turned on she was.

"Prove it."

She gasped as her cheeks heated even more. They were in the front of a crowded restaurant, and he wanted her to prove she wasn't wearing any underwear. How the heck was she supposed to do that without getting arrested for indecent exposure? "H-how?"

He must have read her mind because he chuckled. "Not the way you're thinking, Pet. Turn around, nice and slow, and let me feel if you have any panty lines."

He put his hand on her hip, and she made a complete turn, his hand staying in contact with her body the entire rotation, across both hips, the top of her buttocks, and her lower abdomen. When facing him again, she glanced around and was relieved no one was paying them any attention.

"Very good, Pet. You saved yourself from additional punishment, although I'm sure I'll find something else to add to the count before the night ends."

She was grateful to have his teasing interrupted when the hostess chose that moment to approach them, and Devon gave his name, which the reservations were under. It allowed Kristen to get her heated body back under control and inspect her date. He wore dark-gray dress slacks, black loafers, and a white button-down shirt with the sleeves folded up to the middle of his forearms. His shirt wasn't tight but the perfect cut to showcase his physique. He wore no jewelry besides a black dive watch on his left wrist. The look was simple yet classic, and he could have graced this month's cover of *GQ* magazine and had millions of women drooling over him. And those thoughts gave her pause. The man could be dating a supermodel if he wanted, so what was he doing here with her? She glanced around and noticed, now that he was facing the other patrons, several women were gawking at him in obvious interest.

She tamped her jealousy down, and when the hostess told them to follow her, Devon motioned for Kristen to walk in front of him. She felt as if he was ogling her ass the whole way across the restaurant as they made their way to a table against the far wall. The thought made her smile, and she put a little more sway in her hips. She could have sworn she heard a low growl, and she giggled to herself.

When they reached their table, she was surprised he pulled out a chair for her to sit on before taking his own seat across from her. The gesture made her feel like a lady. She couldn't remember Tom ever holding out her chair for her. She watched as Devon draped her coat over the back of the empty chair next to him before the hostess handed them their menus and excused herself. Although there were only two place settings at the table, it could seat four people, which Kristen was happy about. She hated tables for two because there was never enough room, and she always seemed to knock over a glass of wine or water. The last thing she wanted tonight was to look like a klutz.

A smartly-dressed waiter approached their table and filled their water glasses. "Good evening, my name is Kevin, and I'll be your waiter. Can I get you anything from the bar while you look over your menus?"

Devon looked at Kristen and arched his brow in question. "Would you like a glass of wine or something else?"

"White wine, please—a Riesling, if they have it."

He nodded, then turned back to the young man who stood waiting. "A Riesling for the lady, and I'll have tonic water with lime. Thank you."

"You're not having any alcohol?" she asked after the waiter left to get their order.

"No, I don't drink."

"Ever?" It sounded like it was the weirdest thing she ever heard, but she didn't know any men who didn't at least have the occasional beer or two.

"No."

The way he said the one word made it clear to her that it would be best if she changed the subject. She opened her menu and began perusing the choices. Everything sounded so delicious.

"So, what's good on the menu since this is my first time here? What are you getting?"

When he didn't answer right away, she glanced up and saw a sexy smile on his face. "Well, since what I want to eat isn't on the menu," he paused, and her face heated, "I'm having the steak pizzaiola. It's one of the chef's specialties. What do you prefer—beef, chicken, veal, seafood, or pasta?"

"I pretty much eat anything, but I'm leaning toward either the veal piccata or the mushroom-crusted salmon. Which do you recommend?"

"I've never had the salmon, but I can assure you, you won't be disappointed with the veal."

Kristen giggled. "You sound like a car salesman."

Devon laughed at her comparison. The waiter returned

with their drinks, and they placed their dinner orders. A few minutes later, they were enjoying Caesar salads and warm, fresh Italian bread.

"So, Ms. Kristen Anders, tell me about yourself, other than what's in the short biography I read on the back of Jenn's book."

She took a sip of her wine. "What would you like to know?"

Shrugging his shoulder, he picked up a black pepper mill and added some to his salad. He held the mill up toward her, and she shook her head.

"I don't know—tell me about your family, where you grew up, what you did before becoming a romance writer. Things you've told other guys on a first date."

"Well, since I've only had a few first dates in my life, and my last first date was over four years ago, I'm not sure I remember what I talked about on them."

Devon stopped his salad fork halfway to his mouth and stared at her in surprise. "Okay, explain, please, because I find it hard to believe you aren't beating men off with a stick."

Kristen blushed, which she did a lot around him, and stared at her own salad like it was the most exciting thing in the world. He put his fork down, reached across the table, and placed two fingers under her chin, lifting it until she looked at him again. His eyes were a deeper blue tonight in the low restaurant lighting. "Talk to me, Kristen. Believe it or not, I've never said this to a woman, but you fascinate me, and I want to know everything about you."

She doubted it was true, but it did prompt her to start talking. "I was a bookworm through high school and college—kind of nerdy. I was shy around guys, I guess, and didn't date a lot. I had one serious boyfriend my sophomore year of college, but he got tired . . ." She paused, not wanting to finish the sentence.

"Tired of what, Pet?"

She didn't know what it was about that one word, but it made her heart pound faster, and she liked the nickname. It felt intimate, though she doubted she was the only woman he used it on. "He got tired of me telling him no." She'd lowered her voice, so he was the only person who could hear her. She couldn't believe she was telling him this ten minutes into their first date, but she couldn't stop the words. "I was a virgin on my wedding night two years ago. I met Tom my senior year, and although we fooled around, something in me wanted to wait. I know it sounds silly in this day and age, but it was important to me."

"It's not silly at all, Kristen. I think it shows what a strong woman you are—one who knows what she wants and doesn't. And you're willing to fight for what feels right to you. There's nothing wrong with waiting for the right guy, and I respect you for doing it." He paused when a look of disbelief appeared on her pretty face. "What?"

The corners of her mouth twitched as she held back a smirk. "I find it hard to believe you respect my long-term virginity when you own a sex club."

He let out a small snort. "Okay, I can see your point, but what I said was true. Guys have no trouble losing their virginity and having sex with any willing woman, but women are wired differently. Sex is more emotional for them . . . well, most of them. I hope my niece waits for the right guy, and don't even think of making me believe she is anything but a virgin."

"Yeah, well, in my case, the right guy didn't come along. My ex-husband had been cheating on me the whole time we were dating and while we were married. But I didn't find out until it was too late. The skanks he preferred wouldn't look like a good wife for a respected stockbroker, like the goody-two-shoes I was."

"What an asshole—excuse my language."

Kristen couldn't help snickering at him. "Let's see, you've told me you want to fuck me on a table and spank my ass, so calling my ex an asshole is rather tame."

He laughed along with her. "All right, enough about your ex-fudge pecker. Tell me about *you*."

"Little ol' me?"

Devon pointed his fork at her before digging into his salad again. "Yes, Pet. Little ol' you. Start talking, or I'll add to the count of thirteen."

"You wouldn't." She gaped.

"Fourteen."

"All right, all right. Has anyone ever said you would make a good interrogator?"

"Fifteen."

"I was born in a log cabin . . ."

He rolled his eyes. She was pushing her luck. "Sixteen."

"No, it's true. I was born in a log cabin. My parents went to my dad's family's cabin in the Poconos a month before my mom's due date. They figured it would be the last chance they had to get away, just the two of them. The next morning, Mom woke up in full-blown labor. She didn't realize she'd been in labor for over twenty-four hours because the contractions weren't that strong until, all of a sudden, she felt the need to push. Before my dad had a chance to get her to the car, I started crowning, and, whoops, there I was. Dad was a cop, but he'd never delivered a baby before. He did fine until the ambulance got there. After he let the EMTs in, though, he passed out, hit his head on a table, and needed ten stitches. He always said that's why I was an only child."

They laughed as the waiter replaced their salad plates with their dinners. Devon asked the young man for another round of drinks before turning his attention back to her. "I think I would've done and said the same thing. I've seen a lot in my life, things that would scare the hell out of most people, but delivering a kid would send me into a panic—and I never panic." He paused as a busboy stopped and refilled their water glasses. "So, okay, you're an only child. Are your folks still around?"

She nodded and picked up her knife and fork. "Yes. They divorced when I was ten. Mom, Elizabeth, was an elementary school teacher and never learned how to live with a cop who was always called into work on days off and holidays. His rotating shifts didn't help matters. Although he's always been a good father, Mom said Dad wasn't even close to being a part-time husband. Looking back, I'm surprised their marriage lasted as long as it did. As divorces go, it was friendly. No fighting over who gets what or those sorts of things. Dad, his name is Bill, got remarried when I was fifteen to a nice lady named Susan, who works in the courts. He retired from the Philadelphia police department two years later. He's now teaching criminal justice at the community college. Mom and my step-dad, Ed—he's an insurance adjuster—eloped to Vegas three months after my wedding and moved to the Jersey shore a few months later. I have two older step-brothers, but we barely know each other. They live near their mom, about an hour from where we lived."

"So, did you always live in Philadelphia? When did you move here?"

"Actually, we lived a few miles outside Philly in New Hope, and then I lived in Ridgewood, New Jersey, after I got married. I only moved here a few weeks ago after my divorce was final."

"Why here?"

Kristen chewed and swallowed a piece of veal before answering him. "My cousin, Will, has lived in Tampa for six or seven years, and I loved the area the few times I visited him. I wanted a new start, so here I am. What about you? Have you always lived in Tampa?"

"No. My brothers and I were born and raised in Charlotte, North Carolina. After the Navy, Ian and I decided to open our security business here. Mitch was raised here, and like you, we visited a lot and liked it. We were still getting our security firm on its feet when Mitch approached us about the club, and the rest, as they say, is history."

"It must've been difficult and expensive. The club is beautiful, and I can't imagine what it took to transform the place while starting another business. And, oh my God, it sounds like I'm trying to find out how much money you have. Don't answer—I don't want to know. I'm just going to remove my foot from my mouth." She was babbling but couldn't stop. It was a bad habit which occurred when she was embarrassed.

Devon didn't look upset—instead, he seemed amused. He held out a piece of steak and peppers on his fork. "Here, replace your foot with this."

When she reached for the fork, he pulled his hand back. "Uh-uh, Pet. Open your mouth and close your eyes. I want to feed you."

* * *

Kristen's eyes widened before she leaned forward and did as he requested. He eased the fork into her mouth, taking care not to stab her with the tines. When she closed her lips around the fork and moaned as the flavors hit her tongue, he would have sold his soul at that moment to replace it with his throbbing cock. He eased the fork out of her mouth, allowing her to chew and swallow the food. "Mmmm, it's delicious."

Clearing his throat, he shifted in his seat. "Glad you like it. I'd offer you more, but I think if I did, I'd come in my pants."

Her eyes flew open again, and she had to see the desire in his eyes. Swallowing, she shifted her gaze back to her plate. "Um . . . so . . . um . . . what about you? You said you have a brother, Ian. Any others? Are your folks still in Charlotte?"

Devon paused for a moment. He always found it difficult to talk about his brothers. It was also one of the reasons he never dated outside the club. With a submissive, they didn't need to know him beyond the surface, beyond what he was willing to give. He rarely mentioned John to people who inquired about his family since it always made the conversation depressive and awkward. "We have a younger brother, Nick. He's in the Navy stationed in San Diego. Ian's the oldest. Mom and Dad are still based in Charlotte but travel a lot. My dad, Chuck, is in real estate and has done well for himself. He has a corporation now with a board that runs it for him when he's out of the country with Mom—Marie. She's a plastic surgeon, although now she only practices in Charlotte enough to maintain her hospital privileges. She has a small stake in a practice with four other doctors, but her main focus is working in third-world countries for Operation Smile."

"Isn't Operation Smile the organization which offers surgeries for kids with cleft lips or palates?"

He nodded and took a sip of tonic water. "Or other facial deformities, yes. When we were young, my brothers and I traveled all over the world with my folks, and by the time I went into the Navy, I was on my third passport. We spent every summer digging wells, building schools and huts, and everything else we could do to help."

"Wow, that's amazing!" She sounded impressed, and it pleased him even though it hadn't been his intent. "I've never been out of the United States except for Jamaica on my honeymoon. And the most I ever did when I was younger was volunteer at the animal shelter five minutes from my house."

He could imagine a younger Kristen playing with, and caring for, a bunch of animals looking for forever homes. She probably cried after each one got adopted. "Yeah, well, it was fun when we were younger, but by the time we were in junior high, we wanted to stay home and hang out with our friends and girlfriends—typical teenage selfishness. When we hit high school and started working, my grandparents on my mom's side would spend the summer at our house, so my folks could do their thing. Nowadays, though, Ian and I try to take a week or so a few times a year to meet up with my parents in whatever country they're in. We do what we can to make some poor village a little less desperate for the people there."

* * *

Kristen could tell how much he loved his family by listening to the affection in his voice. Although her parents and step-parents got along well, and she loved them all, she sometimes wished her folks were still together and had given her a brother or a sister.

"Kristen."

She looked up, realizing her mind had wandered as the waiter was clearing their plates while Devon stared at her.

"I'm sorry, what?"

"Did you want coffee or dessert?"

"Oh, no thanks. I'm full." *And I want to leave for The*

Covenant and jump your bones—but she wouldn't say that out loud. Too bad they weren't allowed to play at the club.

"We'll take the check, thanks," Devon told the waiter, who nodded before taking their plates to the kitchen.

As he reached into his pocket for his wallet, Kristen jumped and grabbed her evening bag. "Let me split this with you."

She froze when he let out a low growl. "If you take anything other than lipstick out of your purse, I will pull you across my lap right here and spank you until the cops show up."

Stunned by his fierce expression, she left her purse on the seat beside her. "I just thought since this was our first date, and I was the one to ask you out—"

He held up his hand. "Do not finish the sentence. Under no circumstances will I let you put a penny toward our dinner. You may have asked me out, but it was only because I thought you were seeing Brody. Otherwise, I would have done it. I've never allowed a woman to pay for dinner, and I won't start now."

"Isn't that a little sexist?" She sat back and placed her hands in her lap, a little put off by his reaction.

He leaned forward, his arms resting on the table. "You may have written a book based on BDSM, but you still don't completely understand the lifestyle. Let me explain something about Doms to you, Pet. We like to . . . no . . . we demand to be in charge when it comes to certain things. Aside from the sexual aspect, we want to ensure our sub's safety and comfort. To treat them as if they are the most precious thing on this earth. I know a few Doms who will tell you their favorite part of a scene is the aftercare because it's when their subs need them the most. It's when they connect the most.

"We care for our subs, giving them everything we can and wishing we could give them the moon if they asked for it—whether for one night only or a long-term relationship. We don't do it because we're sexist or think they can't care for themselves. We do it because it pleases us in a way you can't imagine. We crave it beyond the basic human instinct and need to have sex. The lifestyle is so much more than kinky sex and giving up or taking control. And all we Doms expect from our subs in return is respect and obedience . . . well, that and their orgasms. Now if you want to argue with me about money, I will be more than happy to continue the count. I believe we're at sixteen."

She'd tilted her head as she listened to all he said. She'd been looking for this when she'd gone to The Covenant for research. There was only so much she could find on the internet, but what she hadn't been able to comprehend was the passion and need for a Dom to take control. Now she understood that part of BDSM, but she still had to discover why a submissive needed to give up control. "No, it's fifteen. You said sixteen when you thought I was lying about the log cabin."

"Well, now it's back to sixteen for arguing with me about the count and the check."

"That's not fair," she huffed, crossing her arms like a petulant child.

Devon chuckled, and when the waiter returned with a small leather folder, he handed over his credit card. "Whoever said life is fair, Pet, wasn't a Dom."

CHAPTER SEVEN

The assassin took a swig of whiskey and watched as Eric Prichard rounded the corner onto County Road #32. The former Navy SEAL was starting the fourth mile of his evening run with four more miles to go. It wouldn't be dark for another forty minutes or so, and the target would be turning around at a bank of mailboxes a little further up the road to backtrack toward his home. But if the coast was clear this time, he wasn't going to finish those last four miles. The assassin had been observing the man's habits for the past week, looking for his opportunity to strike.

After locating Prichard, he realized he would have to do the job away from the man's residence. The former SEAL and his wife had four children, and even though the assassin killed people for profit without a second thought, he drew the line at murdering children. It was the only time his conscience wouldn't let him kill unless necessary, but oddly enough, the moment a kid turned eighteen, they were considered expendable. Had his earlier target's eighteen-year-old daughter been home when he broke into their house and shot her parents six months ago, she would have been a third body the police found. A slumber party saved her from certain death.

It'd been three months since his last kill for the man paying him because the bastard didn't want to get his own hands dirty. The first kill on the list of seven men occurred six months ago. His temporary employer wanted them spaced out, so no one would notice a pattern. Seven dead former Navy SEALs from the same team would raise a lot of questions, but by that time, there would be no one left who could figure out the hows and whys. After he took out Prichard, the assassin would head to Tampa to track the last four names on his execution list—Ian Sawyer, his brother Devon Sawyer, Brody Evans, and Jake Donovan. He would have to find a way to take them out together while still making it look like an accident since, according to the files he had been given, they worked and hung out together along with two other former SEALs. He might be able to take out one or two before they realized they were targeted and went underground, making it much harder to kill the rest of them.

Stalking men who had been trained to do the stalking themselves was a delicate job. Over a week ago, he'd found a used car dealership two towns over from the bum-fuck town in Iowa where his target lived. The business lacked decent security, so he'd picked the lock to the office in under a minute and helped himself to the keys to their available vehicles, some of which were kept in an overflow lot a few blocks away. Using a different car and different disguise each day, he was able to keep his target from spotting him, but there had been a few moments when the man seemed to sense he was being watched, so the assassin had to be smarter than his prey.

Finishing a count to three hundred, the killer-for-hire put the car in gear, took one last sip from his flask, and pulled out from behind an abandoned laundromat. By now, his target would be running back toward town on a straight-away while facing oncoming traffic. Although the man ran along the narrow shoulder, he didn't flinch when cars drove past. He'd passed Prichard twice this week on his run, but there had been cars with witnesses on the road.

Taking the turn Prichard had disappeared around minutes before, the assassin straightened the steering wheel and accelerated to the posted fifty-miles-per-hour speed limit. His target was where he expected the man to be, unknowingly running at a decent clip toward his tragic death.

One hundred yards. He could see the target's black shirt, military green sweatpants, and white sneakers.

Fifty yards. He could read the yellow lettering, spelling out "U.S. Navy" on the man's chest.

Twenty yards. The target looked at his watch and upped his pace.

Ten yards. The dead man running made eye contact with him a split second before the assassin swerved.

A half-hour later, he dropped off the used and now damaged car, wiped it clean of prints, and retrieved his own vehicle. He typed off a one-word text on his burner cell —*Done*—then pulled out onto the road leading to the interstate, where he would dismantle the phone and throw a part out the window every few miles.

CHAPTER EIGHT

Once they were on their way to The Covenant, Kristen became nervous again. She had been twisting her hands together until Devon reached over, took hold of her left hand, intertwined their fingers, and rested them on her thigh. His thumb was now brushing her thigh, below her hemline, back and forth. With those soft, reassuring caresses, she tried to settle into the comfortable silence and let her mind wander.

She hadn't thought she would be interested in BDSM, but after her interaction with Devon earlier at the club, she wasn't sure now. She'd been so turned on she'd ended up masturbating in the shower before Kayla and Will got there. And instead of Master Xavier urging her on, this time, it'd been Master Devon.

"I meant to ask you earlier, but we got a little sidetracked. Did you bring your limit list with you?"

Kristen turned her head to examine his profile as he drove. "Yes, it's folded in my purse. I also reviewed the protocols."

He nodded and glanced at her before returning his attention to the road. "Good. I'll look over your list when we get to the club. Do you have any questions about the protocols?"

She thought back to the papers she had read. Most of the rules were pretty straightforward, but she still wanted to clarify a few of them. "Yes, I do. Some rules were listed under the heading 'High Protocols' while others weren't. How do I know when to follow the 'High Protocol' rules?"

* * *

Devon had been happy when she agreed to leave her car near the restaurant and ride to the club with him. He left the convertible top closed, not wanting the wind to ruin her styled hair. He wanted to save the pleasure for later when he got a chance to run his fingers through those soft brown curls. "Most members follow the relaxed protocols unless we have an event requiring the more rigid ones, and everyone is notified of those in advance. A few Doms insist their subs follow the stricter rules, but if one approaches you, I'll let you know. If it does happen, remember to keep your head bowed, do not make eye contact with the Dom or their sub, if they have one, and ask my permission to speak before saying anything to them. Never be rude to a Dom in any situation. You'll be next to me most of the time, but if for some reason I'm not there and a Dom is bothering you, immediately look for a Dungeon Master who wears a gold vest or a security officer who wears a red, button-down shirt with a black bowtie, and let them know. Just because you're a submissive does not give a Dom or another submissive permission to harass you for any reason. Most of our members are not a problem, but like every large group, it has its jackasses and bitches."

"What's the difference between the Dungeon Masters and the security officers?"

He squeezed her hand before releasing it, needing both

hands to navigate the sharp turn from the highway ramp to the road leading to the club. He missed the warmth and reclaimed her hand as soon as possible. "The Dungeon Masters are experienced Doms who keep an eye on the scenes throughout the club. I think we have a total of thirty-two of them. They ensure all play at the club is safe, and keep the subs from getting injured, in case a Dom overlooks something, such as a restraint too tight or a sub not using their safeword when they should. The security officers keep an eye on everything else and are the club's bouncers."

A confused expression came over her face. "Why would a submissive not use their safeword when it's obvious to a monitor they should?"

Devon sighed as he stopped two cars back from the guard shack at the entrance to the club parking lot. The lead car must be either a newer member or a guest the guard didn't recognize because he checked the driver's ID with a hand-held computer. It was another one of Brody's toys the club used regularly. "Sometimes what a sub thinks they want isn't what they need, and not saying their safeword can be destructive behavior. How can I explain it?" He paused. "Do you know what 'cutting' is?"

"I've heard of that. Isn't it when a person, sometimes teenagers, cut their arms with razor blades?"

The line of cars was moving again, and the guard waved at Devon as he passed. "People who cut themselves to feel whatever they are looking to feel don't cut deep enough to bleed out, but it's still dangerous. They feel compelled to cut themselves, for whatever reason, causing damage to their bodies, and they usually can't stop without psychological help. It's what a sub who doesn't use their safeword when they should, is doing—damaging themselves to feel whatever it is they are trying to feel. A good Dom needs to know how to find the fine line between what a sub needs to make them feel good and what's going too far and damaging the sub's psyche and body. If a DM thinks a sub is pushing himself or herself too far, to the point of severe injury via a Dom, the sub is referred to one of our contracted psychologists and can't play again unless they get an okay from the doctor. It doesn't happen often, but we're serious about our submissives' safety here—physically, psychologically, and emotionally."

He'd parked his car a few minutes earlier and finished his explanation before opening his car door. When she reached for the latch to open her own door, he stopped her. "Do not even think of opening your door. Stay there until I come around, or I'll add to your spanking count."

She laughed out loud, and he couldn't help but grin at her amusement. "Is this something that brings you pleasure, Master Devon?"

God, how he loved how she combined his title with his name. He'd heard it from the mouths of hundreds of subs over the years, but never had a woman gotten him hard by saying those two words—until now. "Yes, my little subbie, it is. Now stay there."

He adjusted himself as he walked around the back of his car and then opened her door. Putting his hand out to help her up from the low seat, he couldn't tear his eyes away as the hemline of her dress crept further up her legs when she exited the car. He was almost tempted to push it up a little further to see whether she was bare between her legs. Bare was his personal preference. "Didn't your ex ever open your door for you?"

"Now that you mention it, no, he didn't."

"Well, there's another reason to hate the selfish prick-bastard."

Kristen laughed at him again as she tugged her skirt back down, which wouldn't go further than the middle of her thighs. "You don't know him. How can you say you hate him?"

Reaching into his pocket, he retrieved the item he had placed there earlier. "Easily, Pet. Any man who would cheat on, disrespect, and leave a beautiful woman like you deserves to be despised and degraded by the rest of his gender." He held up his hand and let the object dangle from it so she could see it. "This is a training collar, Pet. You'll wear it while you're here at the club with me. It'll let the other Doms know you're spoken for, and they're not allowed to try and negotiate with you or demand you follow a certain protocol without my permission. I may order you to kneel, but another Dom would have to get my approval for them to tell you to do the same, except in extreme cases. Some Doms like to tease the subs, and it's not considered rude here unless it's insulting, and I will not allow anyone to insult you. If I have to leave you for some reason, I'll ask a DM or security to watch you until I return. Understood?"

"Yes, Sir." She nodded and turned around, lifting her hair so he could fasten the collar around her neck. It was a simple black leather band, and he regretted not having a nicer one to give her. He'd never had a sub wear one of his collars for more than a weekend, but this time, he didn't want to think about un-collaring her when they were done playing tonight.

When she turned back around, fingering the leather band, he found his hands reaching up to cup her face. Looking into her hazel eyes, he lowered his mouth to hers, a scant inch at a time, waiting for her to stop him, to let him know she didn't want this. But she didn't stop him, and he sent a silent thanks to whomever or whatever brought this woman to him.

The second his mouth touched hers, her eyes fluttered

shut. The kiss was light, a soft brushing of his mouth against hers until she sighed and her lips parted, granting him entry. He deepened the kiss, darting his tongue into her mouth to tangle with hers, dying for a taste of her. He savored the sweetness of her wine, the tartness of the lemon from her dinner, and something delicious and unique to Kristen. And for tonight, she belonged to him. He just didn't know how he would be able to let her go when they were done playing.

Mine.

When her hands began to move up his arms toward his neck, he grabbed her wrists and put a reluctant end to the kiss. Her eyes reopened as if she was waking from a long slumber, and he smiled. "Sorry, Pet, but if I let you touch me, I'll go off like a rocket."

He pressed his hips to hers to make his point. He gave her another quick kiss before releasing her wrists, turning her to his side, and tucking her one hand under his arm. Thankfully, it was normal to see men walking around the club with hard-ons because his wasn't going down anytime soon.

Moments later, they were standing in the lobby at the front desk, which was being attended by a slight but toned man who was about Kristen's age. He was shirtless but wore black dress pants and a red bow tie with gold trim. The man smiled and nodded at her before speaking to Devon. "Good evening, Master Devon. How are you tonight?"

"I'm good, Matthew. And you?"

"Very good, Sir, since I'm scheduled to scene with Mistress China later."

Devon winced, knowing the sub's cock and balls would be tortured before the night ended. It wasn't something Devon could imagine subjecting his man parts to, but the younger sub enjoyed it.

"Matthew, this is Ms. Kristen, my guest this evening. Kristen, Matthew is one of the club's long-time employees, and he's also a submissive. If you ever have any questions, he can answer them from a sub's point of view."

When she nodded, he took her arm and extended it outward over the desk so that Matthew could place a yellow band around her wrist. When he was done, the sub patted her hand. "It's nice to meet you, Kristen. This indicates you're a guest and not allowed to participate in any play. And Master Devon is right. If you have any questions, I'm an expert on club protocol. By the way, love your dress."

Kristen smiled at his friendly manner. "Thank you, and it's nice to meet you, too."

Devon tucked her hand under his arm again before leading her to a large man dressed in black slacks and a red button-down shirt standing next to the wooden doors leading into the club. "Kristen, this is Tiny, the head of security. Tiny, this is Kristen."

SHE TILTED HER HEAD UP . . . AND UP . . . AND UP. GOOD LORD, the man was tall . . . and broad. He was about six foot eight and two-hundred-seventy-five pounds of solid muscle. His neck was too thick to close the top button of his shirt, so he was without a bowtie. Bald with a goatee, he reminded Kristen of a wrestler from the eighties who became an actor, Mr. G, or something like that. The only thing he was missing was the gold chains. "Tiny?"

The man laughed and gave her a wink. "Yes, ma'am. My real name is Travis, but I've gone by Tiny since I weighed thirteen pounds at birth. It's a pleasure to meet you."

Before she could reply, Devon spoke again. "Tiny, would

you be so kind as to keep an eye on my sub for a few minutes while I run and change? I'm afraid she'll cause a riot inside if I leave her unattended."

"Absolutely, Master Devon. I don't doubt she'd cause trouble in there. The Doms will fall all over themselves the second they spot this cute little thing." Tiny stepped to the left and revealed a stool she hadn't known was behind him. "Have a seat up here, Ms. Kristen, and I'll keep the big, bad Doms from killing each other trying to get at you."

She doubted that would happen but still smiled at his compliment. "Thank you, Master Tiny."

"Uh-uh, Ms. Kristen. It's just Tiny since I'm not a Dom, nor do I participate in the lifestyle. I only work here to check out pretty ladies like yourself and pound on the occasional idiot who gets out of hand."

She laughed and relaxed again. "I get the feeling you're nothing but a big teddy bear."

"Hey, I like it. Tiny the teddy bear."

Devon helped her up on the stool before giving her a fast kiss on the lips. "Take out your list and hand me your purse. You won't need it inside, so I'll put it in my locker for safekeeping." She did as he requested and handed him both. "I'll be right back, Pet. Stay here with Tiny, and you'll be fine."

"Yes, sir."

He grinned and then disappeared through the big wooden doors leading into the club. The pounding music increased in volume before becoming a dull beat when the door closed again. She felt a little self-conscious sitting on the stool and turned toward the big man beside her after tugging at her dress to keep from flashing him. "So, how long have you worked here?"

He opened the door to allow a couple to walk in and

waited until the music died down before answering her. "Ever since the club opened. Have you met Master Jake yet?"

Jake was the man who met Devon at the pub the day before while they were making their dinner plans. "Yes, I think so, but only briefly, and I didn't know he was a Dom then."

Tiny leaned against the wall, crossing his arms over his massive chest, and Kristen couldn't help but wonder what size shirt the man wore. "Jake and I go way back to our high school football days. After I got injured in the pros, I ended up doing bodyguard work in Hollywood. Then a few years ago, while I was down here visiting family, I ran into Jake, and he recommended me to Ian and Devon. When they offered me a job, I moved as fast as possible from L.A. I still do occasional bodyguard work for them when needed, but mostly I'm in charge of the club's security."

She found it odd he was working in a BDSM club yet not participating in the lifestyle and told him so.

The big man shrugged. "To each his own. Even though it's not for me personally, it doesn't mean I find anything wrong with the lifestyle. Like I said earlier, at least I get to see a lot of pretty girls in hot outfits. And just when I thought I'd seen it all, something happens that makes me laugh. It can be pretty entertaining working here."

"I'll bet. I'm glad you found a job you enjoy." Kristen watched as Tiny opened the doors to allow three women in various states of dress to enter the main club and thought she was a little overdressed. One woman was wearing a black leather mini-skirt and a matching bustier which left her midsection exposed. The shortest of the three had on a red satin and sheer teddy which stopped an inch above her knees, while the last one wore a sheer, black dress shirt over a bra and thong set. Two of them wore ballet-type slippers instead of shoes, but the blonde in the skirt had removed her slippers and held them in her hand, opting to go barefoot. Although two of the women were on the skinny side, the one wearing the teddy was a size or two larger than Kristen, and she wondered if she would be as confident looking as the other woman had she been wearing a similar outfit.

After the door closed again, she looked back up at Tiny. "Do you miss playing football?"

He tilted his head as if thinking about his answer before verbalizing it. "Yeah, I do, sometimes. But unlike some guys who go pro, I knew I wouldn't play forever. And when life hands you lemons . . ."

"You make lemonade," she finished the cliché for him.

"If you have a lemonade stand, little one, I'd be more than happy to stop by for a taste." A deep, male voice startled her, and she tensed before turning to find a strange man standing a little too close for her comfort, although he wasn't touching her. "I'm sure anything you have to offer would be the sweetest of fruit."

She gaped at the man who was now devouring her with his gaze. This was what she had expected Master Mitch to look like when she met him. If she had to guess, the man was in his fifties, with a pointed nose, narrow eyes, and a mustache. His black hair was graying at the temples and upper lip. Slender, he stood about six-foot even and was dressed in a black dress shirt and leather pants with black boots. Never taking his leering stare off her, he addressed the large security guard. "Tell me, Tiny, who is this gorgeous creature? I see she has a collar. I may have to challenge her Dom to a duel to win her favor."

Was this guy for real? She looked up to see Tiny smiling down at her, and she relaxed only a fraction when he winked again at her. "Good evening, Master Carl. This is Ms. Kristen, a guest of Master Devon."

The older man sighed and frowned before he took a small step backward. "Such a pity since he can kill a man in many ways, I'm sure. Master Devon is a lucky man, but please find me when he removes your collar, girl. I would love to play with you for an evening. I guarantee I'd make it most enjoyable for both of us."

An involuntary shudder passed through her body as she watched the man disappear through the club doors. She didn't like how he'd said, *"when* he removes your collar," instead of *if,* and reached up to touch the thin band wrapped around her neck, not wanting to think this might be her only evening with Devon.

"Unless you're into a great deal of pain, you might want to avoid Master Carl. He's actually a nice guy but a sadist."

Kristen's eyes widened, but before she could respond to Tiny's comment, the doors next to him reopened, and Devon stepped back out into the lobby. Her mouth watered at the sight of him. He'd changed out of his dinner clothes and was now wearing a tight, black T-shirt that showed off his defined arms and torso. A pair of black leather pants hugged his lower body like they had been painted on. Replacing a zipper, the crotch was laced up and showcased the large bulge behind it.

He grabbed her hips and helped her off the stool, pulling her close so their lower bodies made contact. "Ready?"

"I-I think so."

Tiny spoke up at the tremble in her voice. "She met Master Carl a minute ago."

Devon rolled his eyes. "Wonderful. He really needs to stop scaring the new subs." The sarcasm was evident in his voice, but then he became serious. "Relax, Pet. You're safe with me. No one will touch you in there except for me. If you have any questions, just ask. And if something makes you uncomfortable, tell me. I won't be upset if something bothers you, but I will be if you keep it from me. A major portion of this lifestyle depends on verbal communication between a Dom and sub."

The tension in her shoulders eased slightly, but she was still worried. "What if I make a mistake?"

He brought his hand up to cup her chin. "You're bound to make a few mistakes, and it's expected. Everyone in there was new to the lifestyle at one point, and mistakes happen. Okay?"

When she nodded, he frowned and raised his brow. It took her a second to figure out what was wrong. "I mean, yes, Sir."

Taking her hand, he nodded at Tiny and started for the doors. "Besides, mistakes lead to punishment, and punishment leads to pleasure for both of us . . . eventually."

Kristen's mouth dropped at his evil yet amused tone of voice. What was she getting herself into?

Devon stood next to Kristen at the balcony railing and watched her face as she took in the sights, sounds, and smells of the club. Despite the early hour of nine-thirty, the club was close to being full, but due to the square footage of the building, there was still plenty of room for members to walk around without having to fight their way through a crowd. Many of the activity stations in the pit were occupied, and the sounds of spanking, flogging, and ecstasy battled with the music filling the air. The beat of an instrumental version of the Rolling Stones' "Satisfaction" pulsed throughout the club. Ian had found a company that made elevator music from every possible genre. Wednesdays and Sundays, the music tended to be sensual jazz. Thursdays leaned more toward punk, techno, and Goth, while Fridays and Saturdays usually had classic rock mixed with heavy metal pouring from the hidden speakers. The genre was subject to change if they were having a theme night, which was about once every two months.

When they first walked into the bar area, several members greeted them, and he introduced the Doms and subs to Kristen. She'd been polite to everyone even though there were several times he knew she was trying hard not to stare at some of the states of undress. If they weren't used to it, people tended to have difficulty talking to a naked or almost naked person's face while their private body parts were exposed. It was like being a virgin who'd never seen a naked body, walking through a nudist colony—you didn't want to stare, but it was hard not to.

As he watched her try to look everywhere at once, he breathed in deep the aromas of leather, citrus, and sex, but it was the fresh, enticing scent of the woman next to him which held him captivated. He glanced around the upper floor and spotted several members of both sexes giving Kristen appreciative and interested looks. For the first time in his life, he fought the emotion of jealousy that was running through his veins. He wanted to strip her naked right where she stood and fuck her like a wild beast staking the claim of its mate for the entire world to see.

The thought of another Dom collaring her after he moved on to another sub like he always did, made his stomach clench in pain. These feelings were new and strange to him, and he didn't like or know how to deal with them. He didn't do relationships, and he'd nothing to offer her beyond an introduction to his lifestyle and a weekend filled with intense pleasure and orgasms. The rules may state they weren't allowed to play at the club, but he had every intention of taking her back to his place, at some point, where there would be no restrictions other than her hard limits. But the notion of sending her away at the end of the weekend felt like a hot poker to his chest.

He watched as her eyes widened at the screaming of a female sub coming hard somewhere in the pit below them. Her nipples were distended, pushing at the fabric of her dress, and he could sense her arousal. He wanted to dip his fingers under her dress and run them through what he knew would be her soaked folds. It appeared his little pet was a voyeur, and he couldn't wait to let her observe a few scenes tonight. While in the locker room, he'd looked over her soft and hard limit list and been pleased with most of her choices, but he did have a few questions for her about them later.

Her tongue darted out to moisten her lips, and he wished she was on her knees in front of him, using that same tongue to taste and tease him. He was torturing himself with his fantasies of her, and it took all his strength not to drag her off club property and fuck her silly. "Would you like something to drink? Since we won't be playing here, I can get you another glass of wine, or would you prefer something else?"

"Water would be fine, please." The two glasses of wine she had with dinner were all she could tolerate and still be able to keep her wits about her. She wanted to be able to take in and remember everything she saw tonight so she could recall it all while writing tomorrow. She planned on letting Master Xavier and Rebecca have some wild monkey sex in the next chapter.

Devon stopped a bow-tied waitress walking by and grabbed two bottles of water from her tray. "Thank you,

Cassandra," he said before sending the girl on her way again and handing one of the bottles to Kristen. "Bottles of water are the only beverages allowed in the pit. Many of the subs walk around barefoot, and we don't want them to risk being cut by any broken glass."

She looked down at her shoes. "Should I take these off?"

Taking her hand and leading her to the grand staircase, he smiled. "Usually, I prefer subs to be barefoot, but I love how sexy those killer heels make your legs look, so I want you to keep them on unless, of course, they start to bother you." And yes, he was definitely going to fuck her at some point while she was wearing nothing but those shoes.

He nodded at one of the security guards at the top of the stairs and pointed to Kristen's yellow bracelet before walking past the man. As the owners, Devon, Ian, and Mitch were the only three people who didn't have key cards, which needed to be checked before descending into the pit, and her wristband indicated she wasn't allowed to participate in a scene.

As they descended the stairs, Kristen held onto his arm with one hand and the banister with the other. "I've always loved to wear high heels. I'm so used to them and can wear them for hours before I want to rip them off." She'd discovered designer Manolo Blahnik's shoes to be extremely comfortable, despite the height of the heels, and she owned a few pairs. They'd become her one major indulgence after the sales of her books had increased, giving her a tidy savings account. It hadn't surprised her that Tom never asked how much she had in the account, which was in her name only. He couldn't imagine her books would ever be popular to the point she could live off the sales and still have money to splurge on a few indulgences. Boy, was he shocked during their divorce proceedings when he found out.

When they reached the bottom of the stairs, Kristen noticed a woman, a few years older than herself, hurrying toward them. She was wearing a hot pink bra and short pleated skirt that were only a few shades lighter than her bright pink straight hair, which fell below her shoulders. The petite woman stopped right in front of them and opened her mouth to say something to Kristen, but then her eyes widened a fraction, and she closed her mouth again. Turning toward Devon, she lowered her gaze to the floor. "I'm sorry, Master Devon, forgive my impatience. May I please have permission to speak to your sub?"

He smiled at the sub. "Permission granted, and by the way, happy birthday." He then looked at Kristen and nodded. She took it to mean she was also allowed to speak.

"Thank you, Sir." The pink-haired girl turned back to Kristen and began talking with exuberance. "Oh my gosh! You're her . . . you're you . . . you're Kristen Anders. I recognize you from your promo pictures."

Realization struck Kristen. "Are you Shelby?"

"Yes! I can't believe we're finally meeting. I mean, we've been chatting online for so long I feel like we're already friends, but it's so awesome to meet you in person."

She always enjoyed the online conversations with the beta-reader, but now she found she liked the woman even more. She had such a bubbly personality which made Kristen think of rainbows and puppies. "It's so nice to meet you, and happy birthday. I can't thank you enough for putting me in touch with Master Mitch. He gave me a lot of information to help me with my next book."

"I'm glad I could help. Did you start writing it yet? Who did you pick for the hero?"

Kristen laughed at her enthusiasm. Her beta-readers had been trying to get her to nail down the lead character for *Leather and Lace* for several weeks now, but she hadn't told them yet whom she chose. "The winner is Master Xavier."

Shelby squealed and clapped her hands like an excited child. "I knew it! I fell in love with him during the scene you had him do in the pool with Master Greg and Annette in *Satin and Sin*. He sounds like the ultimate dreamboat."

As the two subs chatted, Devon looked up to see Brody approaching with a broad smile. The geek wore his usual dark T-shirt, snug blue jeans, and brown cowboy boots. He preferred the well-worn jeans over leathers, saying they were more comfortable since he'd been born and raised in Texas ranching country.

Stopping next to him, his friend clapped Devon on the shoulder. "You're a lucky man, Devil Dog." He tilted his head toward Kristen. "She's hot, but there's got to be something wrong with her since she picked your sorry ass over mine. When she shot me down, I thought maybe she played for the other team. I must admit, though, I was a little surprised when Jake mentioned you were on a date tonight. I didn't think you knew what the word meant."

Devon smacked the man's shoulder with the back of his hand. "Knock it off, Egghead."

His buddy chuckled and changed the subject, but Devon knew once Kristen was out of hearing distance, Brody would continue to bust his chops. "Have you spoken to Marco today?"

Keeping an eye on the women next to him, still chatting

about Kristen's books and her recent move, Devon shook his head. "No, I haven't. How's his sister doing?"

Brody's face became somber. "Not good at all. The doctors told them this morning to bring Hospice in as soon as possible. She's only got a few weeks left at the most." Marco's sister, Nina, had been battling inoperable brain cancer for over a year, but a month ago, they discovered it'd spread to most of her major organs. Now Devon knew they would need to give their friend a leave of absence so he could spend as much time as possible with her. "The only reason he's here tonight is for Shelby's birthday. She asked us last week if we would tag-team her tonight to celebrate, and you know how much I like that. The little girl right there has one of the most talented tongues I've ever had the pleasure of licking my dick."

Both men laughed, and then Brody interrupted the women's conversation. "Hey, birthday girl, your spanking bench is almost ready. Why don't you go over there and keep Master Marco company for a few minutes? Give him a little sass so he can look forward to your birthday whacks."

Shelby's grin lit up the room. "Yes, Master Brody." Before she headed to the station reserved for her scene, she hugged Kristen and then turned toward Devon. "Thank you, Master Devon, for letting me talk to your sub. Besides Master Brody and Master Marco playing with me tonight, I think it was the best present I could get."

Devon reached out and gave the girl's pink hair a gentle tug. "It was my pleasure, little one. Enjoy your birthday."

As Shelby turned, Brody smacked the girl's backside, and she yelped but walked away with a smile. Brody then looked at Kristen and winked. "I'm a little offended you picked my boss here over me. I don't think it's ever happened before, but I'll get over it sooner or later. If you ask Master Devon,

I'm sure he'll let you watch our scene with Shelby in a little bit. She'll get her birthday whacks, along with a few birthday orgasms."

Kristen's eyes widened, and she bit her lower lip as her cheeks flamed red. Brody laughed at her expression. "Master Devon, I do believe your sub likes the idea. Bring her over in about ten minutes to the last bench, and I'll save a place for you upfront."

Devon was focused on his sub as he agreed with his friend. "I think you're right. She does like the idea. We'll be there in a little bit." He continued to stare at her as Brody left them standing a few feet to the left of the staircase. When she licked her lips again, he sensed her need and took the water bottle from her hand, unscrewing the cap before handing it back to her. "Drink up. You'll find it easy to get dehydrated in here."

She took a sip and then must have realized how thirsty she was because she guzzled some more. After she drank half the bottle, he took it from her again and replaced the cap. "We'll walk around on the way to their scene toward the back. But before we do, the locker rooms are right around the back of the stairs. Would you like to use the restroom?"

Now that he mentioned it . . . "Yes, Sir. I think I will."

He lifted his hand to cup her cheek and used his thumb to brush her plump bottom lip. "I like hearing the word 'Sir' from your lips. I can't wait to hear you say it while begging me to let you come." Her mouth gaped open at his statement, and he took the opportunity to push his thumb between her lips and rub it along her bottom teeth. Her tongue poked forward and licked the tip of his finger, and heat flared in his eyes. His dick hardened painfully, and he placed his other hand on her hip and pulled until she was flush against him from their chests to their thighs.

Bending forward, he replaced his thumb with his mouth and tongue. He didn't start the kiss as slowly and gently as he had in the parking lot. This time, he plunged right in, taking her intense passion as he gave her his. Their tongues dueled, first in her mouth and then, to his surprise and delight, in his, as she explored and tasted him. He took her arms, placed them on his shoulders, and left them there as his hands traveled south. One hand stopped to cup the weight of one of her breasts while the other went to her ass, and he squeezed her lush flesh. It took everything in him not to lift the bottom of her dress, pick her up, and impale her on his rigid cock.

He was about to grind his throbbing erection into her clit when the sound of a single tail whip split the air, followed by a low moan. The loud crack startled Kristen, and she jumped back, her mouth tearing away from his, her breath coming in hard pants which matched his own. As much as he wanted to draw her to him again, he knew if he did, he'd be in danger of breaking his own club's rule of no playing with guests. Kissing was one thing, but he wanted to do so much more to her than just that.

As they both recovered their breath, he took hold of her shoulders, turned her toward the door to the women's locker room, and gave her a gentle push. "Hurry back, Pet. I'll be waiting."

CHAPTER NINE

As Kristen disappeared into the locker room, Devon heard his name being called by someone coming down the stairs. Looking up, he saw his brother and cousin approaching him with amused grins. Both wore similar leather vests without shirts and leather pants, but where Ian's leathers were black, Mitch's were dark brown. Devon rolled his eyes at their expressions, knowing what was coming and there was no way to avoid it.

"So, little brother, I hear you went on a date tonight. Do you even know what to do on one of those?"

Of course, Mitch had to add his two cents. "I don't think the boy does, Ian, considering his date appears to have abandoned him."

"She's in the bathroom, ass-hat." It was times like this he hated being so close to his family. They never missed an opportunity to give him, or each other, a pile of shit.

"So, who's the lucky lady who managed to get you to pay for dinner before you screw her?"

"Fuck you, Ian."

"No thanks, I'm a pussy lover."

Devon growled, and Ian relented. "All right, all right, I'll be good. Who is she?"

"You remember the girl typing away on her laptop last week when we were at the pub?"

"The cute brunette you were drooling over in the mirror?" Of course, Ian would have noticed since the man never missed much. Devon rolled his eyes again and nodded. "Very nice. Mitch told me how you ran into her here earlier. Just be careful you don't end up being written into a chick-lit book. Everyone will find out about your small Irish dick."

His brother and cousin laughed again, and Devon was about to tell them both to fuck off when the door to the women's room flew open. He expected Kristen to walk out, but instead, a shy little sub named Colleen came running out, her eyes wide in panic.

"Master Mitch, Master Ian, hurry, please help!" She turned around and ran back into the locker room with Ian, Mitch, Devon, and one of the nearby bouncers following on her heels.

Ian and Mitch managed to get through the door first, and before he finished rounding the corner of the partition, Devon heard his brother bellow in his loudest Dom voice, "Stop!"

The female screeching and yelling in the room came to an abrupt halt. They hadn't been able to hear the commotion outside the locker room due to the pounding music.

Confused, Devon took in the incredulous scene before him and tried to figure out what the hell was going on. A sub named Heather was face down on the floor with Kristen sitting on her back. His date had the other girl's arm jacked up behind her back, and her hand was clenched around a mass of the redhead's hair. Another sub, Michelle, was sitting on the floor holding her stomach, trying to catch her breath, while Colleen was now standing in a corner to Devon's left, her eyes still wide and her hands covering her mouth as she stared at the other women. Although they were all quiet now, he could still hear the heavy breathing from the women on the ground.

While Mitch and the bouncer were as confused as Devon, Ian was downright pissed. Mitch managed The Covenant, but Ian was the head Dom, and Mitch often deferred to his cousin taking the lead in situations like this. The men watched as the three subs got to their feet, with Kristen taking two steps back to avoid Heather's swinging arms which were now loose again. "You bitch!"

"Enough!" Ian boomed, his anger evident. "Knees!"

Without faltering, Colleen, Heather, and Michelle dropped to the ground and presented themselves appropriately—on their knees, which were shoulder-width apart, their heads bowed, and their arms behind their backs, hands clasped around the opposite forearm. The only sub still standing was Kristen, who was staring at the other three in apparent shock.

Devon stepped forward, and her gaze swung up to meet his. He told her in a low, controlled voice, "I know this is new to you, Pet, but I suggest you drop to your knees as fast as you can." She hesitated. "Now."

OH CRAP! KRISTEN KNEW SHE'D SCREWED UP BIG THIS TIME. She fell to her knees, mirroring the other subs' postures as best she could. Once she was in position, she heard Devon whisper, "Sorry, Ian, this is new to her."

"Then she better learn fast, or her ass will be red for a month."

Is he serious? Yup, he probably is. Can this get any worse? Yup, it can.

She realized if it moved up another inch, the hem of her dress would give everyone a glimpse of her bare crotch. She was desperate to adjust it, but since she was in enough trouble, she let it stay where it was and prayed it didn't move. She kept her gaze on the floor in front of her, yet she was dying to look up to see what was going on but didn't dare. The door leading out to the club opened again, and she heard Tiny's voice.

"I got this in here, Anthony. Wait outside and keep everyone out. Kent is upstairs doing the same." The door closed again, blocking the music blaring out in the main room.

The man, Ian—she recognized him as one of the Sexy Six-Pack from when she'd first noticed Devon—spoke in a deep tone she had begun to refer to as a Dom's voice. "Does someone want to explain what the hell is going on here?"

Kristen and the girl in the corner, who was now crying quietly, didn't say anything, but the other two began talking over each other.

"We were just talking, and this bitch comes out of nowhere..."

"She attacked us for no reason..."

"She tried to break my arm..."

"Quiet!" Ian barked, obviously having reached the end of what little patience he had. "Michelle and Heather, go get your Masters and wait for me outside the office upstairs. I advise you to hurry because you do not want me to get there before you." Kristen didn't look, but one of the two must have tried to speak again as they got up because Ian added, "No. Upstairs with your Doms. I won't tell you again."

As the two women ran barefoot out the door, another

man walked in and looked around. Through her lashes, Kristen saw him drop to his knees and pull the crying girl into his arms to comfort her. The man appeared to be in his late thirties, while the girl was younger than Kristen's twenty-six years, but she thought they made a cute couple.

"What the hell is going on, Ian? Why is my sub in here crying?"

"I'm about to find out, Reggie." Ian closed the distance between himself and Kristen, and she saw his feet stop a few inches in front of her. His voice wasn't as harsh as it had been when he spoke, but she could tell he was still pissed. "Eyes up, sub."

She tilted her head back until she could see his face but remained silent as his eyes bore into her.

"Do you want to tell me what this is all about?"

Kristen's gaze went from the man looming over her to the young girl sobbing in her Dom's arms and back again. "No, Sir, I don't. Not at the moment."

She waited for him to yell at her, but instead, Ian raised his brow at her words and then proved he was astute. "Tiny, would you take Colleen to the office and wait with her inside, away from the others, please?"

Tiny stepped toward the couple as they got to their feet. "Come with me, Ms. Colleen. I'll take care of you until Master Reggie can join you again."

Colleen looked at Kristen, then at each of the Doms, tears still falling from her pretty eyes. Her lips trembled. "Please, Master Ian. It wasn't her fault. She was helping me."

Ian looked over his shoulder at the sub, and his voice softened. "Go upstairs, little one. Everything will be all right. I promise."

The girl started to say something else, but Master Reggie quickly kissed her before handing her off to the head guard.

"Go with Tiny, love. We'll get this all straightened out. I'll be upstairs in a few minutes."

After the young sub and head bouncer left, Ian took two small steps back, and his voice sounded weary. "Stand up, girl, and tell me what happened, although I have a feeling I already know."

Kristen stood, tugging the hem of her dress down as she did, and peered at the four Doms in the room staring back at her. She tried not to be intimidated, but it was no easy feat with their stiff postures and stern faces. Ian, Mitch, and Devon stood similarly, with their arms crossed and their feet shoulder-width apart, while Reggie had his hands on his hips.

She swallowed hard and took a deep breath. "I'm sorry, Sir. I didn't mean to cause any trouble, but when I came in to use the bathroom, those two bit . . . I mean, those two women had the girl, Colleen, up against the lockers, and the redhead had her hand around Colleen's neck holding her there."

"Fuck!"

Kristen's eyes widened and shot toward Master Reggie, who held up his hand apologetically. It was obvious the man was keeping his anger in check for her benefit. "Forgive me, girl. Go on."

She nodded and kept her gaze on the man. "I didn't want to say this in front of her because she's upset enough as it is. They were in her face, and I didn't hear everything they said, but the gist was they thought she was too fat and ugly to keep her Dom happy, and if it weren't for her daddy's money, she wouldn't have a Master."

She winced as Master Reggie exploded in rage. "They said what? Fucking cu . . ." He cut his vulgar insult short when he remembered there was a woman in the room. "God damn it,

Ian! I've had all I can stand from those two bitches. I want their asses out of here tonight!"

Ian's stare never left her face. "Reggie, calm down. I don't need you having another asthma attack in my club. The last time we had to call the EMTs to the lobby, I think one of them creamed his pants when Shelby walked by, then cried when Mistress China threatened his manhood because she thought they weren't working on you fast enough."

With those words, the tension rolling off the four men was released, and to her amazement, Mitch and Reggie began to laugh. Devon's posture eased a bit, and he leaned back against the wall, the corners of his mouth trembling as he held back his own laughter. She had a feeling he would be laughing out loud with the other men if he hadn't been so mad at her. Ian stayed where he was, looking at her. "Is that everything, little one?"

Kristen nodded. "That's when I stepped in, and well, you know the rest."

Ian's lips twitched, but he didn't smile. "Reggie, go upstairs to Colleen, and we'll be right behind you. After I mind-fuck those two, their memberships will be terminated."

Rather than heading toward the door, Master Reggie approached her and took her hand in his. "What's your name, girl? And whose collar are you wearing?"

"Kristen, Sir. And it's Master Devon's collar." She swallowed, and her eyes flashed to Devon before returning to the man before her. Well, she wouldn't be wearing it much longer, she guessed.

Master Reggie's brown eyes softened. "Thank you for sticking up for Colleen, Kristen. I'm grateful you were here and stepped in to protect her when I couldn't."

Her heart swelled at the gratitude in his eyes and voice,

and she smiled at him. "I'm glad I was here at the right time. I hate bullies."

"So do I." He let go of her hand and walked toward the door, passing the other men. "As a favor to me, Devon, please don't be too hard on your subbie's ass tonight."

Kristen bit her bottom lip when Devon said nothing and only nodded at the other Dom. He was no longer looking at her. Instead, his gaze was on the floor, and she knew she was in so much trouble.

"Little one." She looked back to Ian, who no longer seemed to be pissed—at least, not at her. His voice and blue eyes, so similar to Devon's, had softened as he spoke to her. "I don't condone fighting in my club, but every once in a while—very, very rarely, I might add—I'll admit there's a good reason behind it. This is one of those times. However, please try to alert security or a DM next time, and don't take on the bullies yourself. This time you had the upper hand, but it may not always be the case, and I'd hate to see you get hurt. Now, if you'll excuse us, Master Mitch and I have some things we need to tend to, and I'm sure my brother is thinking up ways to punish you for putting yourself in harm's way."

Without waiting for a response from her, Ian turned and walked out of the room, followed by Mitch, who winked and smiled at her before he left. She stood there waiting for Devon to say something to her. He still wasn't looking at her, and she began to fidget, knowing she'd spoiled what was left of their date.

"If you give me back my purse, I'll call a cab to take me back to my car."

His eyes whipped toward hers, then narrowed as he studied her. With his head tilted to the side, he took slow and deliberate steps toward her. "Why do you want to leave?"

She twisted her hands and fingers together in front of her. "Well, I obviously ruined the rest of our evening. I know you must be furious with me for having a catfight in your club."

Devon stepped inside her personal space, but she managed not to move backward, not that there was much room between her and the lockers. Grabbing her hands, he brought them up to his lips, kissing the back of one and then the other. She watched him, stunned he was being so gentle with her when he should be kicking her out the door. "Where did you learn to do that, Pet?"

She was confused, and her heart rate sped up at his closeness. "Do—do what?"

"Kick subbie ass when it was two against one."

Really? Was he serious? "Um . . . I told you my dad was a cop. A few female officers he worked with ran a program for teenage girls to teach them how to defend themselves, and I was a fast learner. Look, I'm sorry, Devon . . . I mean, Sir. I didn't mean to cause trouble and get them kicked out of the club. I saw what they were doing to her and snapped, I guess."

She watched in amazement as his head fell back on his shoulders, and he began to laugh. And it wasn't a short, light laugh but a full-blown belly laugh.

"Oh, Pet. How you fascinate me. You didn't start the trouble, but you ended it, and I'm proud of you. We've had a few complaints about those two harassing other subs, and they've been given fair warning their days here were numbered. The only reason they hadn't been kicked out before this was because their Doms are well-liked. I would've loved to have been a fly on the wall to see Heather's and Melissa's faces when you went all girlie-ninja on them."

"Girlie-ninja?"

"Uh-huh. My own personal ninja-girl. I kinda like it. That might be your new name for when we're not playing."

His smile faltered a fraction, and he hoped she didn't notice. He had to stop saying things like that—things which sounded as if they'd be spending time together past the weekend. Before they took anything further, he would have to tell her this thing between them was only temporary—a few days of mutual pleasure until he fucked her out of his system and then moved on. He wouldn't have that conversation here in the club's women's room, but he had to explain it to her soon. "If we hurry, we can still catch the end of Shelby's birthday scene. I mean, if you want to stay."

* * *

Of course she wanted to stay! She wanted to shout the words but tried to remain calm. "I'd like that."

He squeezed both her hands before dropping one and tugging on the other. "Great. Come on."

Kristen took two steps forward and then came to an abrupt stop. Devon looked back at her with a questioning look. "Something wrong, Pet?"

"Um . . . I never got a chance to use the facilities."

Laughing, he let go of her hand and made a grand sweeping gesture toward the other room where the toilets and showers were. "Be my guest. I'll wait for you outside. Try not to get into trouble in the next three minutes, hmm?"

CHAPTER TEN

Devon rushed his sub past several scenes. There would be time to return to watch them at their leisure, but he wanted Kristen to see Shelby's scene. A ménage was on her soft limits list, and he wanted to see her reaction. The birthday girl's ass would have been spanked crimson by now, but there should still be enough time for his pet to catch the end of the scene, and he knew it would be a good one.

A Brody and Marco tag-team scene was pretty popular with the unattached subs, but because there were times one or both were working on an assignment, it wasn't always a weekly occurrence. With Marco spending a lot of time tending to his sister lately, Devon didn't think the two had done a scene together in over two months. Some ménage Dom duos never did solo scenes, but Marco and Brody didn't need each other to enjoy a woman, which they did more often than not. It didn't mean they still didn't enjoy their threesomes when an opportunity arose.

Easing their way through the crowd which had gathered around the area the trio was using, Devon managed to find a spot where, if he placed Kristen in front of him, she would have an excellent view. He knew the moment she realized what she was watching because he felt rather than heard her breath hitch as he held her back to his chest. He peered over her shoulder and saw her eyes were wide, in awe more than shock, he thought. The pulse at her neck quickened as her breathing increased and her face flushed. He put his mouth next to her ear and whispered, "Like what you see, Pet?"

KRISTEN SHIVERED BUT DIDN'T ANSWER DEVON BECAUSE SHE couldn't find the words. In front of her was the most erotic thing she had ever seen. She'd never watched porn before, and even though she owned a *Playgirl* calendar, thanks to Will, she'd never looked through the pictures in a sex magazine. The R-rated movies she watched never showed a sex scene like this. Shelby was bent at the waist, her upper torso resting on a red leather bench. Completely naked, her ass and upper thighs were as deep red as the bench. She was tied down, shackled to the bench, unable to move her arms or legs. A wide strap across her lower back held her flush against the leather padding beneath her. The girl was sweating, moaning, and writhing as much as the restraints allowed, which wasn't much. But the two men with her held Kristen's attention, their bodies moving in tandem with each other and the music pulsating overhead.

A man, she assumed was Marco, was standing behind Shelby, his leather pants unlaced, and he was thrusting his condom-covered penis deep inside the girl's core. His feet were apart enough to keep his pants from falling further. Their current position bared the upper half of his ass, which was hard as granite. He was huge in front, and Kristen couldn't help but wonder how he fit without ripping the sub in two. Despite the din around her, Kristen was able to hear the slapping of Marco's exposed hips against Shelby's buttocks, and she was shocked to realize her own clit was throbbing in concert with the sound.

At Shelby's head stood Brody. While both men were tall and built, they were complete opposites regarding hair and skin tone. Marco was dark Italian with hair almost as black as Devon's, while Brody looked like a combination surfer-Norse god with his blond hair and tan, yet fairer skin. Both men had removed their shirts, and their upper bodies had the same sweaty sheen as the woman they were servicing. Rubbing her bare upper back with his hand, Brody's jeans were unzipped and hanging low on his hips as he plunged his cock into Shelby's welcoming mouth. He wasn't as thick as his counterpart but was still well-endowed.

Shelby's moans got louder, and Marco glanced at his friend. "She's about to come a fourth time, man. You better finish up soon if you don't want to visit the ER tonight."

Kristen watched as Brody nodded and increased the tempo of his hips. She turned slightly toward Devon but didn't take her gaze off the threesome. His mouth was still near her ear, and he must have anticipated her question. "Shelby tends to come hard, and when she does, she usually clamps her teeth together—it's an involuntary response for her. The Doms know this and back off on fucking her mouth when they sense she's about to come. Marco will slow down a little to keep her from going over the edge, and Brody will come before she does, so he doesn't need his dick surgically reattached."

Brody grabbed a handful of pink hair. "Come on, Shelby, take it . . . take it all." The girl's cheek hollowed as she sucked him harder, and Brody threw his head back, tensing and roaring his release. Not a drop of semen fell from the sub's lips as he slowed his hips and then pulled out of her mouth. Her lips were red and swollen, while her eyes were half closed and glazed over. Not bothering to zipper his jeans after he tucked himself back in, Brody dropped to his knees next to the sub, petting her head and talking to her in a voice too low for others to hear. She gave a slight nod of her head, and Marco increased his own pace again while reaching around to finger Shelby's clit in a hurried motion. Her moans became louder, then turned into cries of jumbled words. Marco's hips and fingers never slowed, but it wasn't until he slapped her ass hard with his other hand that she screamed with such an intense orgasm it should have brought the roof down on top of them. As she went over, she took Marco with her, his body rigid as he came inside the latex barrier.

Around her, Kristen heard words of appreciation and praise for the trio. The scene had been watched by many, and she almost expected them to break out in applause. She felt Devon's hard erection as he pressed his hips against her bottom, and her empty vagina clenched with need. Her body was so aroused by what she'd seen it wouldn't take much to set her off. One, maybe two swipes of her clit, and she would be flying. The thought surprised her. She could've never imagined being so turned on watching other people have sex. But it hadn't just been sex, she realized. It'd been a sensual and erotic exchange between the three individuals involved and shared with the people watching them. She couldn't think of the words to explain it. It hadn't been crass and dirty but carnal and beautiful—a sensual dance as old as time.

The crowd started to disperse as Brody and Marco began to unshackle the limp and satisfied Shelby, rubbing her limbs to revive her slowed circulation. If she hadn't been mumbling in response to the questions the men were asking her, Kristen would have thought the sub was unconscious. There were "happy birthday" wishes called to Shelby as people walked away, but Kristen didn't think the girl heard them, and she wondered if this was the subspace she'd read about during her research.

While Brody stayed with Shelby, Kristen watched Marco step a few feet away from the bench and dispose of his used condom, tossing it in a nearby receptacle. He relaced his pants, then took a blanket someone handed him. With Brody's help, he eased Shelby up and wrapped the blanket around her naked body. He then picked the petite girl up in his arms without effort, turned, and left the area with his charge. It was only after the sub was being cared for by his friend that Brody took a moment to zipper his jeans before he began cleaning up the area.

A female club employee, who wore a red and gold bow tie with a black bra and miniskirt, the club's uniform, stepped forward to help him. The employee took a towel and spray bottle and wiped down the spanking bench. The scent of oranges, faint earlier, now flooded Kristen's senses. She'd read somewhere the smell of citrus fruit could be an aphrodisiac, and now she understood why. It complemented the scents of leather and sex without being overbearing.

After tidying up the area, Brody grabbed his black duffel bag, which was his personal "toy" kit, and walked over to Marco, sitting on a nearby couch with Shelby on his lap. She was sipping from a bottle of water the dark-haired man held for her. Dropping the duffel bag at his feet, Brody sat down next to them, pulled the sub's legs across his lap, and began massaging them. When she was done with the water, Shelby rested her head on Marco's shoulder and closed her eyes.

Kristen hadn't moved from where she stood and felt Devon shift his weight behind her a second before she felt two fingers drag against her soaked pussy lips. It had been so unexpected, she tensed for a moment before moaning at the delicious sensation, but the fingers left her body as quickly as they'd appeared. Turning around, she watched him place the wet fingers in his mouth, sucking and licking them earnestly. His eyes flared with heat. The sight stunned and aroused her even more, which she hadn't thought was possible.

After he had consumed every last drop of her cream, he removed his fingers and leaned toward her. "Just because we can't play doesn't mean I can't touch what belongs to me, and the collar you're wearing says you're mine tonight." He licked his lips, and all Kristen could do was stare at him. "You taste so sweet, Pet, like the purest of honey. I want to spread your legs and eat you for hours until I've had my fill. It pleases me so much that their scene turned you on."

If his hands hadn't moved to hold her waist, she would've melted to the floor in a big pile of goo. Her eyes shifted downward, and her flushed face became even redder. Devon took the two fingers, which had been in his mouth a moment before, and placed them under her chin. She could smell her scent on him.

He applied gentle pressure, forcing her to look at him again. "Don't be embarrassed, Pet. Your arousal is nothing to be ashamed of, just because it doesn't follow the norms of society. Here, in this world, it's normal. Here, there's no right or wrong way for Doms and subs to enjoy sex and all its possible facets, as long as they're safe, sane, and consensual. Understand?"

She nodded. "Yes . . . yes, Sir, but . . ."

"But what, Pet?"

Although she whispered, it was loud enough for him to hear. "Did she really come four times?"

* * *

Of all the questions he expected her to ask, that hadn't

been one of them. Devon let out a bark of laughter before answering her. "I'm sure she did, and each one was probably as intense as the one we saw. Haven't you ever had multiple orgasms before?"

She shook her head, probably embarrassed, thinking she wasn't like most women. "No, Sir."

Her denial didn't faze him at all. He recalled her limit list and the question mark she had placed next to "Coming on Command."

"Okay, here's another question, and I'm not asking you these to make you uncomfortable. I'm learning what I need to know in order to take proper care of you when the time comes. And I guarantee the time *will* come, and so will you." Her chin fell toward the floor, but she didn't say anything. "Have you ever had an orgasm during intercourse?"

When she shook her head, he frowned. "I need verbal answers, Pet. I don't ever want to guess what you mean or have any miscommunications between us. You have to tell me in plain English. Have you ever had an orgasm during intercourse?"

Kristen tried to look away from him, but he wouldn't allow it. "No, Sir. Not during intercourse. The only orgasms I've ever had are the ones I've given myself when I'm alone. My ex said it was because I was frigid and couldn't relax during sex."

Devon growled. "And yet another reason to despise the low-life pile of cow shit you were married to."

Her amusement was evident in her smile. "Do you realize every time you mention my ex, you call him something else?"

"No, I didn't," he said with a chuckle. "But since I've developed a rather colorful language over the years, I'm sure I won't run out of new things to call him for a while. For now, though, I don't want to talk about him anymore. I don't want him between us tonight or any other time. So I want you to forget you were ever with him. I'm going to treat you like a virgin and start from scratch. I'm going to seduce you, arouse you, and by the time I'm done, you'll know exactly how non-frigid you are. You'll also know what it's like to have multiple orgasms because I won't stop until I'm completely satisfied you have nothing left to give me."

* * *

Devon spent the next hour or so escorting Kristen around the pit. They'd been pulled into a few conversations, and introductions were made, but after a few short words, he was able to keep them moving while still being polite, so she could see as many scenes as possible. He wanted to observe her while she watched the different scenes to get an idea of what interested her and compare it to her list of limits.

He found a flogging scene and another spanking which obviously turned her on. A wax scene had intrigued her despite the wariness on her face when she first saw the hot wax being dripped onto the female sub's large breasts and abdomen before it landed on the woman's clit, causing her to scream as she came. When they watched Mistress China whip a sub tied to a St. Andrew's cross, Kristen had winced as the single tail left red lines up and down the man's nude back, ass, and upper thighs. Devon sensed it was a little too much for her during her first visit, so he didn't let her linger.

The most interesting reaction she had was when they stopped to watch a new scene start. The female sub was sitting naked on a bondage chair as her Dom plucked her nipples into stiff peaks, prepping them for the alligator clamps he had in his other hand. When the Dom placed the clamps on his sub, Kristen had paled and began to panic, her breathing becoming rapid. Devon was about to pull her away from the scene when he saw her hands move to her breasts as if she was trying to push away unseen clamps from her own nipples.

He grabbed her shoulders and jerked her away from the scene. She hadn't gotten upset until she noticed the clamps, and her negative response to a standard piece of BDSM equipment bothered him. There was a story behind her reaction, and he was determined to get it out of her after he calmed her down. Until then, the best he could do was hold her until her breathing slowed and the panic receded.

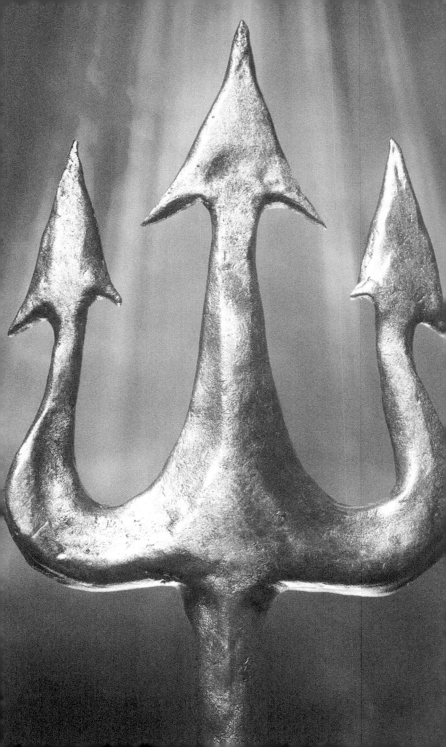

CHAPTER ELEVEN

Kristen tried to get her breathing under control as Devon held her tight against his body. He must think she's an inexperienced wimp. She thought she could handle watching the Dom put clamps on his sub's nipples, but as soon as the girl cried out in pain, something in Kristen flipped. It didn't matter that the girl was now moaning with pleasure. If Devon hadn't pulled her away from the scene, she was sure she would've vomited all over the place or, at least, passed out—which was so not the way to make a good impression.

She let him lead her to a sitting area closer to the middle of the room and was surprised when he sat in a wingback leather chair and pulled her down into his lap. The chair was situated so she couldn't see the scene which had upset her, and she knew he had chosen that one on purpose. He adjusted her hips until they were both comfortable before signaling a nearby waitress to bring him a bottle of water. Taking the bottle, he uncapped it and held it to her lips, allowing her to take only a few small sips at a time. "Easy, Pet. Don't drink too fast, or it'll make you sick."

She nodded before taking a few more sips as the bile, which had risen to the back of her throat earlier, subsided. "I'm sorry. I don't know what came over me or why I reacted like I did."

"I think you do."

Her eyes flashed up to his, then away again, but he wouldn't allow her to hide. With a tender touch, he cupped her chin and turned her head so she had no choice but to look at him. She could tell he wasn't angry but concerned.

"Tell me, Pet. Tell me what happened to you."

She tried to shake her head as her eyes filled with tears, but he still held her jaw. "I can't."

His concerned eyes softened in sympathy. His voice was deep—demanding, yet kind. "You can, Pet. Trust me. There isn't anything you can say that I won't understand. Tell me, so I can help you heal."

Kristen blinked several times and took a deep breath. "I can't look at you when I say it. I've never told anyone, and it's embarrassing."

He caressed her cheek before pushing her head to rest on his shoulder. He turned his head, then kissed her forehead. "Don't be embarrassed. I've been in this lifestyle for over a decade, and I've pretty much heard everything. Not much surprises me anymore. Close your eyes and take your time. No rush, but you will tell me before we get up again. I don't care if your ass falls asleep—I'll just spank it awake again later."

She hiccupped, then giggled, as he'd intended, and the tension she was feeling eased. She closed her eyes and settled deeper into his embrace. Taking another deep breath, she began to speak. "I told you earlier I dated a guy in college before my ex. He was the one who got tired of me saying 'no' to actual intercourse, but we still fooled around a bit."

Devon said nothing as he caressed her shoulders and back while nuzzling his cheek against her hair.

"We dated for about three months, and everything was great until we went to a party one night, and Derek had a little too much to drink. Later, we went back to his dorm room alone and started making out and stuff. I had my shirt off, and he'd pulled my bra down, so he could . . . God, this is so embarrassing."

Devon remained quiet, letting her tell him at her own pace.

She took another deep breath. "Anyway, he was sucking and licking my breasts when he started getting rough. He kept trying to get my pants undone. I'd never been afraid of him before, but that night, I guess because of the alcohol, he got aggressive, and I was scared. I tried to push him away, and he bit my nipple hard. I think if I hadn't screamed at the top of my lungs and hit him in the head, he would have bitten it off."

She didn't know when she began crying, but the tears were pouring down her cheeks, and she paused to catch her breath. Devon's hands never stopped as they caressed her back, legs, and arms, and the constant motions helped calm her. Despite being in a crowded club, she felt as if it was just the two of them, far away from anyone else. He was murmuring words of sympathy for her ordeal and praise for telling him about it as his lips brushed against her forehead. She felt the tension in his body with the obvious anger he had toward the man who'd hurt her, but he kept it in check.

"I grabbed my shirt and ran back to my dorm room. Thank God my roommate had gone home for the weekend. When I looked, his teeth marks were deep enough to make me bleed. It hurt so badly, and I cried all night. I was in pain for almost a month. I couldn't stand to wear my bras because my nipple was super-sensitive. But it was worse without them because my shirts constantly brushed against it, so I wore my padded sports bras until it healed, but it still hurt. And to make everything worse, Derek came to see me the next day when I wouldn't answer his calls or texts. He didn't even remember doing it. He said I must've been cheating on him because he didn't do it, and he would tell everyone I was a cheating whore if I reported it."

"So you never told anyone? Never went to the doctor?" He spoke the words into her temple as he continued to pepper her with the sweetest touches of his lips.

She shook her head. "I know I should've, but I was so scared and mortified. Anyway, I broke up with him right then. I was glad we didn't have any classes together, but I still saw him on campus, and three days later, he had a new girlfriend. I never talked to him again. When Tom and I started dating, and I wouldn't let him touch my breasts, he asked why. I told him they were overly sensitive, and he didn't push me after that. I can touch them, and eventually, I got to the point where I could let him touch them as long as he was gentle, but I would freeze up if his teeth made contact. I guess it's one of the reasons I'm lousy in bed. I don't think I'll ever be able to relax enough to make a man happy."

Without warning, Devon grabbed her hair and pulled her head back so that he could look her in the face. He was frowning, his eyes flashing in anger, and this time it was aimed at her. He wasn't hurting her, but a sliver of fear raced through her. "Pet, I'm only going to say this once, and if I ever have to repeat myself, I'm going throw you over my knee and make sure you can't sit for a week. I will not tolerate you putting yourself down, *ever*, especially because you're experiencing a version of PTSD. Do you know what that is?"

She'd heard of Post-Traumatic Stress Disorder, but she thought it only happened to soldiers in combat or people who witnessed a murder or something just as bad. He was waiting for a response, so she nodded her head the best she could while he still had a firm grip on her hair. "What happened to you was not your fault. It was not safe, sane, or consensual. No one, and I mean *no one*, should have to go through what you went through. You were violated by a man you should've been able to trust, and he took your trust and destroyed it. I never want to hear you say you're lousy in bed or can't make a man happy. What you experienced between those two cocksuckers may have buried your passion and your trust in men, but I've seen glimpses of your passion, and I know it's there, waiting to come to the surface. That dick hurt you physically and mentally. And the fucking amoeba you were married to never took the time to learn about you —your body and mind. He didn't learn what pleases and frightens you as a lover should.

"When I'm with a woman, her pleasure, her desires, her needs, and her orgasms are what matter to me the most. My need for sexual release is at the bottom of a long list. It's almost an afterthought, and I will not allow it to happen until my sub is thoroughly and completely sated and she can't take anymore. My satisfaction comes after I've given her everything I can, and I've taken everything she has in return. I want to be the man who can make you trust again. I want you to see and feel how good sexual play can be.

"Stay with me tonight . . . for the weekend. I want to be the man who gives you orgasms you never knew existed. I can't give you more than that. I can't offer you forever—it's not in me—but for this weekend, I can offer you the chance to learn what pleases you and how incredible sex can be with a man who places your needs and pleasure before his. I want to teach you what it means to feel cherished. Tell me now if it's not what you want, and I'll take you home. But don't deny yourself the chance to explore your sexuality. Don't ignore what I can see in your eyes and body language that you crave. If it's not with me, find someone you can trust and make it happen."

Kristen stared at the man who held her captive, not only with his hands but with his words. She knew he was right. She was a passionate woman, but it was buried deep within her, and no other man had looked for it and put her before himself—until Devon. Did she want him? No question about it, she did. Did she trust him?

She didn't know why, but the answer was yes—yes, she trusted him with her mind and her body. She only hoped she didn't lose her heart to him because she couldn't endure the pain again. This is what she'd told herself she wanted last week—a friend with benefits, nothing long-term. And if he were willing to teach her and let her explore, she would take whatever time he offered her. And when the time came, and they went their separate ways, she would thank him for everything he had given her.

* * *

Devon could almost hear her brain process everything he'd said. He wanted her more than he'd ever wanted a woman, but this was her decision, and he would abide by it, even if it killed him. She looked into his eyes, and his cock stirred when he knew she'd made up her mind. He knew what her answer would be, but he needed to hear the words, and he refused to proceed without them.

"Teach me, Sir."

CHAPTER TWELVE

Devon stood and set Kristen on her feet, holding her hips until he was sure she was steady. Grabbing her hand, he almost dragged her up the grand staircase, across the bar area, and out the double wooden doors. He didn't say a word to her or anyone else on the way, and several people barely managed to step out of his path before he ran them down. He wanted to strip her naked, and he couldn't do it here, not with the rules they had in place. As they crossed the lobby toward the front door, he heard her say from where she trailed behind him, "Devon, wait, I need my purse. It's still in your locker."

He didn't slow down but turned his head so she could hear him. "You won't need it. We'll get it tomorrow morning." He was too impatient to stop for anything. He wanted to spend hours proving his words to her. She would be satisfied many times over before he found his own release, or he would die trying.

Throwing open the outside door, he reduced his pace a little, so she wouldn't lose her balance on the stairs while going down with her stilettos on. Instead of heading toward his car, he turned toward the gate in the fence separating the club from the rest of the compound. As they approached, Beau, Ian's large lab-pit mix, came running to greet them, happy to see someone who would play with him.

Sorry buddy, Devon thought, *I've got bigger plans tonight, and they don't include a rubber ball covered in dog slobber.*

"Where are we going?" Kristen eyed the black canine, who was now bouncing his big body off the other side of the fence. "Does he bite?"

Devon placed his hand on the security scanner, which would unlock the pedestrian gate instead of the drive-thru one. "My apartment is in the last building, and he only bites when we tell him to or if one of us is being threatened."

Before he pushed open the gate, he addressed the excited mutt, "Beau, *pfui, fuss,*" the foreign words being pronounced as "fooey" and "fooss." The dog quieted and sat while the two humans walked into his territory, and his favorite one closed the gate again. The dog's impatience was obvious, and his stubby, little tail twitched while the rest of his body remained still. As the two began walking across the compound, he fell in step, almost attaching his furry body to his human's right leg.

Kristen was a dog lover and watched the animal in amazement as she kept pace with Devon. "What did you say to him?"

He slowed his pace a little when he realized she was almost running to keep up with his long stride. "Beau is his name. The other two words are 'no' and 'heel' in German. Ian found him as a pup and had him trained by a guy specializing in protection and security dogs, and his commands are given in German, so bad guys can't give him a command. He only knows a few words in English from being around us, and they're all harmless."

Kristen was impressed. "That's so cool. I might have to remember that for one of my books." Devon stopped short, and she almost stumbled past him before he grabbed her arm and steadied her. "What's wrong?"

His face was serious and borderline angry. "I want to make something perfectly clear. This thing between us, what we are about to do, is not research, Kristen. It's real. I don't want to be a story in one of your books. If that's why you're with me, tell me now. Because if I find out later you're using me for that reason, I swear there'll be hell to pay."

Is that what he thought she was doing? Before she lost her temper, she took a moment and thought about it from his point of view. Yes, she had come to The Covenant for research but returned with him because she wanted to. Because she wanted him.

She brought her hand up to his cheek and saw his stern face relax. "I can see how you might be worried, and I can't say I won't unconsciously recall how you've made me feel tonight while I'm writing, but I would never use you or anyone else that way, Devon. I swear to you, I'm here because I want you, and not for research for my books, but to discover the woman I hope . . . I *believe* is hidden deep inside me."

He leaned down and took possession of her mouth—hard and fast. Clutching her hips, he pulled her to him until there was no denying how much he wanted her. When she moaned into his mouth and rubbed her body against his, he ripped his mouth from hers, grabbed her wrist, and began pulling her along again. "Come on, woman, before I throw you to the ground and fuck you right here. I wouldn't mind, but I'm sure you'll be more comfortable in my bed."

Giggling at his impatience, she followed him into the last warehouse through a ground-floor door, which he also opened using a hand scanner. Again the exterior of the building belied the interior. A wooden apartment door was a few steps in from the outside door. Brown carpeted steps to their left led to a second-floor landing and another door. The sheet-rocked walls had been painted a soft beige.

Devon pointed to a much smaller door to the right of the first-floor apartment door and spoke to the dog. "Beau, *geh rein*," he instructed the canine pronouncing it "gay rine," "Go inside. Your boss will be home in a bit."

The dog reluctantly but obediently approached the door, and a red light on a small black box at the top of the door turned green. Ducking his head, Beau pushed open the top-hinged door and disappeared while the door fell back in place and the green light returned to red.

Taking Kristen's hand in his, Devon led her up the stairs. He stopped at the second-floor door and used yet another hand scanner to unlock it. She looked toward the floor and smiled when she noticed another doggie door set in the sheetrock. Devon opened his apartment door and gestured for her to go in first. Looking around his living room, she couldn't believe they were in an old warehouse. The walls and ten-foot ceiling had all been enclosed with sheetrock, and the spacious room was comfortably decorated. The walls were painted a pale moss green, while the furniture was made using dark-stained woods. A large, L-shaped, brown leather couch took up two living room walls, with two recliners in a muted fabric completing the sitting area. The large framed pictures on the walls, a coffee table, end tables, lamps, and throw pillows on the couch were well coordinated.

Two large horizontal windows were located high on the outer wall, above the shorter end of the couch, allowing plenty of light to come in while preventing anyone on the outside from seeing in without a ladder. Window treatments in the same fabric as the throw pillows framed the glass. Across from the longer length of the couch was a huge entertainment center, which contained a sixty-inch flat-screen TV, a complicated-looking stereo, a gaming system, and an assortment of photos of family and friends. Beyond the large sitting area was a six-seat bar, although no liquor bottles were on the shelves.

Attached to the living room, but still its own open space, was a dining area with a teak wood table and chairs with seating for eight and a matching buffet table and china cabinet. Two beautiful wrought iron chandeliers, similar to the ones in the club, hung from the ceiling over the dining area and living room. Past the dining area was a huge eat-in kitchen with stainless steel appliances, oak cabinets, and black granite countertops. The walls in there were painted ivory. Opposite the front door and between the living and dining areas was a hallway that led toward the back of the apartment, where she assumed there were bedrooms and at least one bathroom. The entire apartment looked bigger than the three-bedroom home she grew up in.

Turning, she saw Devon had been watching her. "Your place is beautiful."

His grin was sheepish. "Thanks, but I can't take any of the credit. I mean, come on, I'm a guy who spent most of his adult life living on Navy bases and sleeping on the ground in places you couldn't imagine when we were on assignment. Can you see me picking out curtains or couch pillows? When my mom saw my card-slash-dining table and mismatched couch and folding chairs, she hired an interior decorator to come in and give it a major overhaul. The result is what you see, and it finally got Mom's approval. At least Ian's place wasn't much better than mine then, and he got the royal treatment, too."

He took a few steps toward the hallway and added, "Make yourself comfortable, and I'll be right back."

As Devon disappeared into the back of the apartment, she continued to look around. She spotted the photos again and approached the entertainment center to see them better. There were two pictures of the Sexy Six-Pack. In one, they were all dressed in military camo fatigues and holding some huge weapons, while in the other, they were playing a three-on-three basketball game. The photo looked like it was taken outside in the compound.

There was a picture of Mitch, Ian, and Devon dressed in their club leathers in the lobby of The Covenant. They looked a few years younger, and she wondered if it was taken when they first opened the club. She moved to another group of pictures. The first one was of a much younger Devon in his Navy dress blues flanked by an older man and woman she assumed were his parents.

Behind her, she heard him come back into the room and was about to turn toward him, but something stopped her. Looking at the picture again, she focused on the older man who looked so familiar. Devon stopped next to her, and she realized he'd changed into a pair of sweatpants, and his feet were now bare. "Those are my folks, Chuck and Marie."

The names didn't ring a bell, so she moved on to a photo of four boys, three of whom were in their teens. Two of them looked like twins, and she thought one of them was Devon. She pointed to the boy on the left. "Is this one you?"

* * *

Devon nodded, took her hand, and led her to the couch, where they sat down. "Yeah, that's me. Right before Ian left for basic training."

"What about the other two? I take it they're your other brothers."

Turning toward her, he ran a finger up and down her bare arm while the fingers from his other hand played with her hair. "John's the one who looks like me, and Nick is the little guy."

He knew nervous tension was behind her questions rather than her curiosity, but his family wasn't something he talked about often. If he didn't take command of the situation, her brain might override what her body obviously wanted. When it looked like she was about to ask another question, he plunged his fingers into her silky strands before grabbing hold and pulling her mouth to his. "I don't want to talk anymore."

Then he slammed his mouth down on hers and took what he did want—her.

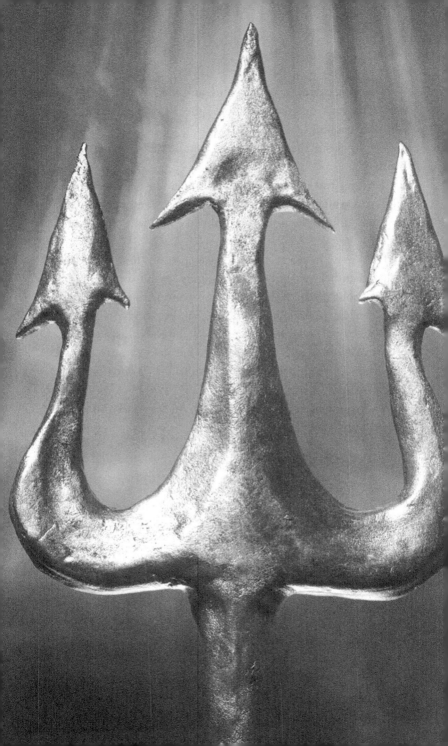

CHAPTER THIRTEEN

He inhaled her, and Kristen loved every second of it, but he drew away again when she tried to move her body closer to his. Without a word, he stood and pulled her up next to him before leading her down the hallway to his bedroom, which she barely noticed was decorated like the rest of his place. What she couldn't miss was the room's main focus—a stained black oak, four-poster bed with a gray-and-maroon patterned comforter on it.

Devon let go of her hand, leaving her standing next to the bed while he sat down on it and leaned to the side, resting his upper body on one elbow. "Undress for me, Pet. I want to see all of your luscious body and your eyes on mine the entire time. Unzip your dress and let it slide slowly down your body, revealing one delicious inch at a time. Don't think. Follow my orders and feel. Feel how beautiful you are to me. You have no idea how much I want you, but you will soon."

She swallowed and felt her pulse increase. His seductive voice was mesmerizing. She could do this. After all, it's what she told herself several times she wanted. Hesitating only a second or two, she reached up to the dress's side zipper and lowered it. Slowly. Her eyes remained focused on his blue ones, and she realized his stayed on hers in return—he wasn't looking at her body but into her mind. Her confidence went up a few notches. When the zipper stopped at her waist, her hand went back up to the thin strap holding the dress up, and she pulled it down her right arm, inch by torturous inch. His nostrils flared as if searching for her scent, yet his gaze never left her face.

As the fabric of the dress dragged across her excited nipples, making them even harder, her breath caught, and a rush of arousal moistened her inner thighs. By the time she got the dress down to her waist, she wanted to rip it the rest of the way off, shove her hand between her legs, and relieve herself of the intense pressure peaking there. She used both hands to shimmy the dress over her voluptuous hips, and once it cleared them, the garment fell to a heap on the floor. Taking one step to the side, she toed the discarded fabric out of the way.

It was only then, when she stood completely naked in front of him, Devon's eyes lowered as he took in every inch of her. "Turn all the way around."

This was more disconcerting than when she had done it fully clothed in the restaurant. However, this time it wasn't his hands touching her, but his hungry stare. When she completed the rotation, Devon got up and held his hand out to her. Without hesitation, she placed her hand in his and let him help her climb onto the big bed. "Lay down on your back in the middle of the bed, Pet—legs together, straight out. Put your hands above your head, grab the posts in the headboard, and keep them there. Your trust so far has me humbled, but I don't think you're ready for me to restrain you in this setting. However, if you remove your hands without permission, there will be consequences. Understand?"

She licked her lips and nodded after positioning herself as he'd ordered. "Yes, Sir, I understand."

"Good girl. You're absolutely beautiful, Pet."

She blushed as she watched him grab the hem of his shirt and lift it over his head, tossing the tee on top of her dress. Her eyes widened at the sight before her, and she licked her lips again. She couldn't help it. His torso was sculpted perfection. If he'd lived in the time of Michelangelo, the statue would be called *Devon* instead of *David*.

He and his friends might forever be the Sexy Six-Pack in her mind, but the man before her had a sexy eight-pack. It wasn't a body gained only in a gym, although he obviously spent time working out with weights. His muscles had fluidity when they moved, which came from swimming or other cardio activities. She'd bet he loved to mountain climb or some other extreme sport. When he saw her interest in the black script tattoo over his heart, he rubbed his hand over it but didn't explain the letters and numbers.

Leaving his sweatpants on, even though they did nothing to hide his erection, he crawled onto the bed and stretched out on his side next to her so he was at eye level with her chest. Placing the fingers of one hand on her stomach, he began to rub in small, sensual circles, which gave her goosebumps. Heat emanated from his fingers into her body as he gradually began to make the circles bigger until he brushed the underside of her breast and the top of her shaven mound, never quite touching her where she wanted him to.

Even though he was watching his hand and where he was touching her, he knew the instant she closed her eyes. "Eyes open, Pet. Follow my hand. Watch how your body responds to my touch."

She did as she was told and noticed the heaviness of her breasts and how the throbbing in her clit intensified. She tried to rub her thighs together to create some much-needed friction between her legs, but his hand lifted from her abdomen, giving her a sharp smack on one of her thighs. Her hips jolted in surprise. "Don't move, Pet. You don't give yourself pleasure here. That's my job, and I'll do it in my own good time."

The impact hadn't hurt beyond the initial sting, but it did startle her, and so did her increased arousal. Before she could process it, his hand dragged up her torso and cupped the weight of her breast closest to his face. Devon lifted the orb, massaged the flesh, and ran his fingers around its base before moving his hand over to do the same to her other one.

While he was tending to her second breast, he pursed his lips and blew on the nipple of the first one from about two inches away. The sensation sent lightning bolts to her clit, and she involuntarily arched her back. He then took his index finger and began to draw lazy circles around her breasts, switching from one to the other, starting at their base all the way toward her nipples, yet stopping short of touching the hardened points. Kristen was almost panting, and for the first time since her horrible experience in college, she wanted to beg a man to touch her nipples.

Devon didn't stop what he was doing. "Take your left hand, run your thumb and forefinger through what I know is your soaking wet pussy, and coat them with your juices. Do not touch your clit or put them inside you. Just get them nice and wet."

She removed her hand from where it had been and did as he ordered. Moaning, she ran her fingers through her folds, gathering as much of her moisture as she could. He gave her further instructions when she held up her fingers for him to see. "Now, take them and play with your left nipple. Roll it between your thumb and finger and pull on it."

Her mind flashed to a similar command she'd dreamed Master Xavier giving her, and her breathing increased along with the aching need in her pussy. And, oh, how she remembered how that scenario had ended. The second her wet digits closed around her left nipple, Devon's moist tongue swiped at her right one. The combined sensations had her crying out for more, and all thoughts of the fictional Master X fled her mind.

Devon's tongue licked her nipple repeatedly, keeping pace with her fingers pleasuring her other one. If she sped up, he sped up . . . if she slowed down, he slowed down. He may have been the one issuing commands, but she was starting to understand the control she had too.

"Wet your fingers again. After you put them back on your nipple, I want you to do the same with your other hand and take over this one for me."

She did as she was told, and after she was in control of both breasts, Devon slid further down the bed. "Don't stop playing with them, Pet, and spread your legs wide for me. Eyes on me and what I'm doing."

She separated her legs, and he climbed over her right before settling between them. He pushed her ankles toward her hips until her knees were bent to his liking with her feet flat on the bed. She was now so exposed that nothing was left for him to imagine.

She watched as he ran his calloused hands up the insides of her thighs and stopped at her unprotected core, framing it with both thumbs and forefingers. His mouth was only inches away from where she wanted it the most. Tom had only touched her there, he'd never given her oral sex, and she knew Devon was about to do something she had only experienced in her dreams. She waited and waited . . . wanting to beg him to do something other than stare between her legs while her fingers continued to pluck and pinch her nipples.

His eyes lifted to hers. "I love how your pussy is bare, Pet. It's so beautiful. My mouth is watering. Tell me, how long have you been doing this?"

"D-doing what? Waxing down there?"

"Yes, how long have you been waxing your pussy? Did you do this for the donkey scum-sucker, or am I the first to see you like this? I want an honest answer, Pet."

Her empty vagina clenched in desperation, searching for something, *anything* to fill it. "I tried it for the first time six months ago for research. I liked it and kept getting it done. So the answer to your question is—you're the only person who has seen it."

His grin was almost evil-looking. "I'm so pleased to hear that, Pet."

He closed the gap between them and stiffened his tongue to lick the length of her dripping slit. She screamed his name, and her hips sprung from the bed, but he grabbed them and put them back where they belonged. "Stay still, or I won't let you come. And I didn't tell you to stop playing with those gorgeous tits of yours."

"Y-yes, S-Sir," she panted. Her fingers began to move again, and this time when he licked her like she was an ice cream cone, she barely managed to keep her hips still.

"Mmmm, straight from the source. This is so much better than licking your sweet nectar from my fingers, not that I didn't enjoy it immensely. You may come whenever you need to, Pet."

Devon continued to pleasure her with his tongue, alternating between impaling and swiping her with it. As his thumb began to rub the hood covering her clit, she moaned.

The first time he plunged his tongue inside her, her eyes rolled back into her head as her body began to climb. Oral sex was better than she'd ever imagined. He'd said earlier he wanted to eat her for hours, and right now, she'd let him.

He shifted his hands, resting one above her mound and using his fingers to expose her little jewel to his mouth while he took two fingers from his other hand and thrust them inside her hot, wet channel. His probing fingers searched and found the spot where it felt like he was rubbing her clit from inside her womb. The three-pronged assault on her nipples, clit, and G-spot proved too much for her to take, and she screamed as she came apart at the seams. White lights flew before her closed eyes. Her body shook as her legs quivered. The muscles of her vagina clenched his fingers in a hard grip, refusing to let them go. Devon's tongue lapped at her faster to catch every drop of her release, and moments later, she went over the edge again, screaming even louder this time.

As she began descending back to Earth, his mouth returned to her clit, and his fingers began to work to send her airborne for a third time. She was shocked to feel her body begin to climb once more. She didn't think she could handle another orgasm if it were as intense as the first two. Her hands had left her breasts sometime during her first release, and now both fists clutched the comforter as she pleaded with him. "N-nooo, not again, please!"

"Yes, Pet," he growled into her mound. "Again!"

His mouth and fingers were relentless, and whether she wanted to or not, she was soon coming again. Her third orgasm was the strongest yet, and she would be surprised if it didn't kill her. If it did, it would be a helluva way to go.

Ten minutes or so later, Kristen's fuzzy mind began to clear as she lay cuddled in Devon's arms. In less than one hour, the man had proved her asshole ex wrong. She was far from frigid. In fact, she was a raging volcano in the hands of a man who knew how to please a woman. From where her head rested on his chest, she looked down the length of Devon's body and saw he still had his sweatpants on with his hard-on bulging inside them. She realized, despite her three powerful orgasms, he had yet to come. "Devon . . . I mean, Sir?"

He kissed the top of her head. "Yes, Pet?"

"You didn't . . . I mean . . . don't you want to . . . um?"

He let out a low chuckle. "Don't worry about me—the night is still young. Have you come back to Earth?"

Picking her head up, she smiled down at him. "Yes, and I have a request."

"Anything, sweetheart."

Suddenly she felt shy and blushed. "Teach me how to please you?"

* * *

Although Devon smiled at her vague request, he wouldn't let her off the hook. "Please me, how? You've been pleasing me all night."

She rolled her eyes, and his hand on her ass pinched her flesh. "Ow! That hurt!" Her eyes flashed in annoyance.

"Then don't roll your eyes at your Dom." He tried to sound stern, but she was so cute when irritated with him. "Now, what is it you want, Pet? In plain, simple, and dirty English."

"Fine," she huffed. "I want you to teach me how to give you a blowjob. Is that plain and dirty enough for you?"

It was all he could do not to laugh at her petulance. "Plain enough, yes. Dirty enough, no. But we'll work on expanding your naughty vocabulary later. For now, before we go any further, you have a punishment coming to you."

She squealed as she sat up. "Now?"

Pushing himself into a seated position, he placed a pillow between his back and the headboard, making himself comfortable. "Yes, Pet, now. I waited because I wanted your first few orgasms to be only the result of pleasure. Since I've proven you're not unresponsive as you've been told in the past, it's time for your spanking. Come lay across my lap."

She hesitated, and he gave her a moment to come to terms with what she was about to let him do. He knew she would comply with his order but was new to BDSM. This was her first punishment in the world of sexual play, and it had to be her decision whether or not she wanted to take the final step forward. When she finally accepted what she wanted, she crawled over and lay across his thighs with her ass in the air.

He rubbed the pale flesh of her ass and squeezed her cheeks to warm them up. "The count is sixteen, Pet. I'm going to let you choose this one time. After the first eight, you can choose for me to give you the remainder now, or your second option is to receive the other eight when we wake up in the morning because you will be staying in my bed for the rest of the night. Is that clear?"

He could hear the nervousness in her voice when she responded, "Y-yes, Sir."

As soon as the words were out of her mouth, he lifted his hand and slapped it back down on one cheek.

Smack.

He was pleased when she yelped but didn't move. Her ivory skin turned pink, and he momentarily held his hand to it to keep the heat in.

Smack.

That one landed on her other cheek. Again, she let out a little cry but remained in place. He knew after the sting registered, it would begin to morph into something she couldn't explain at this point.

Smack. Smack. Smack.

Those were a little harder, and she squealed and began to squirm. His hand on the middle of her back kept her from going anywhere. He aimed the next three along the creases where her ass and thighs met.

Smack. Smack. Smack.

He paused as she began to sob, and he smoothed his hand over her red buttocks, giving her a chance to get her breathing under control. Despite her cries, she'd kept her hands in front of her with a tight grip on the comforter. It pleased him she resisted what would've been a natural response for a new sub to reach around and try to protect her flesh from his punishment. He dipped his fingers between her legs, and she moaned when he found what he'd expected—she was very aroused. "That was eight, Pet. Should I continue or save them for the morning?"

* * *

Kristen was so confused. Her ass was on fire, and all she could think about was how much she wanted him to thrust his cock deep inside her and fuck her. She was soaked. Even though tears were falling from her eyes, she wanted to get this over with and move on to the point when he would let her come again. Waiting to receive the other eight until morning would only make her anxious all night. "I-I'll take them now, Sir, please."

"Very well, I'll make them quick."

The next ones were harder than before, and although she was crying from the pain, she was also panting and getting wetter by the second from the heat that followed. When the last spank had been delivered, she breathed a sigh of relief. He let her rest as he caressed her tender skin. After her breathing was back under control and her tears were no longer falling, he helped her up, and she knelt next to him on the bed, not wanting to sit yet.

Devon brushed her damp hair from her face. "I'm proud of you, Pet. You did very well for your first spanking. Now, the reasons for your punishment have been erased, and we can move on to more enjoyable activities. I believe you asked me to teach you something."

Her tear-stained cheeks creased when she smiled at him. "I did, Sir. I asked you to teach me how to give you a blowjob."

* * *

Devon shifted his hips until he was reclining a little bit and shoved the elastic waistband of his sweatpants down over his aching cock. "I'll be more than happy to, Pet. Scoot down on the bed and pull my pants off the rest of the way."

After she removed his clothes, he spread his legs to give her room. "On your knees between my legs. I want to see your red ass in the air while you pleasure me. Get comfortable."

When she was in position, he fisted his cock hard and pointed it toward the ceiling. A drop of pre-cum oozed from its slit. "Lick it."

He watched as she leaned forward, extending her tongue to swipe the head. She savored his taste before licking him again and then again. Her inexperience was obvious, but rather than turning him off, it made him harder. "Take your hand and wrap it around me."

He removed his hand as hers took its place. "Tighter. Aaaahh, yeah. Like that. Now take the head between your lips while pumping your hand up and down slowly."

Shit! Her innocence would be the death of him. "That's it. Now take me into your mouth as far as you can. Watch your teeth." She dragged him in and out of her mouth, taking his cock further each time, and her confidence grew with each pass. "Use your tongue on the way out. Fuck! You're a natural at this, babe. I'm not sure I'll last long."

She increased her pace without being told, and his eyes nearly rolled back into his head. "Take your other hand and roll my balls in it gently." He fisted his hand in her hair and thrust his hips up, sending his dick to the back of her throat. She gagged and then instinctively began to breathe through her nose. Without a doubt, the woman was going to kill him with bliss.

"Pet, I'm not going to last much longer. No matter what, I promise I'll get my cock in your sweet pussy tonight, but if you don't want me to come down your throat, you better tell me now."

Refusing to stop, she tightened her grip on his shaft and balls and sucked him harder and faster. It was all the encouragement he needed, and he roared as he came deep inside her mouth. He felt her swallow several times, and the movement of her throat extended his orgasm, forcing a long groan from his mouth. Despite his release, he was still hard.

Reaching down, he surprised her by grabbing her under her arms and pulling her up until she was straddling his hips. He leaned over and grabbed one of the condoms he'd placed on the nightstand when he changed his pants earlier. She lifted onto her knees, and he rolled it on before lining his cock up with her opening. As soon as his head was inside her, she lowered herself all the way down onto him. She was so tight, but her wetness eased his entry. He grabbed her hips and began to rock them up and down in time to his own. "Oh God, sweetheart. You feel so fucking good."

* * *

Kristen couldn't believe another orgasm was building up

inside her. Never in her life had she known sex could be so incredible. This was what women bragged about and what she wrote in her books. She clenched around him, and he groaned, so she did it again. His finger found her clit, and when he pressed down, she screamed as waves of ecstasy flowed through her. Before she knew what was happening, Devon flipped them so he was on top of her and began to pump his hips feverishly.

Holy crap! There was no way she could come again. But he proved her wrong, and, this time, she took him with her, and as one, they flew over the edge.

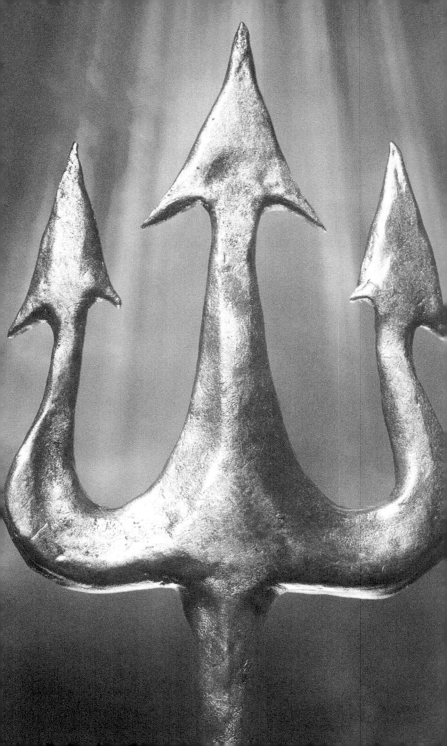

CHAPTER FOURTEEN

Devon sat in his office, waiting for Boomer to join him. The team's youngest member had sent him a text telling him he was running about ten minutes late due to a flat tire on his Jeep. Devon's desk had files and paperwork on it that needed attention, but his mind was on the brunette he woke up next to this morning. He couldn't remember the last time he spent an entire night in bed with a woman, but it had been many years. Thinking back, it must've been while he'd been in the Navy, and not in his own bed, but one in a hotel. No other woman, aside from Jenn, his mother, Aunt Marsha, and the interior decorator, had ever been in his apartment here in the complex. All his sexual encounters occurred at the club—until last night.

He'd awoken to Kristen's seductive hand grazing across his chest and abdomen before she began to explore lower. Instead of letting her know he was awake, he'd kept his eyes shut for a few moments enjoying her touch. She'd been about to wrap her soft hand around his hard dick when he surprised her by flipping her over to her stomach, grabbing a condom, and sliding into her from behind.

It had been quick and carnal and somehow not satisfying enough because he took her again a few minutes later in the shower. But not before taking his time to soap up and touch every inch of her luscious body, making her scream at the top of her lungs as she came for him again. He wondered if Ian had heard her in his own apartment below, despite the soundproofing they'd installed in the walls and ceilings of the units.

In one night, and early morning, he'd given her eight or nine orgasms—he'd lost count at some point—and found his own release four times. And yet he wished she was here in his office so he could fuck her silly on his desk. Kristen may be many things, but frigid was not one of them.

He couldn't get enough of his Ninja-girl librarian. The woman had so many different layers to her, and he didn't think he would ever discover them all if he tried for the rest of his life. For some strange reason that he couldn't explain, he hadn't removed her submissive collar after he'd dropped her off at her car this morning. He'd noticed she touched it often as if it grounded her, and the thought pleased him more than it should.

She'd been so eager and responsive last night that it blew his mind. He couldn't remember a time when a woman's innocence had turned him on the way Kristen's did. He also couldn't recall ever being so at ease with a woman he had sex with. After she left The Covenant yesterday afternoon, he'd looked through her background check Marco had done several days earlier.

He'd been surprised to see she hadn't sought alimony during her divorce, even though her ass-monkey ex, Tom Rydell, made a good living as a stockbroker, and the goat-fucker would've deserved it if she had. Most women would've taken their revenge against a cheating husband out of his bank account. Kristen hadn't. In addition to being a beta-reader herself for other authors, her books earned her decent money, which she could live off of in comfort. She was making her own way in the world and was proud of it.

Devon had never found a woman so enticing beyond a basic sexual attraction, and despite his thoughts, or maybe because of them, he couldn't wait to see her again tonight. They'd made plans for a late dinner at his place and even later dessert since he would be working until around seven. He would have to retrieve his toy bag from his locker at the club because he knew what her next lesson would involve.

He heard a knock on his door and lifted his head to see Boomer walk in and sit down in one of the leather chairs on the other side of his desk. "Hey, Devil Dog, sorry I'm late. I must've run over a nail last night. Damn tire was flatter than a piece of road-kill this morning."

Devon glanced at the small clock inside a brass anchor on his desk, noting the time. "No problem, man. Shit happens. We still have a few minutes before we have to leave for the airport to meet up with King Rajeemh and his lovely offspring."

He said the last three words with sarcasm and an eye roll. King Rajeemh was the ruler of the small North African country of Timasur, near Mali. The man owned several homes worldwide, but the nearby Gulf-front Clearwater Beach mansion was one of his favorites. He and his family visited several times a year and used Trident Security to assist his personal bodyguards while they were there. For royalty, the king was a laid-back man and kind to anyone in his employ as long as they didn't insult or betray him. His son, Prince Raji, the heir to the throne, was exactly like him. But his daughter, Princess Tahira, was a completely different story.

The exotically-beautiful twenty-three-year-old was a spoiled brat, plain and simple. She treated her minions as if they were bugs on the bottom of her shoe—unless she wanted something from them. She also had a thing for American men and had unsuccessfully propositioned every man at Trident, along with the company's contract employees they brought in when extra manpower was needed. And damn, could she pout and get revenge when she didn't get what she wanted.

The last time she was in Florida, it was Brody who she'd blatantly hit on when her father's back was turned. After the geek shot her down for the third time one morning, she dragged him and the rest of her security detail to every shoe store within a fifty-mile radius. She then spent five hours trying on every single pair she liked—not once, not twice, but three times, asking the former SEAL his opinion on each pair, as if Brody knew the difference between a pump and kitten heel. Devon didn't know the difference either, but later the same night, Brody had gone on a half-hour rampage, bitching about the little princess and her fetish, so they'd all gotten an unwanted lesson on women's shoes. They'd finally begged Shelby to scene with him to shut him up, not that the sub had minded.

"Why am I stuck on this assignment again?" Boomer had been complaining for the past two days since they found out the royal party was making a last-minute change in their itinerary after visiting New York, where King Rajeemh had been attending a conference at the U.N.

"Because it's your turn in the princess rotation."

"And why are you and Ian not in the rotation again?"

Devon smirked. "Because we sign your paychecks, ass-hat."

The younger man frowned. "I knew there was some

fucked-up, bullshit reason. Can you just shoot me now and put me out of my impending misery? You know how much I hate shopping unless it's for a new gun or toy for the club."

Devon chuckled before Boomer's frown turned into an evil grin as if a thought had suddenly occurred to him. "So, speaking of the club..."

Uh-oh.

"Tell me about this..." He snapped his fingers a few times. "Um, what did Egghead call it? Oh yeah... a date. That's it. Tell me about this date you went on last night. I heard she was smokin' and kicked some serious ass in the locker room." Boomer had apparently shown up at The Covenant after Devon had dragged Kristen out of there.

"You went on a date?"

Both men's eyes whipped toward the open office door and saw Paula Leighton standing there. Boomer turned back around so the woman couldn't see him and mouthed the word 'sorry.' The thirty-year-old office manager had worked for them for the last three months after Mrs. Kemple retired to be closer to her newborn triplet grandchildren in Miami. The older woman had worked for them since the beginning of Trident and was a surrogate mother of sorts to all of them. She'd been a godsend when Jenn first came to live with Ian, giving the younger girl an understanding and sympathetic female shoulder to lean on and taking her shopping for things she would need for her college dorm room. They'd thrown her a big party at a local restaurant and given her a handsome severance check when she left them after training Paula, and the gray-haired woman was deeply missed.

Efficiency wasn't Paula's problem. The problem was she was overly nosy about their personal lives and tried to insert herself into them. She also made it not-so-subtly known she wouldn't mind going out with any of the men she saw every day in the office, but it appeared her hopes hung on Marco.

In a way, Devon felt sorry for her because she tried too hard to fit in, making it much more apparent that she didn't. The men tried to be subtle yet let her know they weren't interested in her other than as the woman who ran their office. Even if any of them were attracted to her, none of them were stupid enough to get involved with a company employee. If things didn't change, Devon would have to talk with Ian about letting her go and looking for a replacement.

At the moment, he didn't want to answer her prying question and posed one of his own. "Paula, what are you doing here on a Saturday?"

It was a testament to where his mind had been earlier when he realized he had never heard the alert on his phone, which sounded when the interior gate was opened, not only when Boomer drove up but also when Paula had arrived.

The woman waved her hand as if her unexpected presence was no big deal. "Oh, I left my wallet in my desk yesterday after I paid some bills during lunch, so I swung by to pick it up. I was going to use the restroom before I left. So, who did you go out with last night?"

Standing, Devon picked up his shoulder holster and put it on before placing his SIG Sauer 9mm semi-automatic in it.

"No one you would know." His response was vague on purpose. He grabbed his keys and cell phone off his desk before retrieving the lightweight sports coat, which would conceal his weapon in public, from where it was lying over the arm of his couch a short distance away. They didn't need to leave for another ten minutes or so, but he didn't want to give Paula a chance to ask any more questions.

"Come on, Boomer. Don't want to keep the princess waiting." Passing the woman on his way out, he added, "Have a nice weekend, Paula."

* * *

"Okay, sweet cheeks, lunch orders are in, mimosas are at hand. Start dishing the dirt."

Kristen rolled her eyes at Will and realized she was playing with the leather collar that was still around her neck. She forgot to take it off this morning and didn't want to now. Devon hadn't told her to remove it, and it didn't feel right to do so without his permission. "I have no idea what you're talking about."

"Don't be coy, Kristen, or I'll have Roxy spank your ass."

They all snorted and giggled at Kayla's comment, and Roxy added, "I don't know, honey. I think she might like it too much." The four of them laughed even harder, drawing a few stares from the Saturday brunch crowd at The Gallery. The place was a combination art gallery/restaurant the others had introduced her to. The owners served great food and displayed paintings from local artists for sale. Some of the painters showed a lot of talent, and every time they'd gone there to eat, new ones had replaced paintings that had been sold.

One painting caught Kristen's eye when they'd first sat down, and after taking a better look, she realized it was similar to the art in the lobby of The Covenant. She wondered if they'd been done by the same artist and decided to ask Devon about it tonight over dinner.

Kristen looked at her friends and cousin and was once again grateful for her new life in Florida. Two months after they'd married, Tom had transferred to his company's New York City office, so they'd moved to New Jersey, across the Hudson River from Manhattan. At first, she'd been happy to follow her new husband anywhere, but it wasn't long before she became lonely. Her best friend from high school, who'd also been her maid of honor, had made a permanent move to Arizona after graduating from ASU.

Kristen's other high school and college friends were scattered all over the States with new careers and families. Her parents and step-parents had their own jobs and lives to keep them busy. Most of their neighbors in Ridgewood, New Jersey, had been two-income families, who worked Monday to Friday, nine-to-five or later, so she hadn't bonded with any of them past the point of generic conversations. She'd thrown herself into her writing, and her human contact soon consisted of only her husband when he was home, her family and best friend over the phone, and her editor and beta-readers online, with a few get-togethers with Tom's associates thrown in for good measure.

Now she had face-to-face friends again, and it felt wonderful. "Okay, what do you want to hear about first? Dinner, the club, or after?"

Roxy called out "the club," while the other two demanded she tell them about "after."

She giggled and took another sip. "I'll tell you what—it's easier to go through everything in order." Her tablemates groaned before she lowered her voice so as not to be overheard by other patrons. "Okay, I'll do this part quick. I was thirteen minutes late meeting him, and he promised to spank me for each minute I was late. Dinner was great. I had the veal piccata, and he had the steak pizzaiola. Good conversation, no turn-offs, lots of turn-ons, and one minor faux pas on my part where it sounded like I was asking about his financial status. He didn't seem to mind. Lots of flirting, and he fed me a bite of his dinner. I let him drive me over to the club in his car. Nervous chit-chat, and we arrived safely."

Her companions laughed at her rushed, stunted recap of

the first part of her date. She took a dramatic breath and then a sip of her champagne with orange juice. "Okay, moving on to the good stuff. When we got to the club, he opened my car door for me like a perfect gentleman and then kissed me senseless. And, yes, the man can kiss."

She paused as the waitress dropped off their bruschetta appetizer. "The club was absolutely amazing. It looks so different at night with the mood lighting and all."

Roxy spoke up. "And I'm sure having a bunch of nearly naked people walking around had something to do with the different atmosphere."

Kristen winced, then nodded because that part had been awkward. "Yeah, it freaked me out at first. I was being introduced to all these people, some with all their private parts showing, and I didn't know where to look."

"It does take a while to get used to. When I started taking Kay to clubs, it flustered her more than the scenes. Casual conversation is hard when you're trying not to stare at a chick's who-ha and jugs or a guy's junk."

They all burst out laughing again, drawing even more attention to themselves, but they couldn't help it. Will was almost crying. "Who-ha, jugs, and junk? Are those actual medical terms, Doctor? Yes, Mrs. Smith, your son playing with his junk is normal, and your teenage daughter's who-ha hasn't been popped yet, but she needs to get a bra for those jugs."

Kristen almost fell out of her chair because she laughed so hard her cheeks and stomach ached. The others were just as bad. It took several minutes for them to all regain control because they couldn't look at each without losing it again. She waved her hands in front of her tear-filled eyes. "Oh my God, Will, you did not just say that."

"Of course I did, sweet cheeks. It's what I'm here for . . . to look good for the men and to be a comic relief and fashion stylist for my girls. Now get back to the juicy details, like why you're still wearing his collar. I may not be into kink," he pointed to her neck, "but I do know what one of those means."

"You fucking bitch!"

Startled, Kristen and her friends looked up to see a very pissed-off woman standing over her. She was shocked when she realized it was the redhead whose butt she'd kicked last night. Heather or Melissa—she wasn't sure who was who. Either way, Kristen wouldn't stay in a vulnerable position, so she stood, as did Roxy and Will, who'd been sitting on either side of her, while Kayla looked on from her seat tucked away in a corner.

"Because of you, I lost my membership to the club, you bitch."

There was pure venom in her words and rage in her eyes, but Kristen refused to back down even though they were making a public scene. She'd bested the woman the night before and would do it again today. She kept her voice calm, which would surely piss the redhead off even more. "No, *you* lost your membership because *you* and your cohort were bullying a sweet, innocent girl who was too afraid of you to stand up for herself. It's what bully-bitches like you do. But I told you last night, and I'll tell you again . . . I'm not afraid of you, so if you want to try to take me on, I'll gladly drop you on your fugly face again."

She took a step forward, but Roxy was quicker and moved in front of her, facing the woman who'd interrupted their brunch with her rudeness. If she hadn't learned Roxy was a BDSM top, Kristen might not have noticed the authority in her voice. But now she clearly recognized the low don't-fuck-with-me-or-you'll-regret-it tone of a

Dom/Domme, and she knew she'd never want to be on the good doctor's wrong side. "Heather, I don't know if you remember me, but your friend, Scott, is an associate of mine from the hospital. And I doubt you want me to talk with him about your behavior today because, from the sound of things, I'm sure he's already angry with you. Now, I suggest you leave, or I'll call Scott faster than you can say 'Yes, Ma'am.' Do I make myself clear?"

Kristen watched as Heather paled more and more with every word Roxy spoke. The Domme doctor was a healthy size six and five-eleven in her low heels, so she could be daunting when she wanted to be. She towered over the now-very-intimidated sub, who Kristen expected to pass out or pee in her pants. Without saying anything more, Heather spun around and tore out of the restaurant, leaving two very confused other women to take off after her.

Roxy turned and looked at Kristen, her eyes gleaming with mischief. "Oh, girl, I can tell you haven't gotten to the good parts yet, and I can't wait to hear them."

As the three sat back down, Kayla batted her eyes at her wife and crooned, "I love when you go into your protective Wonder Woman persona. It's such a turn-on." She then stared at Kristen while flagging down their waitress simultaneously. "Start dishing, girl. This is going to be good. Waitress, another pitcher of mimosas, please."

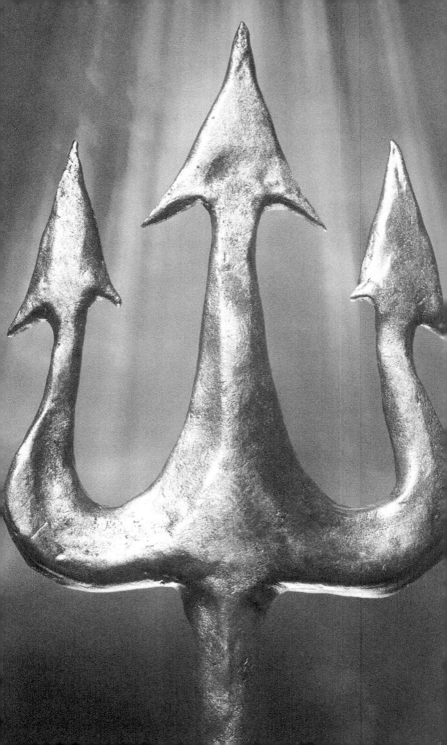

CHAPTER FIFTEEN

At a quarter after seven that night, Kristen was slicing tomatoes in Devon's kitchen for a salad she was throwing together. Across the island from where she worked, the man's broad back was turned to her as he sautéed a skillet filled with penne ala vodka. He was handsome, a good conversationalist, an even better Dom, incredible at sex, and now, he cooked! What more could a girl want?

She hadn't eaten anything since noon, and now her stomach was growling. The rest of brunch had been uneventful as she'd recapped the remaining details of her date for her friends. She'd told them enough to satisfy their curiosity but still kept many aspects to herself.

She felt so at ease with Devon as they prepared and then ate their dinner, and it felt like they'd known each other a lot longer than they actually had. He talked about his day, taking care of the security for a king and some spoiled princess from a small country in Africa, and she told him about her brunch at The Gallery, complete with the run-in with Heather.

At first, he reacted as if he wanted to commit murder but calmed down after she explained how Mistress Roxanne had taken over. "Roxy's wife, Kayla, told me they applied for membership at The Covenant a few months ago. They currently go to another club—I think she called it 'Heat,' but since Roxy is a pediatrician, Kayla said they wanted the increased privacy your club provides."

"What's their last name? I'll tell Mitch to put their application at the top of the list. If there are no red flags, we'll approve it within the next few weeks. It's the least I can do for the way she protected my sub."

Her heart fluttered when he said, "my sub." She knew he didn't mean it as possessive as she thought it sounded, but she still liked it. "It's London, and thanks. That would be so great. They're a really nice couple, and I know they'd appreciate the gesture."

"There's nothing to appreciate. It's my way of thanking them."

They sat down at the dinner table with Devon at one end and Kristen in the seat catty-corner to him. She picked up her fork and pointed it at him before digging into her meal. "So tell me more about your family since I told you about mine last night. You said your parents are Marie and Chuck Sawyer. Can I assume your dad's real name is Charles or Charlie?"

Out of the blue, the name clicked in her brain. Her eyes widened, and the fork slipped from her fingers and clattered against her plate. "Oh. My. God. Your dad is Charles Sawyer? *The* Charles Sawyer? I thought he looked familiar. I read an article about him in *People* magazine. He's like the Trump of the Carolinas and Virginias."

He laughed and shook his head in amusement. "Don't tell

him that. Dad doesn't get along with Trump. He thinks he's too egotistical."

She couldn't believe he was joking about how his *billionaire* father—yes, that was with a *B*—didn't care for another *billionaire* like they were two neighborhood guys who didn't get along. The man in front of her was the heir to a fortune that ninety-nine-point-nine percent of the population could only dream of. *Holy crap!*

She picked up her fork again. "Didn't I . . . didn't I read how he and your mom were raised in middle-class families, and he started with a small real estate agency?"

He took a bite of pasta, chewed, then swallowed. "Yup, it's true. Two years before Ian was born, Dad managed to buy his first apartment building out of foreclosure. The man is shrewd, a quick study, and some would say extremely lucky. By the time I was three or four, he'd made some wise investments and owned a bunch of buildings and strip malls in both North and South Carolina and built his empire from there. He's the CEO of Sawyer-O'Toole, which is Mom's maiden name, but his staff and the board handle the day-to-day operations when he's traveling with my mom."

"Is that how you had the money to start your businesses? Oh, wait! There I go again, don't answer that." She had to stop putting her foot in her mouth because she didn't seem to have a filter around him.

"No, don't worry about it. We grew up more comfortable than my parents did when they were young. But Mom and Dad always made sure we weren't spoiled. We did chores for our allowances and went to public schools. I told you how we worked in the poor countries my parents took us to.

"At fourteen, when we were old enough to get our working papers, we had to either get jobs or volunteer an average teenage work week at a non-profit organization.

When we graduated from high school, we had to choose between a four-year college degree, holding at least a 3.6 GPA, or four years in the military. Dad had served a four-year stint in the Army before marrying my mom and always said that's when he grew up and became a man.

"Dad set us all up with trust funds, but we couldn't access them until we were thirty. At eighteen, we started receiving a small monthly stipend which was only enough for bare-bones living expenses. If we wanted anything more, it had to come from an earned paycheck. Nick hasn't even gotten access to his full trust yet, since he's only twenty-five.

"Anyway, Ian and I used part of our trust money to purchase this compound, start our security business, Trident Security, and the club. My father might have given us the seed money, but he made sure we earned it over the years and knew what it was like to work hard for what we wanted. Life was not handed to you on a silver platter in the Sawyer family. My folks are the greatest and kindest people I know, and they taught us what it meant to have pride in ourselves, our work, and the world around us."

Kristen was impressed with his parents' dedication to raising their sons the right way. "Wow, I went to school with a bunch of spoiled kids who could've learned so much from your parents. Most kids nowadays expect everything to be handed to them with no work involved. So, you and your brothers all chose the Navy over college?"

Sadness clouded his handsome features, and he swallowed hard. He was clearly struggling with how to answer her. Not wanting him to be uncomfortable, she was about to change the subject when he stood, walked over to the entertainment unit, and picked up the photo of the four brothers she'd been looking at the night before.

"Ian went into the Navy right after high school, but I

chose college. The University of North Carolina at Chapel Hill with a business major, in fact. Ian's two years older than me. He was off saving the world while I was partying after class. I still managed a 3.8 GPA my first semester—although it might have been higher if my statistics class hadn't been so early in the morning."

He sat back down next to her and handed her the framed picture. He seemed to forget he'd told her who was who last night and pointed to each of the four young boys in the photo. "This is Ian, right before he left for basic training. That's me, and the little guy is Nick, who was about six back then. And this here is my other brother, John."

The odd tone of his voice when he mentioned John had Kristen studying the photo a little bit more. Devon and John each had one of their arms around their older brother's shoulders while Ian held Nick under his armpits so the boy's feet were hanging in mid-air. All four of them were mugging for the camera. "He looks exactly like you. Are you twins?"

"Many people got us confused, but no, we weren't. We were Irish twins, though, since he was eleven months younger than me." She noticed the past tense he was now using. "And Nick was a surprise. Anyway, John and I hung out with a lot of the same people since we were so close in age, but he was a year younger in school. During high school, we partied like most kids, finding ways to get beer and liquor without getting caught. I knew he was drinking a lot on the weekends, but hell, we all were. For the most part, we managed to keep our parents from finding out, but there were a few times we weren't as careful as we thought which resulted in getting grounded. When that happened, Mom would give the housekeeper a few days off, with pay, and we had to clean the house for her while completely hung over. I didn't know which was worse, the sound of the vacuum on a pounding head or cleaning the bathrooms which five guys used."

He let out a wry chuckle and shook his head at the memory. His meal forgotten, he took a deep breath and continued. "Anyway, John got hooked on alcohol, and I never knew it. None of us did. I didn't think a seventeen-year-old kid could be an alcoholic, but I was wrong."

He sighed but continued, and Kristen got the feeling he didn't talk about this often. Her heart clenched at how he trusted her with his past and emotions. "I'd returned to college for my second semester. Christmas and New Year's had been great. Ian couldn't make it but was able to call home from somewhere overseas—I forget where—on Christmas morning, which, of course, made my mom and Nick's day. I was back at school, settling into my new classes and hanging out with my friends again.

"I'd hooked up with this girl right before vacation, and we picked right up where we left off. We were making out in my room one Friday night after a few hours at a local bar. There was a knock at my door. I had her half-undressed, and we were laughing and having fun like normal nineteen-year-olds, so I yelled at whoever it was to fuck off. The knocking turned into pounding, and I got up to open the door and tell whoever it was to take a hike. It was my dad and my Uncle Dan, Mitch's dad. The look on their faces . . . I assumed it was Ian, but it wasn't. It was John.

"He'd ditched school that morning after Mom, Dad, and Nick left for work and school. I don't recall why, but the housekeeper was off that day too. Dad forgot something in his home office and swung by to pick it up at lunchtime. He found John on the kitchen floor with one and a half empty bottles of vodka. He drank so much he'd passed out, then vomited and aspirated. There was nothing the EMTs could do.

"We found out later his blood alcohol level was four times the legal limit. Here I was having a great time, partying at school, and making out with some girl, trying to get into her pants while my kid brother was on a medical examiner's table." His hand rubbed the left side of his chest. "That's what my tattoo over my heart is—his initials and birthday and the day he died."

Sometime during his story, Kristen had moved her chair closer and now had his other hand in hers. "It wasn't your fault. Alcoholics are usually pretty good at hiding their problems. John obviously hid it well, so you can't blame yourself."

"Part of me knows that now, but part of me will always carry the guilt of knowing my brother was spiraling out of control, and I didn't stop it. I saw he'd been drinking a lot over the winter recess, but I refused to admit he had a problem. Anyway, it took three days to get Ian home from the middle of nowhere, and then we went through the whole Irish wakes and funeral. The night of the funeral, a few family members came back to the house after the service and restaurant get-together.

"I don't know why, but I hadn't cried at all the entire week —I guess I was numb. I was sitting on the patio with Mitch's older brother, DJ—Dan, Jr.—and Ian came out with a couple of beers. I took one sip, maybe two, and threw up all over the place. Once nothing was left in my stomach, I dry-heaved for almost an hour, then broke down and cried. Ian sat on the grass with me and didn't let go of me until I got myself under control. I haven't touched a sip of alcohol since."

Devon took a deep breath as a lone tear fell down his left cheek. Kristen took her hand off his arm and wiped it away with her fingers. "I can't believe I told you all of that. My team knows the basics of what happened, but I've never told anyone the whole story."

She leaned forward and brushed her lips against his before sitting back again. "I'm honored you told me. I'm sorry you had to go through that. I don't have any brothers or sisters, but if I did, I don't think I would've survived the same loss without a complete breakdown."

Obviously embarrassed about crying in front of her, he stood and began to clean up from their meal. "Well, for a while there, I didn't think I would survive, either. I didn't go back to school after the funeral. John had wanted to follow Ian into the Navy. Since he couldn't, I guess I thought I should go in his place. Whatever the reason, it was the best decision I ever made, and I've never regretted it. The Navy gave me a purpose and a way to control my guilt."

Following him into the kitchen, she put away the leftovers in a container he handed her while he tackled the dirty dishes and pots. "Is that why you started playing in the lifestyle? For the control?"

He nodded. "Ian thought it would help me get past it, and in some ways, it did. At least it gave me an outlet to release the grief which had built up over time."

They finished cleaning up in silence, and the domesticity of their actions had her suddenly longing for something more. Something she swore she didn't want, and Devon told her he couldn't give her. Something which would last a lifetime. But she wouldn't have a lifetime with him. She would only have this weekend.

CHAPTER SIXTEEN

Shaking herself from her wayward thoughts, Kristen found him watching her from a relaxed position, leaning against the kitchen counter, his arms overlapping across his gray T-shirt-covered chest and his legs crossed at the ankles. "Where did you go, Pet? I lost you there for a minute."

She tried to brush his question off, not wanting him to know what she'd been thinking. "It wasn't anything important. Do you want some coffee?"

The Dom in him must not have liked her answer because he frowned, and his eyes narrowed. "Strip."

"Wh-what?"

He didn't move from his position, but his posture no longer appeared relaxed. "I won't repeat myself, Kristen. You heard me loud and clear. Either say your safeword or do as you're told."

Hesitating only a split-second longer, she pulled her sleeveless, emerald green shirt over her head and placed it on the counter beside her. His eyes roamed over her body as she continued, and they were the only part of him that moved. She felt his disconcerting gaze as if it was a caress across her skin, giving her goosebumps and increasing her pulse. After removing her sandals and white capris, she stood there in her flower print bra and thong underwear.

It wasn't enough to satisfy him. "All of it, Pet. You've already earned a count of five. Hesitating earned you five more. If you hesitate again, I'll keep adding more."

Crap! Ten wasn't *too* bad, but since he was obviously upset about something, she didn't want to add to it. Her ass had barely recovered from last night's spanking. She got rid of the last of her garments, then stood there waiting for him to say or do something. It was weird to be standing buck naked in his kitchen while he remained dressed. A minute went by . . . then another . . . and he just stared at her in silence. She began to fidget.

When she opened her mouth to ask him if she was supposed to be doing something, he abruptly pushed off the counter, causing her to flinch. "Face the island. Put your chest and stomach on the countertop. Rest your head on the backs of your hands and spread your feet as wide apart as possible."

Following his instructions, she laid her upper body across the island, and the coolness of the granite was a shock to her system. A moment of panic hit her when he left the room and returned with a black duffel bag, setting it on the other countertop behind her. Taking slow, deep breaths to keep from hyperventilating, she heard him rummaging around in the bag and tried to see what he was doing, but she couldn't from her current position.

"Do you know why I'm angry, Pet?"

He wasn't yelling at her, but his voice's flat, low tone was louder to her than any shout she'd ever heard. A shiver of fear mixed with arousal confused her. "N-no, Sir."

"When I asked you where you had gone in your complex brain, what was your answer, word for word?"

Her mind raced—what had she said? "Um, I think I said it wasn't anything important, Sir."

She tensed when he approached and stood behind her widespread legs. She waited for him to touch her, spank her, or do something to her, but he made no contact with any part of her body. The longer he stood there and didn't touch her, the more she wanted him to, in any way he wanted. The suspense of the unknown was killing her. After a minute or so, he spoke again.

"I'm not your ex-lump of cow-turd, Pet. When I ask you a question, I expect an answer worthy of your intelligence. 'It wasn't anything important' was not an intelligent answer. If I wanted you to give me a non-answer, I wouldn't have bothered to ask the question in the first place. For your little lie, you've earned a count of five. Would you like to revise your answer now, or would you prefer I give you your five, then tie your hands behind you? Then I'll leave you standing here for the next hour with one vibrator in your pussy, another in this sweet ass of yours, and a ball gag in your mouth, while I sit on the couch and find a ballgame to watch."

Seriously? "I-I'd l-like . . ." She cleared her throat and tried again. "I'd like to revise my answer, Sir."

"Very well, but I suggest you think about your answer carefully. You only have one chance to impress me."

She was so nervous that it took her a few moments to remember what she'd been thinking about before his big, bad Dom-ness showed up for a visit. What had they been doing? She remembered they'd been cleaning the kitchen and putting away the dishes. *That's it!*

She took a deep breath. "It'd occurred to me, Sir, I've never shared a meal with a man where we cooked and cleaned up together, aside from my dad when I was little. That I was enjoying something so incredibly simple surprised me, and I wanted to do it again sometime. I-I know you . . . I mean . . . we said this was temporary, and I didn't want you to think I was reading into things and wishing things could be different, so it was easier to brush off your question. I'm sorry, Sir."

He placed his hands on her bare back and began to caress her skin from her shoulders to her bottom and back up again. "Now, that wasn't so hard, was it? I may not always like or agree with your answers, but I will not allow you to lie to me. Understood?"

"Yes, Sir. I'm sorry I disrespected you with my first answer."

She couldn't see his face, but she heard the smile in his voice. "Thank you, Pet. And by the way, I also enjoyed cooking and cleaning with you, which surprised me too. I don't think I've ever done that with a woman who wasn't my mother. You never did it with your fucktard ex?"

A little giggle came out of her mouth. "Please, the douche-bag couldn't boil water without a ten-page instruction booklet."

He let out a bark of laughter. "Douche-bag? Very good, Pet, you're learning. Now, let's forget about the ass-nugget and get back to you and me. Let me get you prepped, and then I'll give you your punishment. When it's over, all will be forgiven and forgotten, and then we can move on to some fun for the rest of the evening."

Prepped? What the heck did he mean by that?

"Relax, Pet." She didn't realize she'd tensed up again. "I would never do anything to harm you, you know that, right?"

"Yes, Sir." And she did, although she noticed he used the word "harm" instead of "hurt." Had it been on purpose? It hurt initially when he'd spanked her the night before, but then it transitioned into intense pleasure. She'd been dripping with need by the time he'd finished.

His hands stroked her legs, arms, hips, and back and buttocks in a soothing, circular motion. She began to relax at his ministration and finally let out a deep sigh. She didn't notice when he removed one of his hands until she heard a pop and felt a cold liquid land slightly above her ass before oozing down between her cheeks. It was cold, and her body jerked a little, but she remained in place. The hand rubbing her back eased lower, and his fingers parted her, working the lubricant into the hidden valley and over the sensitive hole within. Her leg and butt muscles tensed, and he slapped her right ass cheek with his other hand. "Don't clench. This will be a lot easier on you if you relax."

Kristen took a deep breath and tried to do as he instructed. He didn't say what "this" was, but she didn't need him to. This morning in the shower, he'd told her he would soon take her in the ass, but he had to prepare her for it first. However, she hadn't expected her preparation to begin tonight. This was one of her soft limits, and he seemed determined to test it sooner rather than later.

As he added more lubricant, one of his fingers stopped at her untried entrance. Part of her wanted to stop him, but the other part wanted to push past her fears and self-imposed sexual restrictions. This man was giving her a chance to explore her deepest, darkest fantasies. Fantasies she would've denied having before meeting him.

"Don't tense up, Pet. I'm going to start putting my finger in. You'll feel some pressure and discomfort, but if it hurts to the point you can't take it, say the word 'yellow,' and I'll ease up and start over. Remember to breathe and bear down. It may take a while, but I promise you will have a plug in this virgin hole of yours before we go any further tonight."

Oh God, she knew he meant it, and his words made her clit throb while her mind raced. She'd never been touched by a man there before, and the feel of him at her anus scared and thrilled her simultaneously. This was what she told herself she wanted. Her Dom telling her what he would do to her, and her only choices were to let him or say her safeword and end everything. Swallowing her fear, she forced her muscles to relax. "Yes, Sir."

"Good girl." His finger rimmed her puckered opening, working in the gel which would ease his entry. He began to push in, and her body naturally fought the invasion. His hand landed on her left cheek this time. "Don't fight it. You will let me in."

She moaned, not knowing if it was because of the heat spreading from where he'd spanked her or the feeling of him easing his finger into her ass. Whenever she started to tighten the muscles surrounding her anus, he retreated for more lubricant and inched back in, a little further each time. He got to a point where she wasn't sure if she could handle the burning sensation flaring through her when he reached around with his other hand and found her clit, pinching it once, hard. The new sensation caught her off guard and switched her mind away from his finger in her ass.

As soon as it relaxed, he pushed his knuckle past her sphincter and lit up the nerves inside her. A flash of pain came and went before it was replaced with a feeling of being filled and wanting . . . no . . . needing more.

She groaned and shifted her hips, looking for something, anything that would give her the relief she desperately sought. The movement earned her another smack. "Stay still," he growled. "You'll take what I give you when I give it to you and not a second sooner."

His finger felt huge as he stroked it in and then out again, never coming all of the way out of her. He'd rotated his knuckle on each outward drag, stretching her a little more. She was panting and sweating, wanting to pull away from him . . . wanting to push back for more. "Please, Sir."

"Please, what, Pet?"

"More. Sir. Please. More." She was reduced to one-word sentences. Anything beyond that would require thought, and she couldn't think, only feel.

"I think you're trying to top from the bottom, sweetheart, but I feel a little generous tonight."

She didn't know what she expected, but it hadn't been for him to remove his finger completely. She cried out at the abrupt loss, and her breath hitched when she felt something larger than his finger at her entrance. He squirted a little more lube on her ass and began to work what she knew was an anal plug into her. It felt huge, and she didn't think he would ever be able to get it inside her. Reaching around her hip, he pinched her clit again, and the plug slid home. The sensations proved too much, and she screamed as an intense orgasm washed over her. White and black spots flashed before her closed eyes, and her body trembled as wave after wave of pleasure pulsated through her while Devon rotated the plug, now seated to its hilt, deep in her anal cavity. Her breathing was heavy as she floated back down.

"Tsk, tsk, tsk. Such a naughty sub, coming without permission. You should know better, and it brings your count up to fifteen, Pet. Now stand there, and take them like the good girl I know you can be. But I feel I must warn you, clenching will make it more . . . intense, but if you relax too much, you risk losing the plug. And trust me, Pet, you don't want to lose it. You won't like the punishment for that offense."

"Yes, Sir," she said, followed by a gulp.

She felt him step away from her and anticipated the first smack, but it didn't come. Instead, she once again heard him retrieve something from his duffel bag. Her mind ran through the possibilities of what he was getting, and none of them boded well for her. She'd been so worried she hadn't heard him approach again until she felt a sharp sting as something struck her ass cheeks. She couldn't help the sudden shriek which escaped her mouth, but somehow she didn't move. Her breathing increased again in short pants. Whatever he'd hit her with, he dragged up the inside of one of her legs and down the other. "In case you're wondering, Pet, it's a riding crop."

Before she could answer him, she felt the torture device strike her ass just above her thighs, and she went up on her toes and clenched her leg muscles. Unfortunately, that reminded her of the plug in her ass. Sensations of pain and pleasure warred inside her, and she couldn't tell which one was winning the battle. The sound of the crop connecting with her bare skin was more of a thud than a slap, but it didn't mean the damn thing didn't hurt. But as the initial sting eased, she felt the increased throbbing in her clit, and she worried she wouldn't be able to hold back another impending orgasm. By the time he reached fifteen, she was one touch away from falling into the great beyond. She heard him toss the crop on the counter behind them before his fingers dipped between her legs, and he discovered how embarrassingly wet she was.

He stroked her folds. "You liked that, didn't you, Pet?

Would you like me to give you permission to come this time?"

"Oh, God, yes! Yes, Sir. Please, Sir, let me come!"

"Since you asked so nicely . . ." One of his fingers moved further and tapped on her clit, and that was all it took to send her over while screaming her throat raw. She'd never thought she could pass out from intense pleasure, but that's exactly what happened next.

DEVON LAY ON HIS SIDE, HIS HEAD IN HIS HAND AS HE LEANED on his elbow. It was four o'clock in the morning, and he couldn't sleep. So, instead, he was watching Kristen as she slept next to him. She was still naked, her lengthy hair spread out on the pillow under her head, and he fought the urge to touch her because she deserved the rest after what he'd put her through the night before. But he needed a connection to her, so he reached out and rubbed a few strands of her brown locks with his fingers.

Reveling in the feel of her silky strands, he thought about all he'd told her last night and was surprised at how comfortable he'd felt about admitting who his dad was. While his SEAL teammates had known about his dad, few others in the Navy had ever been told beyond a couple of his superiors. And no one at the club, except for their teammates, Mitch, and Tiny, had any idea that Ian and Devon's father was *the* Charles Sawyer. Their family and friends called him Chuck—even Jenn called him Grandpa Chuck, to the older man's delight, since she was the closest thing to a grandchild he had at the moment—but to the rest of the world, he was Charles.

He'd further surprised himself when the horrible events

surrounding John's death had poured out of him until all his guilt and grief were laid out in the open for her to see. He'd never told anyone the entire story, and he was still having a hard time wrapping his brain around the fact he'd told Kristen after knowing her only a few hours—their brief encounters before their date notwithstanding. And for Christ's sake, he'd cried in front of her . . . how screwed up was that?

Looking down at her angelic face, he felt how perfect it was having her here in his bed, and the feeling terrified him. He'd told her before they started this . . . this thing . . . that he couldn't give her long-term, but as he listened to her slow, shallow breathing, he couldn't imagine letting her go. The more he thought about it, the more he realized there was no reason to do so. Maybe he'd never had a real relationship because none of the other women had been right for him past a few hours of mutual pleasure. Everything about Kristen called to him on levels he never knew existed. Maybe he'd been biding his time until she came into his life. For the first time, he enjoyed being with a woman on a level other than D/s. The sex was incredible, but besides that, he liked all the talking and snuggling he did with her. Everyday activities were fun with her by his side.

Right then, he decided to see where they went from there and try to have a relationship with her. If, in the end, it didn't work out, he'd still be a better man for having known her. But if it did work out, he was looking at a future filled with happiness . . . happiness he never knew existed before . . . happiness he now craved.

After she'd passed out for a few moments on his kitchen island, he'd picked her up and carried her to his bedroom, then explored her body while he'd waited for her to recover. He'd taken her first while she'd been on her back, sending another orgasm through her before he'd flipped her over, with her knees tucked under her, and entered her from behind. In that position, he could see the red marks he'd left on her butt cheeks and the royal blue plug sitting snugly between them. The marks would fade by the next afternoon, but she would still feel them in the morning. Between his dick and the plug up her ass, she'd been so tight, and it hadn't been long before both of them found their release.

In the master bath, he'd filled his huge Jacuzzi tub with hot water and sat them both in it after removing her plug. At first, she'd been a little embarrassed as he took the soap and a loofah and began to bathe her from her neck to her toes, but she got over it after a minute or two. Four mind-blowing orgasms had rendered her brain and limbs useless, so she'd relaxed and closed her eyes as he'd taken care of her. He chuckled when he thought back to the night before at the club. She'd been astounded when Shelby had experienced four intense orgasms within fifteen to twenty minutes. His pet wasn't shocked anymore.

She began to stir next to him, and her eyes fluttered open. "Mmmm, what time is it?"

Devon's cock came to attention at the sound of her sexy, sleepy voice and the way she stretched her body like a lazy kitten before she cuddled up to him. He kissed her nose. "A little after four."

She closed her eyes again and mumbled, "What? Why are you awake so early?"

"Just thinking."

"Anything good?"

Devon tightened the arm wrapped around her and gave her a quick squeeze. "It's always good when I'm thinking of you."

Lifting her head, she peered at him. "Really? And what was so good about your thoughts of me, hmmm?"

He reached up and tucked a few strands of hair behind her ear before he inhaled deeply and took a leap of faith. "I was thinking how I didn't want this weekend to end." Shifting onto his side so he was face to face with her, he continued, "The last time I spent more than a weekend with a woman was the girl in college. Since then, I've never had time for a relationship; if I did, I never wanted to put effort into one. Any woman I hooked up with knew it was a temporary D/s connection, and come Sunday night, it was over. Monday morning would arrive, and I'd move on without a single regret."

She placed her hand on his bare chest. It was over his tattooed heart, and he didn't want to read into it, but he liked it there. It felt like her hand belonged there.

* * *

"Do I hear a 'but' in there somewhere?" Kristen whispered, not daring to let hope rise within her without hearing his words.

He covered her hand with his own. "Yes, you do. It's Sunday morning, and I have no desire to take the collar off your neck and let you walk out my door for good tonight. You have no idea how much it scares the hell out of me, but it's not as scary as the thought of this being our last day together. Kristen, I know I said this was temporary, and I honestly don't know if it still is, but all I know is I want to see where this thing between us goes. Come tomorrow morning, I want to see you again. Please say yes."

Kristen swallowed the lump in her throat. She realized this was a big step for him since he'd used her name instead of the nickname she'd come to expect. As for his wanting to explore whatever this was between them, she'd been thinking the same thing. She didn't want to walk out his door and never see him again.

"Yes, Devon. Yes, I want to see you again after today to see where we go from here."

He breathed a sigh of relief before claiming her mouth with his.

CHAPTER SEVENTEEN

Late Wednesday morning, Devon sat at his desk, finishing the last paperwork that had been piling up since the week before. It'd been three whole days since he'd seen Kristen, and his frustration was starting to get to him.

They'd spent a few hours at the beach on Sunday afternoon after he made his early morning confession. While wading in the calm waters, they talked some more. He answered her questions about his adventures traveling with his folks to foreign places and his SEAL training. She'd told him she majored in English in college and discovered she could make extra money to supplement her bagel shop paycheck by becoming a beta-reader for other writers.

"I love to read and found out I was a good proofreader. I would proof everything from magazine articles to college term papers to complete novels. I even did a seven-hundred-page history textbook for a professor who was self-publishing it. It was a great way to take something I enjoyed doing and get paid for it, and the extra money helped while I was in college."

She drifted on her back along the water's surface while he stood on the sandy floor and held her ankles so that she wouldn't float away. "So, my little Ninja-girl, how'd you go from beta-reader to writer?"

"One day, I was reading a manuscript from a new client. It was so bad I was ready to rip my hair out by chapter two. It amazes me how some people graduate high school and have no concept of proper grammar, punctuation, and spelling. I was on the phone bitching about it to Will and said an off-hand remark of how I could write a story better than some half-assed author-impersonator, and he said, 'Well, why don't you.' And the rest, as they say, is history. With help from one of my clients, I self-published my first two books before my current editor contacted me, and things took off for me from there."

Tugging her feet, he pulled her further into deeper water, away from prying eyes. He wanted to touch her, but there was a group of children playing in the shallow waters, and he didn't want to contribute to the delinquency of minors. "So what did the dickwhacker think of your writing?"

She giggled. "The whacker thought it was a stupid hobby, and there was no way I would be the author of the next great American novel. He didn't understand that I wasn't doing it to be great. I was doing it because I enjoyed it, and if what I wrote brought enjoyment to my readers, I was happy. After we got engaged, he told me he didn't want his wife to work because he made enough to support us. I refused to give up proofreading because I'd connected with several of my authors and loved helping others develop their stories. He didn't think I could make any money as an author, and it kept me busy, so my little hobby was okay with him."

"Prick-meister. He said that because he was jealous of you. Instead of being proud of you and showing you off to anyone who would listen, he belittled you out of jealousy."

"I never thought of it that way. I just thought . . . Oh, God, Devon, what are you doing?" She moaned as her eyes rolled back in her head.

He smiled. While they'd been talking, he'd pulled her toward him, and her knees were now straddling his hips, and his back was to the shoreline blocking her body from everyone's view. One hand supported her lower back as she floated, while the fingers of his other hand were under the crotch of her bathing suit, teasing her hard little clit.

"I'm playing with my toy, little subbie. This belongs to me, remember? I can play with it whenever and wherever I like, and right now, I like. Now be a good girl and stay nice and quiet. I don't think the parents of those kids by the shore want them to get an impromptu sex education lesson."

Her long hair drifted around her head while he played with her, bringing her to the edge several times and easing off right before she flew over. She begged him and moaned quietly until he relented and gave her what she needed. He watched in amusement as she managed to keep her head above water and covered her mouth with both hands to keep her screams to a minimum as she bucked against his fingers. After she recovered and he managed to get his straining erection under control, they headed back to the beach and basked in the sun for a few hours.

It'd been a wonderful day, but on their way to get something to eat, Devon had received a call from an old teammate who informed him of the death of another former SEAL they'd served with several years earlier. Eric Prichard had been struck and killed by a hit-and-run driver while on his evening run, leaving behind his devastated wife and four children.

Devon had apologized for needing to cut their day short and dropped Kristen off at her apartment, promising he'd call her later. He'd then met Ian at the office to clear their schedules for the next several days and run through their current cases and details, including King Rajeemh's, ensuring their contractors could cover everything for a few days.

Boomer had been thrilled he was being yanked from his princess babysitting duties until he'd heard why.

Early Monday morning, the six former SEALs and their niece boarded a plane bound for Iowa to bury one of their own and assist his family with anything they needed. Devon's heart had broken when he saw Jennifer with Prichard's kids. He knew the sorrow surrounding her must've brought back the nightmare events she had lived through months earlier with startling clarity. But somehow, Jenn had managed to tamp down her own grief and focused on helping out with the four little ones, all of whom were under twelve. Her parents would have been proud of the adult their daughter had become.

The following two days had been long and emotional. After *Taps* had been played at the grave site, and the former SEALs pounded their trident pins into the wood of their colleague's coffin, they all gathered to celebrate the man's life with friends and family. Later that night, they'd coordinated with former teammates to ensure Dana Prichard would have all the support she needed to get through the next few months as a new widow and then headed back to Tampa. Except for Ian, who had flown to Miami for an early meeting the next morning, everyone had gone straight home, completely exhausted. After ten p.m., Devon had pulled into the compound after dropping Jenn at her dorm, and it'd been too late to call Kristen. He hadn't wanted to disturb her since she'd also been busy the entire day at a "Meet and Greet" luncheon, followed by a book signing event for her fans.

He'd been looking forward to seeing her later today, but now thoughts of her were making him hard. This morning, he was the only one in the office besides Paula, and Ian wasn't due back until that night. Devon had made plans for dinner with Kristen over the phone right after he woke up this morning, but he wanted to see her in the worst way. He couldn't wait until later.

He was about to pick up his cell to call her when the thing lit up, displaying Ian's name. "What's up, Boss-man?"

"Hey, Dev, I'm on my way back early. Larry Keon called. He wants to meet with the team about something. I didn't get the details yet because he called while boarding a flight from D.C., but he sounded worried about something. Carter's coming too."

Devon sat up straighter with those last three words. T. Carter was in black ops. Even though the team had known him for the past ten years or so, having worked with him in numerous situations around the world, they still didn't know which alphabet agency he belonged to. Hell, they didn't even know his first name. The man had contacts in the CIA, FBI, NSA, and Pentagon, to name a few—and those were only the domestic agencies. He also had plenty of other contacts around the globe. Devon wasn't sure, but he wouldn't be surprised if POTUS had Carter on the White House speed dial.

If he was coming to them for a meeting in their office, there was something to worry about. It was bad enough the FBI's Deputy Director, the number two man in the agency, who was one of Trident's highest government contacts, was flying in rather than calling. Still, if Carter would be there, something serious had or was about to happen. "Shit, that isn't good. What do you need me to do?"

"Call the team and tell them to get their asses in for a two o'clock rendezvous. Keon's landing ten minutes after me, so I'll wait for him. Oh, and give Paula the rest of the day off. I don't want her anywhere near the place while we chat with our friends."

"Got it. Anything else?"

"No, that's it. I'm walking into the airport now. See you at two."

Ten minutes later, Devon had alerted the team and sent Paula on her way after assuring her several times they could run the office without her for a few hours. He also stressed they didn't need her to take notes at the meeting, and she would still be paid for a full workday. After the annoying woman left, he then took a moment to call Kristen and say hello. She picked up on the second ring. "Hello, Master Devon." He smiled because the woman practically purred.

"Master Devon, hmm? My pet sounds horny."

She laughed. "I'm definitely horny. You spoiled me for three days, and then I went three days without. Yup, I'm horny. Can you meet me for lunch? I can't wait 'til dinner."

Devon's phone beeped with an incoming call, and he reluctantly removed it from his ear and looked at the screen. *Carter.* "Pet, hang on a second for me, please. I have another call I have to answer."

When she acknowledged him, he hit the button to switch the call. "Hey, my friend, I hear you're coming for a visit. Want to tell me what's going on?"

"Not over the phone, Devil Dog. I'm about an hour out. How about meeting me for a bite to eat beforehand? It's been a long morning."

The wheels in Devon's head began to spin, and a thought came to him. Glancing at the clock, he saw he had plenty of time. "I got a better idea if you're up for it. How does a subbie sandwich sound to you?"

There was a pause, and then Carter's deep voice rumbled over the phone. "It sounds tasty, my friend. Where should I meet you, the club?"

"No, we'll be in my office waiting for you. Can you make it thirteen hundred sharp?"

"Absolutely. See you in a few."

After Carter disconnected the call, Devon switched back to Kristen. "Pet?"

"I'm here," she responded.

"Do you remember my librarian fantasy I told you about?"

She giggled. "You want me to do it now, Sir?"

"Uh-huh. I want you to wear a professional but sexy skirt, a white button-down shirt, those stilettos I love, and your glasses and drive to my office. The guard will buzz you past the second gate. Park at the first building, ring the doorbell, and I'll let you in."

"Whatever you say, Master Devon. Will you let me spank you for not returning your library books on time?"

Devon laughed out loud as his dick hardened at her playfulness. "You'll pay for your sass, little girl. Now, I also want you to put your hair up and not wear any underwear, Pet. No one else is here. You have exactly forty-five minutes to ring the bell, and if you're a minute late, you'll end up over my knee. Do you understand?" It would give him fifteen minutes before Carter arrived.

He could hear the excitement and arousal in her voice. "Yes, Sir."

"Good, I'll see you then and not a minute later."

Disconnecting the call, Devon sat back and smiled for a moment before getting up and heading to his apartment for supplies.

A SHORT TIME LATER, DEVON'S PHONE ALERTED HIM TO THE gate being opened outside his office, and he brought the compound's security camera images up on his computer to watch Kristen pull in next to the building. He glanced at the clock and saw she was two minutes early, but as he watched the video feed, he wondered what she was doing—she hadn't gotten out of her Nissan Altima yet.

He watched as she removed a strapless bra she apparently wore to prevent anyone else from seeing her dark nipples through her thin white blouse before she tucked the lacy garment into her purse. She then checked her makeup and hair in the mirror under the car visor but still made no effort to open the door and get out. He zoomed the camera in toward her face and saw her glance several times at the middle of the dashboard where the clock radio would be. Well, well, well . . . his sassy little girl didn't want to be early or on time even. It seemed she wanted to ensure she was a tad late, guaranteeing herself a punishment. He barked out a laugh at her antics. He'd created a subbie monster.

When she finally got out of the car and said hello to Beau, who'd been waiting to greet her, Devon's breath caught, and his cock lengthened. She was sexy as sin, his fantasies come true, in a snug, gray pencil skirt, which landed an inch below her knees, the white blouse with the top few buttons almost obscenely undone, and her kick-ass heels. She'd followed his orders, and her hair was twisted in a tidy little bun. He watched as she put her reading glasses atop her pert little nose and walked toward the main entrance. Standing, he didn't wait for the bell to sound before heading out to greet her.

The doorbell rang seconds before he opened the door to let her in. "You're late, Ms. Anders."

"No later than your library books, Sir," she sassed as she walked past him into the reception area, apparently not too worried he was in Dom mode.

His mouth and hands twitched, and he couldn't wait to

get both on her. "Come with me, Ms. Anders, and we'll discuss the penalties in my office." He turned and walked away, knowing she would be right on his heels.

After they entered his office, he shut the door but didn't lock it. Carter would need to get in. Kristen stood in the middle of the room, and he walked around her slowly, looking her up and down, building her anticipation. He would've liked to have drawn out the suspense a little longer, but he was on the clock to get her where he wanted before his friend showed up. Circling his desk, he sat down in the comfortable leather chair. "Come here, Ms. Anders. It's time for you to pay for your tardiness."

He watched her eyes and nostrils flare before she approached him in silence and stopped at his side. "Pull your skirt up to your waist and place yourself across my lap."

She did as he ordered without argument, presenting her bare cheeks for punishment. He shifted her on his legs until she was off-balance. With her feet in mid-air, she touched the floor with her fingertips to steady herself. The woman had the type of ass most men loved to bounce off of as they fucked their lovers from behind, enjoying the soft cushion of flesh. He rubbed his hand over her enticing globes as he spoke. "It'll be ten, my little librarian, and you'll count out loud and thank me after each one. Understand?"

"Yes, Sir."

He loved the breathy, nervous hitch in her voice. After squeezing her butt cheeks several times to get the blood flowing, he lifted his hand and smacked it back down.

"Ow! One, Sir. Thank you."

Smack.

"Two, Sir. Thank you."

He continued to the count of ten, increasing the intensity with each smack, and then looked at the work of art he'd created. Her ass and upper thighs were bright red, and he could make out several of his overlapping hand prints. He caressed her abused flesh before dipping his fingers between her legs to check her level of arousal. She was dripping. *Perfect.*

He helped her stand before swiveling the chair so he was facing her. "Kneel, my little librarian. Take my cock out and stroke me."

Without lowering her skirt, she dropped to her knees and greedily reached for his zipper, licking her lips as she did so. The gate alarm sounded on his phone, and he glanced at the time, then at his computer, where the security feeds were still up for him to see. Carter was only a few minutes early, but Devon knew the man wouldn't come in until his appointed time.

Devon's hips jolted as Kristen's hands made contact with his stiff cock, and his eyes zipped back to her face. Her stare remained on his as she dragged her clenched fist up and down his shaft, and he grabbed the opaque scarf he'd placed on his desk. Leaning forward, he rendered her temporarily blind and secured the ends of the material behind her head. "Suck me, Pet. Slowly, and don't stop until I tell you to."

Using her hand as a guide, she lowered her mouth to his groin, and his eyes rolled back in his head when her wet lips and tongue surrounded his thick flesh.

Fuck!

The woman hadn't been lying when she said she was a fast learner. She licked and sucked him like an expert instead of a woman giving her second blowjob ever.

Three minutes of sexual torture later, the door to his office opened, and the black ops warrior walked in. Kristen was so into what she was doing she didn't hear him enter and shut the door, but she definitely heard him when he spoke.

From where his friend stood, he couldn't see her or Devon's lap behind the desk. "What's up, Devil Dog?"

Kristen froze, as he'd expected her to, and he grabbed the bun in her hair and growled. "I didn't tell you to stop, Pet." He felt her hesitation before her head began to bob again.

Across the room, Carter's eyes widened, and an amused grin spread across his face as he took several steps toward the desk and peered over the top. "New secretary?"

His friend was joking because he knew Devon would never get involved with an employee, even if it were a quick one-time fuck, which this wasn't. "Nope. This is my naughty librarian, who better start sucking harder before she earns another punishment. Her ass is already sore from her first one of the day."

They both almost laughed out loud when she immediately increased her efforts.

Carter walked around the side of the desk and got a view of Kristen's red backside. "Very nice."

He raised his eyebrow at Devon in a silent question—what was he allowed to do?

For Kristen's benefit, he responded. "One of my pet's soft limits is a ménage. She watched Brody and Marco in action the other night with Shelby, and my little subbie's pussy was sopping wet by the time they were through. Pet, the voice you hear belongs to my good friend, Carter, and I believe he's happy to see your red ass and dripping pussy."

The other man looked down at the blindfolded woman and, in a deep, commanding voice, asked, "Is this what you want, sub? Me, a perfect stranger to you, who you won't be able to see, fucking your sweet pussy from behind while your Master comes down your throat? If it isn't, stop sucking his cock and say your safeword. If you don't want this, I'll turn around and leave. It will be the only consequence of your safeword, and your Master will continue as if I'd never been here. If you don't want me to leave, you must verbalize what will happen if I stay."

Carter was an experienced Dom in high demand with the subs at The Covenant whenever he was in town and had time to stop by. He always made sure a sub knew what she was getting herself into, and there were two options available to her—continue down the road they were going without any detours or stop altogether with no penalties. The submissive held all the control in the scene.

Devon held his breath as Kristen's head slowed, and then she let go of him. He knew she'd taken a moment to digest the unknown man's words and evaluate her thoughts and feelings. "I understand, Sir, and I do *not* want to use my safeword. Please fuck my pussy while I suck my Master's cock until he comes."

Carter grinned at his friend. "How can I refuse such a polite and pretty sub?"

Instinctively knowing he would keep her safe from harm, Kristen took Devon back into her mouth as he watched his friend kneel behind her. Carter gently rubbed his hands over her ass cheeks, hips, and thighs, letting her get used to his touch before going further. After a brief moment, when she tensed at the feeling of unfamiliar hands on her body, she relaxed and renewed her enthusiasm for giving Devon his blowjob. As she lapped and slurped his shaft, her hand reached up to cup his balls, causing him to moan. "Just like that, Pet. Don't stop . . . nice and easy while Carter gets you ready."

Devon opened the drawer beside him and retrieved the condoms and lube he'd put there earlier. He placed them on his desk, where the other Dom could reach them, and then held up one index finger, bending it a few times to let Carter know she wasn't ready for anything other than a finger in her tight ass. Carter acknowledged him as he lowered one hand to her folds between her legs and grabbed the tube of lubricant with the other. He dripped a fair amount of gel into the crack of her ass, then began to work it into the rim of her puckered hole while he plunged two fingers into her soaking wet pussy and fucked her with them.

Kristen moaned around Devon's cock, and the vibrations took him higher. Not wanting to come too soon, he grabbed a handful of her loosening hair and forced her to slow her pace while his other hand caressed her cheek, neck, and shoulder. He worked his way down into her shirt, where her lush, unrestrained tits swayed in time with her movements. Her nipples hardened with a brush of his thumb, and he gently rolled and tugged on them.

Whenever he'd played with her breasts, he distracted her in some other way. He didn't think she was aware of him pinching them with more pressure each time because she was so aroused when he did it that the pain instantly changed to pleasure which shot straight to her womb and aroused her even more. He could now lick, suck, and pinch them without her tensing, but it would be a while before he tried to graze them with his teeth, and he didn't know if she'd ever be able to take the nipple clamps. If she never got over her fear of them, he would accept it, but, for now, he wanted to try and erase every bad memory she had of her previous sexual encounters until only he existed in the far reaches of her mind.

* * *

Kristen's head was in a wild spin. If someone had told her a week earlier, she would be on her knees, blindfolded, sucking Devon's huge erection in his office in the middle of the afternoon, while a complete stranger finger fucked her pussy and ass, she would've said they were crazy. Now, she was the crazy one—crazy with the intense pleasure and sensations running through her body and loving every minute. She knew if she'd said "no," then Carter would've left, and Devon wouldn't be mad or disappointed. However, if she did say it, she would be disappointed for not trying something she'd fantasized about.

She could distinguish the difference between the two men's touch, but she wasn't sure how because it didn't feel like a stranger was touching her. It felt like the other man's hands were an extension of Devon's. In her mind, Devon was the only one touching her, with four hands, not two. Carter's fingers were pretty much the same size as Devon's. In fact, they both had the hands of men accustomed to hard work, yet they were gentle and talented enough to bring a woman extreme gratification.

A brief thought of how the two of them must've done this before with other women popped into her head. But it disappeared just as quickly when the fingers in her vagina moved to rub her fluids over her clit, sending bolts of electricity through her and rendering her mind useless to anything but her four-out-of-five senses. With her eyes covered, her senses of touch, taste, smell, and hearing were heightened. She felt Carter's hands and fingers on her. She savored Devon's taste on the buds of her tongue. She inhaled his musky and masculine scent. And finally, their dueling groans and encouraging words filled her ears, along with the crinkle of a condom wrapper.

Carter pulled his lower hand from her body, and she heard the hum of a zipper. She then felt him align his cock with the entrance to her core as his finger continued to play in her ass. She whimpered as he eased himself into her wetness, his hips rocking back and forth as he progressed a little at a time, giving her body a moment to accommodate his thickness.

"Fuck, she's tight." He groaned in ecstasy once he buried himself deep inside her. "Damn, her pussy feels like heaven, man."

* * *

"I know the feeling. Pet, you have permission to come whenever you need to." Devon let his head fall back against the leather chair and was tempted to close his eyes and just feel, but the desire to watch her take everything they gave her was even stronger. His dick disappearing behind her red, swollen, wet lips was a sight he didn't think he'd ever tire of seeing. She was a pretty woman, to begin with, but in the throes of pleasure, she was stunning.

As she sucked him in and out of her mouth, she swiped her tongue across his purple head on each upstroke, licking drops of pre-cum from his slit. She remembered everything he'd taught her the first time, and her desire to please him brought him more pleasure in return. Her moaning and breathing increased as Carter drove her higher and higher until her orgasm grabbed her and sent her tumbling. She screamed around his dick, and he began to fuck her mouth in earnest. Tightening his grip on her scalp, he held her where he wanted her as he increased the pace of his thrusting hips, plunging into the deep cavern of her mouth and making contact with the back of her throat. When she gagged a bit, he shortened his strokes. "Breath through your nose, Pet. I'm going to come, and you'll swallow every drop."

He felt and heard her acknowledge him with a muffled "um-hmm" and let himself go. Her mouth and throat moved greedily as she swallowed his seed. "That's it, baby. Fuck, you're such a good girl."

As the last drops left him, Carter did something which

sent her over the edge again, with the man following her right after, roaring his own release.

For a few moments, the only sound in the room was from the three of them breathing hard. Then Kristen moaned as Carter slid out of her, murmuring praise. He looked at Devon as he rose up from his knees. "If you've got her, I'm going to run upstairs and take a quick shower."

When Devon nodded, his friend leaned over Kristen's torso and kissed the back of her head while she rested her forehead on her Master's knee, her blindfold still in place. "Thank you, love. That was wonderful. Thank you for letting me share you with Master Devon. You're a beautiful woman, and he's a lucky man."

When he looked back up at him, Devon knew Carter understood this woman was important to him. She wasn't just another sub, and it'd been the operative's honor to participate in her first ménage.

After Carter disposed of his condom in the trash and left the room, closing the door behind him, Devon tucked himself back into his pants and pulled the zipper up. Standing, he leaned down, picked Kristen up in his arms, and placed her exhausted body on his couch. He covered her with a knitted blanket that was draped over the back of the couch —a decorative touch courtesy of Mrs. Kemple. Retrieving a wet washcloth from his office's half-bath, he cleaned Kristen as she fell into a subspace-induced sleep.

He removed her shoes and blindfold to make her comfortable and then took care of himself in the bathroom. Sitting on the edge of the couch next to her, he spent the next twenty minutes or so caressing her from head to toe as she slept. When he heard the gate alert sound from his phone, he sighed and gently roused her. "Pet, are you okay?"

"Um-hmm. Wonderful."

He chuckled at her sleepy, sated voice. "I need to go to a meeting down the hall. I want you to stay here and sleep awhile. The door will be shut, and no one will disturb you. I'm leaving a bottle of water and your purse here next to you. If you need me for anything, text me, and I'll come right back, okay? When I'm finished, we'll get something to eat."

"Mmm-hmm, 'kay. Love you."

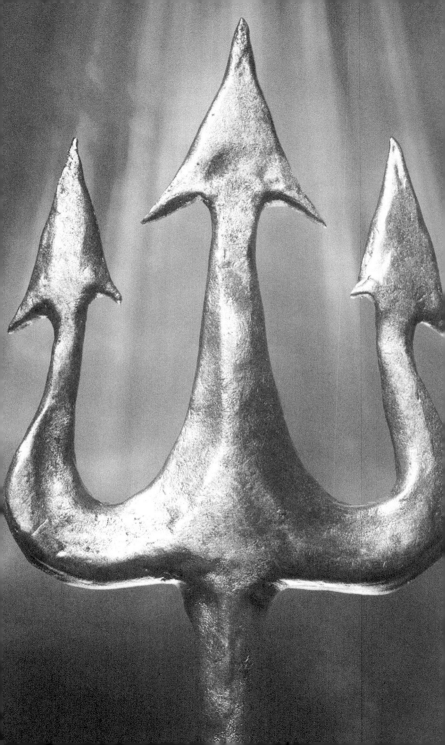

CHAPTER EIGHTEEN

Devon froze at her murmured words, but she'd slipped back into slumber. Did she realize what she'd said? Had she fallen in love with a man who'd never said those words to anyone besides those he considered family? And why was he not running for the hills as soon as he heard them?

A soft knock interrupted his thoughts, and he left her sleeping, grabbed his cell phone, and locked the door, shutting it behind him as he exited. Ian was waiting for him in the hallway. "Just waiting on Carter, Brody, and Marco. Boomer and Jake pulled in right behind me."

"Carter's upstairs—he'll be back down in a minute."

Ian nodded, and his face became grim. "Keon didn't come alone. Two NCIS agents are with him."

Devon's eyes widened. "Fuck. What the hell is going on?"

His brother turned on his foot and began to walk toward the conference room with Devon on his heels. "It's not good. I only heard the basics on the way here. I'll let Keon tell everyone at once."

A few minutes later, Trident Security's six main

personnel sat around the large conference table, along with Deputy Director Larry Keon of the FBI, black-ops agent T. Carter, and NCIS Investigators Nathan Dobrowski and Barbara Chan.

Brody was booting up his laptop while Keon stood and began to hand out identical folders to everyone but Dobrowski and Chan, who had their own copies with them. Chan also had a laptop open, which was hooked up to the large Hi-Def monitor hanging on the wall at the one unoccupied end of the table. Beau had joined them, snoring loudly from under the long table.

Keon remained standing as he spoke. "Information has come to our attention that several recent deaths of former Navy personnel may be part of a larger plot."

Pictures of retired SEALs Eric Prichard, Quincy Dale, and Jeff Mullins popped up on the monitor, along with their death dates or an estimated date in Quincy Dale's case. A round of surprised curses from the teammates followed.

"Are you fucking kidding me?" The rhetorical question came from Boomer. "What the fuck is going on? Did anyone know Dale was dead?"

The others shook their heads as the youngest team member looked at their stunned faces. This was news to all of them. Their former teammate lived in Alaska and had little contact with his buddies since his last tour ended about two-and-a-half years ago. Facial scarring from burns he'd received in an RPG attack had the man living like a hermit.

Keon raised his hand to calm the room down before he continued. "We only found out about Dale on Monday. It's what raised a red flag. Dale's brother hadn't heard from him in four months or so, and, from what I understand, it wasn't unusual these last few years. This past Saturday, Robert Dale finally decided to take a three-hour drive to Quincy's place and found his brother's decomposing corpse in his cabin. The medical examiner estimated he'd been dead for about three months. A nine-millimeter Smith and Wesson was found with the body, and his prints were on the gun. At first, the troopers figured suicide. With Dale's recent history, it wouldn't have been too difficult to believe."

"Except Dale didn't own an S&W nine," Boomer stated with the certainty of a man who'd known his friend's habits well. "He hated them. Said they never felt right to him. The grip and weight were all wrong. I remember him arguing with some grunt about it on his last tour. He would've bought a thousand other guns before he bought an S&W nine."

Keon nodded. "Exactly what his brother said. And someone filed off the gun's serial number, which raised a few more doubts. Robert said Quincy would've never bought a gun with the number missing and wouldn't have removed it himself. Nothing else was out of place—no prints or trace evidence. The state troopers asked the M.E. to scrutinize the entry wound to be on the safe side. The M.E. states the shot to the head was close to, but not quite possible for Dale to have done it himself. The doc said it was an awkward angle, which didn't make sense. It wouldn't have been comfortable to hold the gun so far behind the ear. Suicides by a bullet to the head seem to be a common way to go in desolate areas of Alaska. The doc knows his stuff and ruled it a probable homicide."

Barbara Chan took over. "A homicide death notification of a SEAL, following so closely to the hit-and-run death of another from the same team, made me curious. I ran a list of the team's current and retired members through the VA computer, and Jeff Mullins' name popped up, along with his wife. The burglary-homicide set my internal panic alarm off.

Three members of the same team dead within six months, and all of them are unsolved."

"Someone's hunting SEALs." Devon hated to state what they were all thinking, but it needed to be said.

"And not just SEALs, but Team Four specifically. Prichard knew something was off," Keon said. "Early this morning, I had a local agent go interview Prichard's wife. According to the police report, he was wearing a concealed pistol in an ankle holster when his body was found. The wife said it wouldn't have been unusual when he'd been active with the team, but since they moved to Iowa after his retirement, she didn't think he wore it much anymore—quiet little town and such.

"After a few more questions, she remembered something from a few days before he was killed. Prichard asked her if she'd noticed anything odd or seen anyone in the area she didn't recognize. She hadn't and asked him why. He shrugged it off and said it was probably nothing. It was the last time he mentioned anything to her. I guess, in her shock and grief, she forgot about it. Her eleven-year-old son overheard her talking to the agent and said that the day before his dad's death, the two of them were driving home from the kid's football practice, and Prichard kept looking in the mirrors. He took a long route home, making some turns he didn't need to. He was also slowing down and accelerating for no reason. The kid thought it was weird, and Prichard said he was just checking something out. Nothing happened, and they got home without trouble, but I think it's a good assumption he knew he was in someone's cross-hairs. The questions are—did he know who or why, and why didn't he say something to the sheriff or call someone from the team for backup?"

"I think he was trying to before he was killed." All eyes

turned to Marco. "Curt Bannerman mentioned something to me at the funeral. He'd gotten a voicemail about two hours before Eric was killed. All Eric said was he needed to talk to Curt about something and that he should call him back as soon as possible. Curt couldn't return the call until twenty hundred hours, and by then, it was too late."

Keon sat down and sighed. "You need to talk to Jennifer Mullins and see if anything unusual happened in the days leading up to her parents' murders."

"I agree." Ian quickly texted Jenn, asking her to come to the office in a little while. "I'll have her stop by later, so we can talk."

"The good news is—as if there could be good news in this mess—if the reason these men were killed is linked to a specific mission, and it wasn't only because they were SEALs or, more specifically, SEAL Team Four, then we're able to narrow it down to nine months six years ago. So at least we have a starting point."

Jake's eyes narrowed. "How do you figure?"

"Because," Ian explained, "it was the only time frame when Jeff and Dale were on the team together. Dale joined us nine months before Jeff retired. Unfortunately, according to Dobrowski here, we were active during most of those months, and there's a list of over thirty individual missions. Some lasted only a day or a week, but a few were longer and spanned five countries. Two in the Middle East, one each in Africa, Colombia, and Brazil, and as a team, we're responsible for over seventy confirmed deaths while on those missions."

Chan chimed in again. "We know it's a lot, and other investigators are contacting and interviewing all SEALs active in Team Four at the time. You six are all on the list, and the only ones working together in a large group and still have security clearances, so we came here to pick your minds and review the mission reports with you."

The teammates groaned. Thirty missions with seventy-plus kills could produce an astronomical amount of intelligence, evidence, paperwork, and photos.

"The Pentagon has been working to get us copies of everything since Monday night. I received a call when we got off the plane, and the files will be here first thing in the morning from D.C. I don't need to state the obvious, gentlemen, but I will. This involves highly classified mission reports. Despite your level of clearance, you're all considered civilians now, which means we had to get permission from far up the food chain to get you access to them, even though each of you wrote some, if not all, of them. These reports will not be censored or redacted. This room will be in lockdown as of their arrival at around nine a.m. tomorrow morning. Nathan or I must be present whenever you're in this room with the reports, and nothing leaves this room without our approval. Six MPs will be posted outside in rotating shifts of two. No one, other than the ten people currently in this room, is allowed in here. That pertains to any support staff you have."

Brody laughed out loud. "Paula's gonna go nuts! Ian, can I be there when you tell her?"

With a few chuckles, the tension in the room eased at the thought of their nosy office manager being left out of the loop and banned from the room. If the woman had been a cat, her curiosity would've killed her long ago.

Devon glanced at the individuals around the table, and his gaze fell on one man. "Hey, Carter, how do you figure into this frigging mess?"

The big man's face showed no emotion as he shrugged his shoulders. "I'm just here for the food."

Devon snorted as the rest of the team let out barks of laughter. Years ago, Devon had been undercover for a mission in Rio de Janeiro when he unexpectedly ran into Carter, also undercover, at a swanky gala with over five hundred people. A Colombian drug lord the team had under surveillance was in attendance, and Devon drew the short straw for getting into a black-tie monkey suit. When he'd gotten a brief minute alone with his buddy, he asked a similar question and had gotten the same answer. Every once in a while, the stale joke reared its ugly head when their friend didn't want to lie to them and couldn't tell them the truth. In other words, if he told them, he'd have to kill them.

Keon stood, and the NCIS agents followed suit. "Ian, I don't need to tell you and your team to watch your backs. If you need anything, let me know. I have to head to the Jacksonville office tomorrow for some unrelated business. My time for the next week or so will be split between here, there, D.C., and New York, but I'll be available by cell if something comes up.

"In addition to NCIS, you have the complete support of the FBI. We're involved because the murders occurred in three different states, and they may be the result of any one of the jobs you've done for Uncle Sam, including some sanctioned by the FBI. I didn't know Mullins as well as you, but he was a good man. He, his wife, and the others didn't deserve what they got, and I'll be damned if Team Four loses anyone else on my watch."

After Keon and the two investigators left for a local hotel, Carter stayed long enough to offer his input. "What Larry said goes for me too. A few of my informants are keeping their ears to the ground and listening for any traffic about the team. I'll beat a few bushes and check out a couple of things. If anything pans out, I'll let you know. I've gotten used to your ugly mugs. So stay safe and say hi to Jenn for me. Tell her I'm sorry I missed her, and I'll see her soon." As he passed Devon on the way to the door, he lowered his voice so no one else could hear and added, "Say goodbye and thanks to your little librarian too. I'm looking forward to actually meeting her next time."

The room was silent for a few minutes after Carter left. Ian's phone chimed with a text, and he looked at the screen, then at his team. "Jenn's on her way over. Any ideas of what started this shit storm?"

Jake answered first. "Not off the top of my head, but I must admit I'm worried about Jenn. Not only do we have to question her about the worst night of her life, but is she in danger here with us? Is this going to be easier or harder for her to know it wasn't a random crime and her folks were murdered because of something from her dad's service? The man was a hero to her."

Ian nodded. "I was thinking the same thing. But I think she's mature enough to know there was no way her dad could have foreseen this five years ago. If he had, he would've taken steps to protect his family. And she's safer here with us since we know there's a threat. I'll assign her a protection detail for school, and she'll stay with us for now. Jake, talk to your brother and ask him to take her off the schedule for a few days until we have a better idea of what is going on."

At the other man's nod, he continued. "As for questioning her, it'll be a little tough. I'll call Nelson and see if he can squeeze her in for a session tonight or tomorrow morning." Dr. Brett Nelson was the trauma psychologist Jenn had seen since moving to Florida.

Everyone looked at Devon when he stood. "Kristen's napping on my couch. I'm just going to check on her before

Jenn gets here. Someone want to order some pizzas since we'll be here a while?"

If any of his team was surprised at his first statement, they didn't show it. They couldn't have missed Kristen's Altima parked outside and knew someone else was in the building.

Boomer grabbed his phone. "On it."

There was an immediate chorus of "no anchovies" from the rest of them as Devon walked out the door.

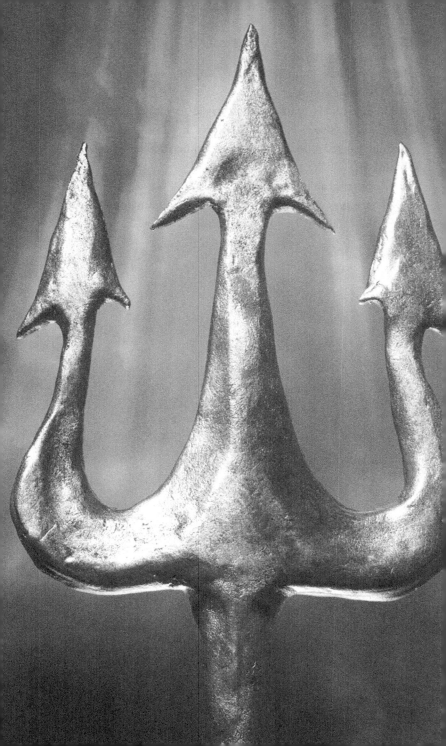

CHAPTER NINETEEN

Kristen was just waking up when Devon entered his office. Her eyes blinked several times before she stretched and smiled seductively at him. "Good afternoon."

He crossed the room and sat on the edge of the couch next to her. "How are you feeling? Did you sleep well?"

"Mmm-hmm. How long was I out?"

He glanced at his watch. "About an hour and a half. You earned it." He chuckled as her cheeks flamed.

"Is he still here?"

"No, Pet. Carter had to leave. But next time he stops by, I'll formally introduce you two." His grin faded. "I have to cancel dinner tonight. Something's come up, but I still want you to spend the night in my bed. I don't know when I'll be back in my apartment, maybe around nine or ten, but you can go over anytime you want. I'll have Brody scan your handprint into the system if you come with me now. It won't get you in every secure area, but it'll open the gate and my apartment for you."

Her eyes and smile widened. "Wow. Is this your version of giving me the key to your place?"

Laughing, Devon stood. "Yeah, I guess it is. And I want you naked as the day you were born when I get there. Now, come on, let's see Brody. We have pizza being delivered in a little bit, so I'll feed you before you go."

A half-hour later, with her skirt straightened, bra back on, and hair down from its bun, Kristen sat in the conference room with Beau at her feet. She ate her pizza and listened as the Sexy Six-Pack and Jenn talked about everyday subjects. It was apparent how close they all were, and their easy banter and teasing were fun to listen to. "I have a question. Why do you call Devon Devil Dog? I mean, it's obviously a play on his name, but is there something more to it?"

Everyone laughed as Devon rolled his eyes and sighed. "It goes back to a parachuting practice/demonstration we were doing right after I joined Team Four. We were doing high-altitude jumping. After jumping, I decided to see how many somersaults I could do before pulling my cord. Normally, it wouldn't have been an issue, but no one told us that Admiral Richardson, a real stickler for protocol and stuff, was watching with a bunch of other big-wigs on the ground. After I landed, the admiral got in my face, reaming me a new asshole. He was beet red, yelling at me, and some of his words were got jumbled. I guess instead of asking me if I thought I was a daredevil, he asked me if I was a devil dog. The next day someone had emptied my locker at the base and filled it to the top with Drakes' Devil Dogs, those little chocolate cakes."

Staring at his way-too-innocent-looking teammates, he added, "I still don't know who did it, but I was eating Devil Dogs for months."

"Yup, and the bastard didn't share either," Brody piped up. "And he wasn't happy with his new nickname for a long time since 'Devil Dog' is a standard in the Marines. Of course, when someone doesn't like their nickname, it pretty much becomes permanent."

Kristen smiled. "I guess he didn't like it because of the rivalry between the Navy and Marines, right?" Devon nodded around a bite of pizza and rolled his eyes again. "So, does everyone else have a call sign?" She thought that was the military slang for it as she looked at Brody. "Yours is egg-something, right?"

"First off, darlin', they're not *call signs* . . . they're nicknames—plain and simple. Call signs are for missions. And, yes, mine's Egghead—a bow to my superior computer hacking skills. By the way, we've already approved yours. I'm diggin' the Ninja-girl tag."

She gaped at Devon. "Seriously? You told them?"

He just grinned and shrugged his shoulders as everyone else laughed. From there, the men went around the table.

"I'm the explosives and demolition man, so I ended up Boomer," Ben told her. "Nothing embarrassing about it."

"Except when we call him Baby Boomer," Jake quipped, making the younger guy groan and flip his buddy the middle finger. "Mine's Reverend. I'm a sniper, and when I first joined Team Four, one of the guys said I was sending my targets to meet their maker."

"Yup, and because everyone feels the need to confess their sins to you, Father Donovan." The room filled with laughter again. "Anyway, I'm Polo."

When Marco didn't explain further, Kristen asked, "Why Polo?"

The room got quiet, and she was confused as everyone, including Jenn, stared at her. Brody deadpanned, "Wait for it."

Wait for what? What's the big deal about calling Marco Polo?

The second her eyes lit up, Boomer chuckled. "Ding, ding, ding ... she gets it, just under the wire."

She giggled. "Okay, so I was a little slow on that one. I get it now. From *The Travels of Marco Polo* and the game. We used to play it in the pool when I was a kid." She looked over at the man who'd yet to answer. "So, Ian, what's your call sign, I mean, nickname?"

Before he could respond, Brody jumped in. "He doesn't have one, at least not any we can say in front of two pretty ladies. We tried several names for him over the years, but nothing ever stuck. Now he's the Boss-man."

Ian smiled, but it didn't reach his eyes. "And don't you forget it, asshole."

* * *

After they finished eating, Devon walked Kristen to her car and kissed her sweetly before he opened the driver's door for her. "I'll see you later, Ninja-girl. And don't forget, you better be naked when I get there."

He watched as she drove away with a wide grin on her face. His own smile faded when her car disappeared through the outside perimeter gate as his thoughts returned to what they now had to put Jenn through. Making her relive the events leading up to her parent's murders would be hard on her, but Doc Nelson agreed to meet with her and Ian first thing in the morning to help her deal with the repercussions.

By the time Devon walked back into the conference room, the rest of them had cleaned up their meal, and Ian had moved to sit next to Jenn, ready to offer his goddaughter the support she would require. Even Beau seemed to sense she would need him because he was now sitting on her other side with his big head resting on her thigh as she stroked his silky-soft ears. The dog's eyes were closed in what had to be canine ecstasy.

They all remained quiet as Ian took Jenn's hand and spoke to her. "Baby-girl, we have to ask you some questions, and I wish we didn't, but it's important."

The young woman's eyes widened at Ian's serious yet gentle tone. "What's wrong, Uncle Ian?"

"We need you to think back to the days and weeks leading up to your parents' murders. Did anything happen that you thought was weird at the time? Was your dad nervous or upset or worried about something? Did he ask you or your mom anything odd? Did you see anyone near your house who was a stranger to you, or was it unusual for them to be there if you knew them?"

They watched as Jenn's eyes filled up, but to her credit, her tears didn't fall. She took a deep breath. "Something else happened, didn't it? Something happened to make you think my parents weren't killed because some burglar didn't expect anyone to be home when he broke in, right?"

Ian sighed, clearly hating what he had to tell her. "We received some information this afternoon that possibly links your parents' deaths to Eric's hit-and-run accident, which we now believe was no accident." He paused, and Devon knew this was killing him. "Sweetheart, Quincy Dale was found shot to death in his cabin. He was killed about three months ago. His brother checked on him after he hadn't heard from him."

Jenn's hand covered her mouth in shock. They'd known she was going to take Dale's death hard. The man had been a big American history buff and always captured Jenn's attention with stories from Christopher Columbus' discovery all the way through to the twenty-first century. Though Dale had withdrawn from pretty much everyone else, he stayed in contact with Jenn through emails and the occasional phone call. She was the only one who could bring a smile to his scarred face these past few years. He'd even left his lonely mountain twice for her—to attend her parents' funeral and then to watch her graduate from high school three months later. Devon realized Dale had probably returned from Jenn's graduation right before he was murdered.

Jenn could no longer hold her tears back. "Oh, no! Not Quincy! I sent him a few emails over the summer, but with the move, school, and work, I just realized he hadn't answered me. He would do that sometimes when he got into one of his funks and then send me a whole bunch of emails at once. Uncle Ian, what's happening? Quincy was the nicest man in the world. Why would someone kill all of them?"

Her questions may have been addressed to Ian, but she turned her head to survey all of them, hoping someone had an answer for her.

Devon spoke to her softly. "We don't know, Baby-girl, but we'll find out, I promise. And you know I don't make promises I can't keep."

"I know, Uncle Devon," she whispered before clearing her throat and speaking up again. "Okay, so let me think. You know I was at my friend's house the night . . . the night it happened. I'd also spent most of the day shopping with Dana, so I only saw my parents that morning. I remember they were talking in the kitchen when I went down for breakfast. Dad said . . . he said something like, if he needed to, he would call you, Uncle Ian, but he wanted to look into something first. They changed the subject when I walked in, and I didn't think anything of it since you two were always on the phone with each other, and Dad had done some research and work for you before. The week before, Dad was also out more than usual and in his home office on the computer a lot. I remember a few nights when he didn't come home until after dinner. When I asked him where he'd been, he said he'd been working on something for you, and it was no big deal."

"For me?" Ian asked with a confused expression on his face. When Jenn nodded, he eyed Devon. "I didn't ask him to look into anything for me. Did you?"

"No." Devon shook his head as the other men denied having asked Jeff to investigate anything.

Jenn sighed. "I'm sorry I don't remember more, but nothing else stands out. It was six months ago, and I was such a mess after."

Ian lifted her hand and kissed her knuckles. "It's okay, Baby-girl. If you think of anything else, let one of us know. For now, though, I want you to stay in your room here. I don't think you're in danger, but I'd rather not take any chances. Tomorrow morning, a few men will be assigned to protect you when you're not with us. I know you can't miss any classes if it can be avoided, but Mike is giving you the next few days off until we get a better idea of what's going on."

Her bottom lip trembled, and six Navy SEAL hearts were breaking for her. "Are you . . . are you all in danger?"

Ian stood and pulled their niece to her feet and hugged her tight. "Nothing's going to happen to us, Baby-girl. You're going to be stuck with us for a long time."

* * *

The assassin answered his vibrating phone from his current perch in a tree a fair distance from the fenced-in compound. "What?"

"How long do you expect this to take?"

The man funding his current excursion sounded anxious after being calm for the past six months. "Why? Has the time frame been changed?"

"The party wants to make an announcement in two

weeks. I want this dead and buried before it happens. Certain things may come to light if any of them are still alive, and I refuse to accept the possibility."

"It'll be done by then. After the rest of my money is deposited into my account, you'll never hear from me again, and this number will no longer be available." He hung up, not caring if the other man had anything else to say.

Picking up his binoculars, he returned to watching the increased activity at the compound. On Monday, the four men he'd been hired to kill had boarded a plane to Iowa to attend the funeral of their fallen teammate, along with the other two and the Mullins girl.

He'd been a little surprised to see her. After her parents' deaths, he'd assumed she would go live with her father's family, but it made no difference to him either way. She cheated death once, but if she or anyone else ended up being collateral damage this time, it didn't matter to him.

Until today, the compound had been quiet, with only one guard at the front gate, allowing him to check the security systems. He'd been pissed when he discovered Trident Security was closely monitored by multiple cameras and sensors stationed inside and outside the fences. Whoever designed their system was good—almost too good. He had yet to find a way past their defenses. There was also a big dog who appeared to be well-trained.

If it hadn't been difficult before, with the number of people going in and out of the compound today, it was damn near impossible to penetrate. Devon Sawyer and the woman, who he'd learned was their secretary, had been the only ones there that morning. Then around noon, the secretary left in a huff, and about an hour later, an unknown woman arrived. He'd wondered if Sawyer was banging them both, but then an unexpected person showed up.

Carter. He didn't know if it was a first or last name. He only knew the man was so dark in the world of black ops that many informants and contacts whispered the guy's name in awe and fear. While he'd never met or dealt with the agent, or whatever his title was, from the stories he'd heard, anyone who'd ever underestimated the man was either dead or missing and presumed dead.

A few minutes before two p.m., it started getting crowded in the compound. The rest of the former SEALs showed up along with three people who carried themselves like feds. Then all was quiet and mundane again for a while. The feds and Carter left, pizza and the Mullins girl showed up, and about a half hour later, the unknown woman drove away. He watched as Devon Sawyer kissed her and knew he had the answer to one of his questions.

The assassin's gut started to twitch again around five p.m. Six more unknown men arrived. Seeing them armed and alert, he recognized that these men were highly trained and intelligent—definitely former military. The Sawyer brothers and Brody Evans joined them outside, and they were obviously talking about the compound and its security system. Two of them even escorted Jennifer Mullins from the second to the fourth building.

Something was wrong. They were increasing their ranks. The question was, why?

DEVON GLANCED AT HIS WATCH AS HE CLIMBED THE STAIRS TO his apartment after checking on Jenn, who was going through some boxes of things from her life in Virginia. She was searching for some family photos of her grandparents and great-grandparents her mom had scanned onto CDs several years earlier.

"Some were my aunt's photos," Jenn had told him, "but she lent them to Mom to make copies for me. I need them for an assignment. We have to do a family tree as far back as possible for my *Sociology and The American Family* class."

He'd leaned against the front door frame as she sat on the floor of Ian's living room with the boxes in front of her and Beau at her side. "Are you okay with doing that, with everything going on?"

She'd sighed. "I think so. My professor and I had a conversation during the first week of school. I had a question about something and stayed after class. We talked for a bit, and she asked me about my family. Dr. Nelson convinced me it was okay to talk about, you know, everything if I'm comfortable with someone, so I ended up telling Professor Palmer what happened. I was glad I did because she really understood. Her brother-in-law killed her sister a few years ago after they got into an argument. He's in prison now. Anyway, Professor Palmer told me if this assignment was too hard for me to deal with, she would understand, and I could do something else instead. But, Uncle Devon, I want to do it . . . I feel like I *have* to do it, and if I don't, I'll let my parents down. Is that weird?"

Devon had smiled at her. "I don't think it's weird at all, Baby-girl. I think it's your heart's way of letting you know it's healing and you're getting better every day. You'll always live with what happened. I mean, how can you not? But the point is you *will* live, not just exist as some people do—people who aren't as strong as you. I know your parents are proud of you, as we all are. I knew someday we would have to start seeing you as a grown-up woman and not a little girl anymore, and I think the day has come. I'll still call you Baby-girl out of habit, though."

After getting off the floor, she stepped over Beau's bulky body and hugged Devon. "I wouldn't want it any other way."

Returning the embrace, he'd squeezed her tight. "Me neither, Baby-girl, me neither."

It was now a little after nine as he opened the door to his own apartment, and his body and mind were suffering from a combination of fatigue and anticipation. The last few days were catching up to him, but all he could think about now was climbing over Kristen's sumptuous body and sinking into her hot, wet core as deep and for as long as possible.

She wasn't in the living room or kitchen, so he walked toward his bedroom in search of her. He knew she'd only gotten there about ten minutes before he did because, like the interior gate, his apartment door also sounded a short, one-note alert on his phone when the door was opened. Walking into his bedroom, he found it empty except for an enticing trail of discarded clothes and underwear leading to the bathroom. From where he stood, he could hear his shower running and smiled. She must've been in a rush when she got there.

He entered the bathroom and saw her naked silhouette as she shampooed and rinsed her hair behind the thick glass block wall separating the open shower stall from the rest of the room. With a silence embedded into him by the military, he stripped, skirted the wall, and grabbed her around the waist from behind. He held tight as she jumped and shrieked. "Oh my God, Devon, you gave me a freaking heart attack!"

He chuckled as he moved the length of her long, wet hair over her left shoulder, giving himself access to the right side of her neck. He lowered his mouth to the area below her ear and began licking and nibbling on her skin. She moaned and tilted her head, inviting him to do more, and he was happy to oblige her. His hands moved as if they had a mind of their own. One lifted to the swell of her breasts while the other inched lower to the treasure between her legs. His cock was erect and hard against her ass, and he mentally cursed himself because he'd forgotten to grab a condom. Oh well, he'd have to enjoy her with his mouth and hands for now, and after he got her into his bed, he would find his own release.

He grabbed the bar of soap from its shelf and began lathering her body. It wasn't the flowery stuff she used, which he loved on her, but he liked knowing he was covering her with the ocean-fresh scent of the soap he used daily. He was marking her body in more ways than one—staking his claim.

"Reach up, put your arms around my neck, and keep them there." After she did as she was told, he asked, "I don't mind finding you naked in my shower, Pet, but why were you so late in getting here? Had I gotten here a few minutes earlier, you would've earned a very thorough spanking because you obviously would've been still dressed, violating my direct order."

Kristen moaned as his hands continued to clean every inch of her. "Mmm. Sorry, Sir. I'd been struggling to get one of the chapters in my book just right. I'd rewritten it several times but still wasn't happy with it. On my way home this afternoon, I came up with the perfect way to write it." She paused and widened her stance as he began to wash her bare pussy with the suds in his hand. "Mmm, that feels so good."

"So, that's why you were running late?" He lessened the length of his stroke while increasing the pace and pressure atop her clit, peeking out from its hood and begging for attention. If the rocking of her hips was any indication, he had her so focused on what the fingers at her mound were doing that she didn't seem to notice the ones playing with her soapy breasts were pinching and rolling her nipples with more pressure than usual.

Soon, she was panting hard, grinding her ass into his groin. "Oh, S-Sir, please. I-I'm going to come."

"But you don't have permission to come yet, Pet." He smiled at her groan of frustration. "You still haven't answered my question, and you know I don't like repeating myself."

As he increased the speed and intensity of his actions, she screamed his name while trying to move away from the insistent fingers on her clit. He then eased back off, not wanting her to come until she answered him, yet keeping her on the edge. "Yes! That's w-why I was . . . I was late. I was s-so into what I was writing, I . . . Oh, God, Devon, pleeeease . . . I-I lost track of time."

He pinched her clit and nipple at the same time. "Come now, Pet."

And she did. She came harder and longer than she'd ever come in her life. If it hadn't been for Devon's strong arms holding her up, she might've melted down the drain with the water. As the last shudders left her body, he rinsed the soap from her skin before helping her sit on the shower's built-in tiled seat. He quickly washed and rinsed his own hair and body before turning off the water and retrieving three towels from the tall cabinet outside the shower. He hung one on a hook on the side of the cabinet and took the other two to tend to Kristen. He held her arm to steady her as she stood, then ran the first towel over her arms and legs before wrapping and securing it around her upper torso. Then he told her to bend forward and flip her hair over her head, so he could towel dry it.

After taking care of Kristen, Devon grabbed the last towel

and took care of himself. *As it should be*, he thought—she deserved to always come first. She was his sub, his woman, his . . . love. His mind seized on the sudden thought while his body followed her into the bedroom, where they dropped their towels and climbed into his bed. Was this love he was feeling? He couldn't be sure since he'd never been in love before, but no other word seemed to fit.

His dad would laugh his head off his shoulders if he knew what was going on in his son's mind. The man had always said, "When you meet the right woman, she's going to have you wrapped around her finger so fast, you won't know what hit you."

His dad was right. In their short time together, Devon had fallen for her hard. He couldn't imagine going back to being the man he'd been a little over a week ago—a man who'd never met her, never talked to her, never touched her . . . never loved her. Yes, it had to be love—there was no other way to describe the fact that she was the other half of his soul.

Wow, go figure—Devon Sawyer, a self-proclaimed bachelor for life, was in love. But he wasn't ready to tell Kristen or anyone else that. He wasn't ready to put his heart and soul on the line. She might not even be ready to hear it since the ink on her divorce papers was barely dry. She'd said she loved him as she fell asleep earlier, but he was certain she didn't realize it and had no clue if she meant it. Neither one of them had spoken about it. But for now, he might not be able to say the words aloud, but he could show her with his body.

He laid beside her and pulled her body beneath his, then proceeded to do something he'd never done in his life. He made love to a woman—his woman.

CHAPTER TWENTY

Devon sighed as one of the two Navy MPs standing sentry unlocked the conference room door. He followed Brody, Jake, NCIS agents Chan and Dobrwski, and finally, Beau into the room before the door was shut behind them again. The others would be there soon to continue the daunting task in front of them. They'd spent over twelve hours yesterday going through boxes and boxes of reports and photos and had barely made a dent in them. Close to one hundred file boxes were piled up around the room's perimeter.

Paired into three groups, each took a different mission and reviewed every minuscule data. Then, to ensure nothing was missed, each assignment was handed off to another pair until the entire team reviewed every file. It was a tedious process, and today they were picking up where they'd left off. As they took seats around the large table, Jake began to hand out the food he'd picked up for everyone at a deli on his way in.

"How many questions do you think Paula will have

today?" Brody quipped as he unwrapped one of his two huge bacon, double-egg, and cheese sandwiches. It was one of the other reasons he'd earned his nickname—the big man was addicted to eggs. He could eat them, prepared any way possible, for each meal of the day, as long as they were accompanied by some form of meat and his favorite hot sauce.

"Shit, I hope not many. Otherwise, I'm going to fire her ass by the end of the day," Devon responded, taking a seat with his own coffee and egg sandwich.

Yesterday, Paula proved Brody's prediction to be correct. She'd been obviously annoyed over not being allowed in the conference room and not being privy to what they were doing in there, especially with armed guards at the door. Of course, she hadn't voiced her displeasure, but throughout the day, she'd knocked on the door, asking the most inane questions over stuff she already knew, just to get a peek over someone's shoulder when they opened the door.

Barbara Chan swallowed a bite of her bagel with cream cheese. "If she pulls that shit again today, I may have one of the MPs shoot her on principle."

The door had opened again, and Ian walked in, catching part of the conversation. "Please don't. The carpets were redone a few weeks ago, and I don't want blood on them," he remarked as he shut the door and grabbed a coffee, sandwich, and seat in that order. "I'll talk with Paula again. I don't want to fire her if I don't have to because none of us have the time or desire to teach someone new how to run the office. Unless anyone wants to volunteer."

His team shook their heads emphatically. "I didn't think so. If things continue, I'll call Mrs. Kemple to see if she can return from Miami for a week or two to train someone else. In the meantime, we've got a killer to catch." He started handing out the bulky files. It was going to be another long day.

Two hours later, Devon's eyes began watering after reading close to a million typed pages. Okay, it wasn't a million, but it felt like it. His phone rang, and he looked at the screen, pleased to see it was Kristen. Answering it, he asked her to hold on while he exited the conference room and walked down to his office, closing the door for some privacy.

"Hi, babe."

"Hi. How's everything going? Did you find anything?"

He'd told her a censored version of what was happening yesterday morning as they shared breakfast in his kitchen before they both left for the day. He might have a bull's eye on his back, and the team agreed that if she was with him, she had a right to know. They doubted she was in danger, but he was still concerned about her safety and had two of their contracted security men watching her. The men excelled at their jobs, and he'd told them he didn't want her to know they were there because he didn't want her to be worried.

Jenn also had two bodyguards taking her back and forth to her college classes. With her parents' murders, there was a stronger possibility she could be a target. In addition to those four and their regular guard at the front gate, there were five other highly-trained and armed men patrolling the compound at all times. They also had people watching Brody's, Jake's, Marco's, and Boomer's places when the men weren't there. "No, not yet. What are you up to?"

"Trying to get my word count in for the day, and I'm almost there. If you don't mind, you were my inspiration for the shower scene I just wrote."

Her voice was low and seductive, and his brain replayed their own shower scene this morning in his head. It had been highly satisfying for both of them, and he chuckled. "No, Pet, I don't mind. In fact, I look forward to inspiring you more tonight. I'll have to think about how I can be your carnal muse. But for now, an idea occurred to me. I want you to bring your laptop with you tonight."

Curious, she asked, "Why?"

"I want you to read me the shower scene you wrote."

"What? Devon, I can't read it to you!" It was one thing if he wanted to read it himself, but something altogether different to read it to him. The scene was so hot, she'd blushed when she wrote it and knew how red her cheeks would be when she said the words aloud to him.

He laughed at her shock and obvious embarrassment. "Sure you can, and you'll do it naked. As your Dom, I'm ordering you to, and you know what happens when you don't obey my orders."

Her aggravated sigh sounded heavy in his ear, and his grin widened. "Fine. Yes, Sir." But she instantly brightened again. "Okay, change of subject. I called to ask if you wanted to go to Clearwater Beach tonight. One of my classmates from high school is touring with an improv troupe, and they're doing a show at a hotel over there at nine. I messaged her on Facebook, and she said she'd hold a table for eight for me if I wanted it. Will, Kayla, and Roxy said they would love to go, and I was wondering if you and three of the guys or maybe Jenn wanted to come with us. I understand if you don't with everything going on, but I figured it was something different to do. You guys could probably use some comedy relief after the past few days."

He had to agree with her. It'd been a long, stressful week, and a much-needed humor break would ease some tension. "It sounds great. I'm in, and I'll see who else wants to go. Why don't you come here at eight, and we'll all drive over together."

"Awesome. I'll message Sara to hold the table and tell the girls and Will to meet us there. It'll be easier for them instead of backtracking to your place."

"Perfect." He glanced at his desk clock and saw he still had hours of tedium left. "Let me get back to work, and I'll see you later. Oh, and don't forget your laptop, Pet."

He smiled as she groaned and could imagine her eyes rolling at his reminder. "Yes, Sir."

A LITTLE AFTER 8:00 P.M., DEVON, KRISTEN, AND JENN climbed into the rear seat of Brody's Ford F-150 while Jake took the front passenger seat. Brody put the vehicle in drive, as did the driver of the Cadillac Escalade, which pulled out behind them. Two guards assigned to Jenn would follow them to and from Clearwater Beach as a precaution.

Jenn and Kristen chatted along the way while the men stayed alert for anything out of place. Devon was aggravated they hadn't found any clues as to why four of their friends were murdered, and his mind continued to search for an answer. It would take at least three more days to go through the files, and he hoped the solution was in them somewhere. He didn't know where they would go from there if it weren't.

Fifteen minutes into their excursion, they were heading down a two-lane highway and began crossing a bridge over a large lake. Behind them, a gray Hummer changed lanes behind the Escalade and accelerated to pass both vehicles on the left. Devon watched as the truck with tinted windows came along the driver's side next to him, and his internal alert system flared up.

Before he could warn Brody, the big truck swerved to the right, smashed into them, and forced the Ford into the metal guardrail, which was no match for the forty-five-hundred-pound pickup. As the women screamed and the men cursed, their vehicle went airborne, falling toward the lake thirty feet below them. The impact of the truck hitting the water hurt like hell, and the driver and passenger airbags deployed when the front bumper struck first due to the engine's weight.

After the vehicle settled, the cab's interior began to fill with water at an alarming rate. Devon shook his head to clear it and swiftly evaluated the situation. He released his seatbelt before reaching over and doing the same for a stunned Jenn and Kristen.

Jenn screamed, "Uncle Brody!"

Devon glanced toward the front seat and saw Jake trying to free their unconscious friend. Knowing Jake could handle Brody, Devon turned around, lifted his feet, and kicked out the back window. If he didn't get them out of the sinking truck soon, they would be going under the water with it.

He grasped Kristen first, since she was sitting next to him, and shoved her out the opening before reaching for Jenn. After both women were safely out of the cab and in the murky water, he turned to help Jake get the still-unconscious Brody into the backseat and then out the window as gently as they could. They didn't know what injuries the big man might have, but any further damage they might do by moving him was better than him drowning.

Devon looked and saw it was about a fifty-yard swim to the shoreline. He grabbed the two women and pushed them toward it. While he helped them, Jake began to swim with his arm around Brody's chest, dragging the man's body in a rescue hold. Devon heard shouts from above on the bridge and from the land ahead of them as they neared the shallower water. Glancing up, he froze when he saw one of their two bodyguards standing at the water's edge, aiming his semi-automatic pistol at them.

Fuck! One of their contractors was a traitor? They were sitting ducks, and he surged forward to put himself between the women and danger just as the man fired his weapon three times in rapid succession. Devon yelled while trying to pull his own waterlogged gun from its holster at his lower back and quickly searched to see who was hit because it hadn't been him. Then he saw what appeared to be a large log floating in the water about ten feet away over his left shoulder. But it wasn't a log—it was an alligator . . . an enormous, very dead alligator.

He looked back at the bodyguard, who'd since lowered his weapon and was now wading into the water to render assistance while staying alert for more gators. Devon breathed a deep sigh of relief and gave their savior a grateful wave.

* * *

Devon saw Ian and Boomer running toward them as the first ambulance pulled away from the hectic crash scene carrying a now semi-conscious Brody and one of the bodyguards for his protection. He'd used a borrowed cell phone to contact them since he and everyone else in Brody's totaled truck needed new ones if they couldn't dry theirs out.

Ian reached the group one step ahead of the younger man and immediately checked on Jenn and Kristen, whose cuts and bruises were being treated by EMTs and paramedics. After he was convinced they would be okay, as well as the bruised and battered Jake and Devon standing protective watch over them, Ian turned his worried eyes to meet his brother's and barked, "Sit-rep."

Devon shifted his stance and grimaced. Wet jeans sucked big time. "Guy came out of nowhere. If he was tailing us, he's good because none of us realized he was a problem until it was too late. The security detail didn't seem to faze him. Gray Hummer, two or three years old, and the plates were covered with dirt, so they were unreadable. Tinted windows, so we couldn't make out any features, but the driver was definitely male, and he was alone. Police have put out an APB, but I'm not optimistic since it was most likely stolen."

Right after their vehicle went airborne, the guard driving the Escalade slammed on his brakes and let his partner out to help the victims, then took off after the Hummer, alerting 9-1-1 in the process. But the brief pause had given the suspect the chance he'd needed to make a clean getaway.

"How's Brody?"

"Got his bell rung, but he was coming around when they left for the hospital. I sent Henderson with him." Doug Henderson was the bodyguard and former Marine sharpshooter who'd prevented them from becoming dinner for the eight-foot alligator. Devon planned on giving the man a bonus for making the difficult and deadly shot into the gator's puny brain.

"Ow!"

Devon's eyes whipped back to Kristen at her pain-filled cry, and he growled at the female EMT who'd obviously done something to hurt her. The woman ignored him as if people growled at her all day long. "I don't think it's fractured, but you're going to have a nice size bruise on your shin."

Kristen glanced at Devon after she was lifted onto a gurney for transport to the hospital. "I can deal with a bruise, considering we were nearly killed."

She didn't look or sound angry as if she blamed him for

putting her in danger, but Devon couldn't help but think she should. She wouldn't have gotten injured if it hadn't been for him and his hazardous past. A cut on her forehead would need several stitches, and she most likely had a concussion. Like the rest of them, she also had multiple more minor cuts and bruises all over her.

He cringed as he thought she could be dead, thanks to him. As her Dom and lover, he was supposed to protect her, and he'd failed. His gut clenched. If she stayed with him, there would always be a chance someone from his past would come to seek revenge on him for whatever reason. And putting her life at risk because he was selfish enough to love her wasn't something he was willing to do. He needed to let her go before she got hurt again or, even worse, killed.

Next to him, Ian grabbed his shoulder in a firm yet gentle grip. When he tore his eyes away from Kristen and looked at his brother, Devon saw the sympathy and understanding in the older man's eyes. Ian leaned toward him and kept his voice low.

"I know what you're thinking, and you need to stop. This wasn't your fault, just like John's death wasn't your fault. Kristen's alive, and you'll do your best to keep her that way. But, brother, she could be hurt walking across a street one day whether she's with you or not. Shit happens. You love her. I can see it, and so can everyone else. And for some unknown cosmic reason, she loves you too. None of us will live forever, Dev, so do you want to be happy or miserable for the rest of your life? I think it's a no-brainer, but then again, you don't have much of a brain. It must go with your small Irish dick."

Devon snorted at Ian's last comments but didn't answer him. He had to give this some thought. His brother had made a point, but it didn't make Devon feel better as his woman was placed in the back of an ambulance. After they loaded her, he climbed in and sat on the bench next to her, clutching her hand because he needed to touch her. He may not have decided on their relationship yet, but no matter what, he would continue to protect her with his life.

CHAPTER TWENTY-ONE

Five long hours later, Devon helped Kristen climb into his bed after getting them both undressed and showering the last of the murky lake water off their bodies. Her body was marred with cuts and bruises, and it was all he could do to tamp down the anger of what'd happened and the fear of what could have happened to her. He'd tenderly washed her hair and skin before toweling the excess moisture away.

The laceration on her forehead had taken twelve tiny stitches to close, but the plastic surgeon did his best to prevent any visible scarring after it healed. While she did have a minor concussion, as he'd earlier suspected, the emergency room physician had assured them she could go home as long as Devon stayed close and monitored her for any related symptoms.

Brody hadn't been so lucky, and after much bitching, the big geek was admitted to the hospital overnight for observation with a moderate concussion. Devon knew the only reason they'd been able to convince Brody to stay, despite the double vision and nausea he was having, was Ian's threat to retrieve a spare set of wrist restraints from his SUV. The boss then told Brody he'd call Mistress China to have her come torture the injured man. Their teammate was now in the capable hands of four rotating bodyguards and one very pretty nurse he'd been hitting on as the others left the emergency room.

Ian was taking care of Jenn in his apartment downstairs. Their niece had suffered a fractured wrist, which was now in a cast, along with her own set of cuts and contusions. When they'd all arrived home, an anxious Beau hadn't been able to figure out which one of his favorite female humans needed him more, but, in the end, the dog had followed the younger woman to her bedroom.

Somehow Jake and Devon had fared better than the others, walking away with moderate bumps and bruises, which would most likely make them stiff and hurt like hell in the morning. Devon was shocked they'd all escaped from the crash with minor injuries. The airbags and seatbelts had done an unbelievable job.

Boomer and Jake were taking refuge in the spare bedrooms above the Trident offices inside the secure compound. Ian had increased the personnel guarding all of them and sent two additional guards to Marco's place. He wasn't taking any chances with his team's lives. As much as Ian and Devon wanted to bring Marco and his sister to the compound, moving Nina, now confined to a hospice bed, wasn't feasible. Devon had spoken to their teammate after he'd first called Ian and Boomer to the crash scene but told him to stay with his sister. He'd only called because he wanted to make sure Marco and the men watching his house stayed alert. The poor guy was torn between staying with Nina or leaving and having her friend take over for him. He didn't want to lose the time he had left with her, nor did he want her harmed by whoever was after the team.

Devon had also contacted Will from the hospital and assured him Kristen was okay but banged up a bit, that she'd be fine, and there was no need for him and her friends to come to the ER because they would only add to the chaos around them. He hadn't wanted to tell the man in great detail what'd happened, but a news crew had shown up as Kristen's ambulance pulled away from the scene, and the story was on the 11:00 p.m. broadcast.

What they'd managed to keep under wraps was that the crash hadn't been an accident. They'd convinced the Tampa detectives who'd arrived to investigate that the other driver must've been a drunk who'd lost control of his car. The last thing they wanted was for whoever was gunning for them to realize they knew someone was targeting Team Four. Despite leaving Tampa's finest in the dark, Ian let the NCIS agents and Keon know what happened, with full disclosure.

After Kristen was settled under the covers, Devon went and retrieved a bottle of water and some acetaminophen, which the doctor said she could take every four hours, and set it on the night table next to her. The doctor didn't want her taking anything stronger with her head injury. Devon ensured she didn't need anything else before he climbed into the bed beside her and pulled her to cuddle against him.

"Are you sure you're okay, baby? I know I've asked you the same question every five minutes since we swam out of the lake, but I need to keep hearing the answer."

She turned her head from its resting spot on his shoulder and kissed his bare chest softly before getting comfortable again. Her hand rested over his heart and tattoo. "I'm fine, Devon, I swear. I was terrified when it was happening, but it's over now, and everyone is okay. I'm relieved and a little sore, but nothing else. It could have been so much worse, but we're alive, and I just want you to hold me."

He picked up her hand and brought it to his lips. "I'm so sorry, Pet. It's all my fault you were hurt. God, when I think about how you and Jenn could've been killed, it makes me want to tear someone apart."

Kristen winced as she shifted and propped her upper body on her elbow until she could glare at him. "How dare you! This was not your fault, Devon. You didn't run us off the road! Some maniac did, and he's probably the only one who knows why. I will not let you blame yourself for another person's evil acts. He may have killed your friends. Are you saying you feel responsible for that, too? Are you saying you could've somehow predicted the future and stopped him before Jenn's parents or the other two SEALs were murdered? Because if you feel responsible for everything that's happened, I'll do what Ian threatened Brody with and call Mistress China."

The tension in his body eased, and he chuckled at her annoyed rant. "Oh, Pet, did you just threaten your Dom?"

Returning her head to his shoulder, she huffed. "Yes, I did, Sir. Because my big, bad Dom was blaming himself for something he had no control over. It seems to be a bad habit of his. And if you think you'll uncollar me and let me go over this—yes, I heard what Ian said to you—then you've got another think coming."

"Thing."

She looked at him in confusion. "What?"

"You said 'another *think* coming.' It's another *thing* coming."

Scowling at his arrogance, she huffed again. "Really, Devon? You're going to argue with an English major? Google it sometime. It's another *think* coming. And why are we even discussing this? The point is, you'd have to come up with a far better reason to make me walk away from you."

Devon's mouth gaped open. The woman never failed to surprise him, and then she did it again. "So, is it true what Ian said? Do you love me?"

Her question shocked him, causing his breathing to hitch before he lifted her chin and looked into her eyes. They were filled with unshed tears, but, more importantly, they were filled with hope and love—for him. "Yes, Ms. Kristen Anders, I do. I love you. I've never thought I'd find a woman who could steal my heart as you have, but I'm so glad I did. I love you, Pet."

"Good, because Ian was also right about something else. I love you, too. After my marriage fell apart, I never thought I would ever say those words to a man again. But I'm glad I did, and I'm glad it's you."

Devon leaned down and kissed her as tenderly as he could. And then he held her close to his side long after they both fell asleep.

* * *

After the late news broadcast ended, the assassin used the remote to change the TV channel from his motel room bed before downing the last of his bottle of whiskey. He was pissed at himself. He'd taken a big chance, something he rarely did, and it didn't pay off. After watching the compound for several days, he couldn't figure out how to get all four targets together. The security had increased, and there was no way in, so he needed an opportunity to get them outside the compound.

He'd set up his own surveillance camera in a tree as close to the monitored fence as he dared. While parked a half mile away from the place, he'd watched on his laptop as three out of his four targets, along with the two women, climbed into a

Ford pickup and tailed them, looking for an opportunity. How they'd all walked away from the crash was beyond him, but they had, and as a result, his job would be much more challenging. If his employer hadn't been calling every day, demanding immediate results, he wouldn't have taken the chance he did. The bastard had shortened the time frame and given him five days to complete the job, or he wouldn't be paid the remainder of his money.

Fuck!

CHAPTER TWENTY-TWO

Saturday came and went with no new information on the driver of the Hummer who tried to kill them, and no leads were found in the boxes of files in the conference room. They were only about halfway through them, and everyone was on edge.

Kristen had only brought one change of clothes with her on Friday night since she'd planned to sleep at Devon's. Instead of allowing her to leave the compound again, he sent one of the bodyguards to her apartment to pick up a few more clothes and a short list of items she'd requested. He wasn't letting her out of his guarded home until this nightmare ended. He liked knowing she was in his apartment, and he could walk over at any time to see her. The thought of asking her to move in with him had crossed his mind several times this morning, but he didn't think either was ready for that big step.

While Devon was with his team, minus Brody, poring over pages and pages of mission reports, Jenn and Beau hung out with Kristen in his apartment. The two women were sore and stiff, so he'd propped them up on opposite ends of his "L" shaped couch with pillows and blankets. He left water, acetaminophen, snacks, the house phone, computers, books, and the TV remote within reach and told Beau to guard them with his furry life before finally heading to the office.

Despite a pounding headache and lingering nausea, Brody managed to get himself discharged from the hospital and was brought back to the compound by his bodyguards late in the afternoon. He immediately crashed in the bedroom next to the one Boomer was using.

Devon had retrieved Kristen's laptop when he grabbed her duffel bag from her car, and she'd worked on her daily word count, managing to write more than she'd expected to. Jenn had several assignments for college, which also kept her busy during the day. Will had called and insisted on seeing that his cousin was okay for himself, so Devon invited him, as well as Kayla and Roxy, over to his apartment for a simple Chinese takeout dinner. It'd been the only option since he wasn't willing to risk leaving the compound with Kristen. Jenn, Ian, and Beau joined them, while Jake and Boomer tended to a woozy and grouchy Brody as they hung out in the rec room above the offices, eating pizza and watching a ballgame.

The two groups of family and friends sitting at Devon's dinner table immediately liked each other, and the conversation flowed. Once Jenn learned Kayla was a social worker, she'd latched onto the woman, asking her all sorts of questions which the older woman was happy to answer. Jenn was still trying to find her future niche in the world and was considering social work as her major.

Roxy and Ian discovered they had mutual acquaintances, and the two had plenty to talk about between them and The Covenant. Despite the man's effeminate mannerisms, Devon found Kristen's cousin funny and easy to talk to. He was surprised to learn Will was an assistant curator at the Tampa Museum of Art because the stuffy-sounding position didn't fit the man's loud and bubbly personality. He'd laughed when Will told him how Kristen referred to Devon and his teammates as the Sexy Six-Pack, which elicited a groan and eye roll from his Ninja-girl.

The evening was enjoyable and relaxing, despite their brush with death a day earlier. However, Devon and Kristen were relieved and exhausted when everyone left a little after nine o'clock. Kristen was grateful Devon had eased her cousin's concerns over her safety and promised to keep him posted. After being there for her when her marriage collapsed, she knew it was difficult for Will to leave her safety in Devon's hands, but her cousin finally decided the man was trustworthy and would guard her with his own life. Will even joked that if anything else happened to her, he would find a way to sneak in and redecorate her Dom's apartment in purple and florescent green with farm animal-themed fabrics.

Less than ten minutes after closing the door behind their guests, Devon had Kristen naked in his bed. Neither one was up for anything strenuous, so he made slow, passionate love to her instead. He skimmed his soft lips over every cut and bruise from her head to her toes. When she insisted she wanted to do the same to him, he made her stay reclined on her back, with her head on her pillow, and by moving and twisting his body, he brought each of his bruises to her mouth. After she was satisfied she'd kissed all of them, he settled himself between her legs and leisurely pleasured her.

They were both so aroused by the time he put on a condom and eased himself between her wet folds, it was only a minute or two before she found her release, with him following a few moments later. It hadn't been the explosive ending they usually reached, but a gentle free-fall over the edge, and what it lacked in physical intensity, it more than made up for in emotional strength. It was a confirmation they were alive . . . and in love.

* * *

The next morning began as a repeat of the previous day, with pages of boredom making Devon's eyes cross. They were getting nowhere fast, despite the fact all six of them were back to reading the reports, along with the two NCIS agents. Brody's double vision and nausea were pretty much gone this morning, and he was sitting at the conference table with the rest of them, his chair tilted back and his sneakered feet upon the table. After the first hour, Ian stopped harping at him to keep his size thirteens on the floor.

They were about to break for lunch when there was a knock on the closed door. No one groaned since it couldn't be Paula who was off for the weekend. From his seat, Ian yelled, "Come in."

One of the MPs swung the door open, and they all froze at the sight of a pale and shaking Jenn, with a wide-eyed Kristen holding the girl's arm to steady her. Jenn's eyes were filled with tears, her chin trembling. "U-Uncle Ian."

Everyone jumped up from their seats as Ian raced to their niece's side. Somehow, he managed to hide the brief flash of panic which shot through him and everyone else in the room. "What's wrong, Jenn? What happened?"

She lifted her non-casted arm toward him, and they saw her holding a thin CD case. It was a blank one that was used to copy files. "I found this in the storage box with my old CDs."

When she didn't say anything further, Ian glanced back at his teammates and saw the same confusion he was feeling on their faces. He took the case from her and opened the cover. "What the..."

Devon watched as his brother's face paled a few shades. "What is it?"

Ian read the words on the surface of the disc aloud. *"Ian—if something happens to me, this is my last will and testament —Jeff."*

"What the hell?" Brody stepped over and took the computer disc from Ian, then brought his laptop out of sleep mode. "Why the heck would this be in Baby-girl's things? Shouldn't this be with his lawyer? I mean, his lawyer had his will, right?"

Ian nodded as he pulled Jenn into his arms and hugged her tight. "I'm sure it's nothing, sweetheart. Your dad's lawyer probably gave him a copy of the will, and somehow the disc ended up with your stuff when we packed everything up." He looked intently at Kristen over Jenn's shoulder.

"Why don't you go back to Dev's with Kristen, and we'll check it out. If it's anything you need to know about, I promise I'll tell you, okay? Kristen, would you mind calling for some pizza for everyone? Order enough pies for the MPs and guards, too. Lunch came around fast, and we're all getting hungry."

Devon was proud of Kristen. She realized Ian was worried about what was on the disc and took command of Jenn by wrapping her arm around the young woman's shoulders. With a reassuring smile and false bravado, she turned to lead the girl back down the hallway. "Sure, no problem. And no anchovies, right?" Before the door shut again, he heard her say, "See, I told you it was probably a copy. Come on, Beau. We'll get you some kibble too."

As he sat down and inserted the disc into his laptop, Brody grumbled, "You know, I never thought I'd say this, but

I'm getting really sick of pizza." His teammates and Dobrowski all crowded around him as the file was scanned. "It's only one file. A Word doc." The document came up on the screen. "Three pages long."

"Print it," Ian ordered.

The nearby printer started spitting out pages, and Ian went to grab them. The rest of them began to read over Brody's shoulder. The computer geek was the first to comment. "Is Jeff fucking kidding me?"

Barbara Chan had remained seated since she couldn't see anything with six big men surrounding and reading the fifteen-inch screen. "What's it say?"

"It's a list of SEALs he worked with over the years and what he bequeathed them upon his death."

The agent looked puzzled and shrugged. "So? What's wrong with that?"

"Well, he left me his snow blower and a pair of snowshoes. When was the last time it snowed in Tampa? He left Ian his collection of shot glasses from around the world—I didn't know he had one—and a paperback copy of *Uncle John's Bathroom Reader*. Prichard was supposed to get a surfboard and one of those singing mounted fish, which is ridiculous since the man lived in fucking Iowa."

Boomer chuckled, reading over his friend's shoulder. "It's not as bad as what I got. A dancing reindeer and his old combat boots. My feet are two sizes bigger than his. What the hell am I going to do with those?'

Pointing to a name on the list, Jake started laughing. "Oh man, Urkel must have pissed him off at some point. He left the guy a collection of used jockstraps and a deflated basketball." Steve "Urkel" Romanelli had been their Heavy Weapons Operator and the man to beat on the basketball court when they played one-on-one.

"The whole list is like this—it's fucking nuts," Brody added. "Did Jeff have a fucking screw loose, and we didn't know about it?"

Ian had sat across the table and shuffled through the pages he'd taken from the printer. "No, it's a coded message. Do you see how the names aren't indented, but the rest of the entry is?"

"Yeah."

"It looks like the names are in random order. They're not alphabetical or in order of service dates or how he was closer to some more than others. Devon doesn't show up on the list until the bottom of the second page, and he's listed as *Sawyer, Devon*. Marco is two above him, and he's down as *Marco DeAngelis*. By the way, Reverend, he left you his ugly Christmas sweater and a yellow rubber ducky. At some point, you'll have to tell us what that's all about."

Jake rolled his eyes as Ian flipped one of the pages over and grabbed a pen. "He's using some first names, some last, and some nicknames. Start reading the names, Brody, exactly as he has them."

"Okay, You're first. 'I.' Next is *Archer, Pete . . . Neil Radovsky . . . Boomer . . . Urkel . . .*" Brody continued down the entire list, then eyeballed Ian, along with everyone else.

"Ian, bury me in the place I hate the most—Jeff Mullins." While the rest watched in total confusion, Ian jumped up from his chair and started searching the content papers taped to the front of each box they hadn't gone through yet.

Dobrowski hurried over to help. "Which one?" he asked.

"Colombia. Ernesto Diaz."

"It's over here, I think." The agent sidestepped to several stacks of boxes under the giant video screen on the wall. "Yeah, here it is. Four boxes."

Ian rushed over and grabbed the top cardboard box, with

Dobrowski picking up the second. Devon scratched his head in confusion. "Um, Boss-man, you going to clue the rest of us in?"

Dropping the box on the table, Ian threw the lid off and started removing the large files, tossing one at each team member. "Don't you remember how much Jeff complained about being in the jungles down there? Said he'd rather be any place else on Earth. He hated it there. It was his last mission with us, and he was bitching because it had to be with all those damn mosquitoes and creepy crawlers."

Ian kept a file for himself and retook his seat. "Jeff figured something out. Something that had to do with this mission, and for whatever fucking reason he had, he was investigating it himself. He needed to give us a starting point but couldn't risk the hint being found if something happened to him. Anyone looking at the list would think the guy was joking around or, like Egghead said, just plain nuts. Whatever evidence or notes he had were probably stolen, with the rest of the stuff taken to make it look like a burglary gone wrong. The answer we're looking for is somewhere in these four boxes."

"Son of a fucking bitch." Like the rest of the team, Devon grabbed the file which had landed in front of him, sat down, and started poring over every little detail of the month-long mission.

CHAPTER TWENTY-THREE

The assassin was back in his tree for the second day in a row, watching the compound. He'd been there since dawn, covered in camouflage to escape detection. He took a sip of warm, brown liquid from the flask he'd brought, annoyed that it only had a few drops left. Adjusting the sniper rifle resting on his legs, he went back to scanning the area a few degrees downhill from his position with his high-tech binoculars.

The first thing he'd done was calculate the distance between his roost and the door to the building where his targets had all gathered again. Even though he had two days left to eliminate them, he was getting nervous and wanted to get the job over with, so he could head to the tropics and lose himself in his four Ws—whiskey and a warm, willing woman.

The hair on the back of his neck had been standing up for the past hour, but he couldn't figure out why. He didn't see anything in the compound or the surrounding wooded area which would trigger his unease, yet the feeling wouldn't leave him.

He saw the two Navy MPs leave the building after their

replacements arrived and glanced at his watch as they drove from the compound. Nineteen thirty hours. It shouldn't be long now. Four quick shots would end their lives as soon as his targets were out in the open. He was out of options. Short of dropping a bomb on the compound or bringing in some help, this was his last resort.

After his failed attempt two days ago, the men were now alert and would do everything they could to thwart further efforts to eliminate them. He had a stolen motorcycle stashed on a bike trail about a third of a mile behind him. With the panic and confusion and no gate in the fence on this side, he would have enough of a head start to get away without any problems. Putting away his binoculars, he readied his rifle. As he peered through the high-powered scope, he took a deep breath and waited.

* * *

Eight hours, eight pizzas, and a lot of coffee and bottles of water later, there were two points they all agreed on, and neither identified who wanted them dead. One, Polo and Boomer were probably not targets, and two, Prichard's name was on the killer's hit list out of pure circumstance. The first two hadn't been on that particular mission. Boomer had been sidelined with a broken ankle, while Marco's grandmother, the woman who'd raised him and his sister, had passed away in New York a few days before they left on the mission. He'd taken a hardship leave to help his sister with the funeral and aftermath of settling the crotchety old woman's meager yet messy estate.

Unfortunately for Eric Prichard, he'd taken Marco's vacated spot for the mission—a spot that wound up getting him killed. A fact that was getting to Marco more and more as they pored through the files.

Only a team of seven had been sent to Colombia for a

month to gather intelligence on drug lord Ernesto Diaz. The man had his hands in a few pots besides the one containing his cocaine empire. Among them were a sex-slavery ring and arms trade. He was killed in a raid on one of his warehouses while making a high-grade weapons sale with members of Al Qaeda. Team Four had been a part of the raid six months after their original mission. Due to a diagnosis of rheumatoid arthritis with increasing symptoms, Lt. Jeff Mullins had ended his time in the field after the mission they were now reviewing and accepted a promotion to a base position in Little Creek, VA. He hadn't been on the raid, so that file wasn't with the ones they needed to search.

Although sitting there reading wasn't a strenuous activity, they were all exhausted and bug-eyed when Ian finally called it a day. "We'll pick up again first thing in the morning. I know it's here. We just haven't found it yet. Keon sent me a text earlier. He'll be here around ten a.m."

As the team cleaned up the pizza boxes and coffee cups, the two NCIS agents gathered their things with a promise to bring breakfast in for everyone around eight. Sometime within the past hour, the MPs had changed shifts, and two new men stood in the hallway. After everyone else exited the conference room, the door was locked again behind them.

It was still light outside as they poured out into the parking area, stretching and inhaling the fresh air. Devon was anxious to see Kristen and check on Jenn. He and Ian had gone to Devon's apartment earlier with one of the pizzas for the two women and to tell their niece what they found on the disc. Of course, they'd downplayed it as a comical last will and testament of things her dad wanted to leave to the men he'd worked with and loved like brothers. She'd accepted their explanation, but they could tell she was still bothered by her find.

After exchanging a few fist bumps with his team and verbal goodbyes with the agents, Devon turned toward the apartment building when a single shot from a high-powered rifle rang out, echoing through the air around them. Almost as one, with adrenaline surging through them, the team, agents, and men guarding the compound dropped to the ground and unholstered their weapons, searching for a target. Whoever was after the team was getting desperate if he was firing on the heavily-armed compound.

Time seemed to stand still as they all tried to assess the situation. No other shots were fired as everyone scrambled for cover. As the echoed report faded and silence ensued, Ian called out more calmly than any of them felt, "Anyone hit? Sit-rep!"

As everyone responded that they were all okay, nobody was hit, and the shot had come from the northwest, outside the fence line, Devon's cell phone rang. Thinking it was Kristen or Jenn, scared out of their minds, he answered the call without looking at the screen, but it wasn't one of the two frightened female voices he expected to hear.

An unruffled and familiar deep rumble came over the line. "Tango eliminated—half a klick from your eleven. I'll be in after I'm sure he was alone. Call Keon for clean-up."

The call was disconnected, and a stunned Devon stared at the phone in his hand for a moment or two. Translated, the brief, one-sided conversation meant their enemy was dead about a third of a mile almost straight ahead of Devon's position, and the deputy director was needed to cover up what'd happened. The only problem was Devon had no clue what *had* happened.

He yelled for everyone to hear, "Stand down but stay alert. Tango's been taken out by one of ours. He's clearing the area before he comes in."

Devon eyed the confused faces of the NCIS agents and his teammates, and in a much lower voice, he simply said one name, "Carter."

* * *

Three hours later, the FBI's Deputy Director strode into the conference room of Trident Security and sat down with a heavy sigh. After receiving Ian's call, Larry Keon got the next available flight from Jacksonville and had a local agent pick him up at the airport instead of waiting for a rental.

Personnel from the FBI's Tampa field office were swarming the woods behind the compound and processing the scene, which included a corpse missing a good portion of its skull and brain. The dead body was thanks to Carter and his trusty MK11 sniper rifle, which was now hidden in the trunk of Devon's classic Mustang. The man wasn't taking any chances the local feds would try to confiscate his baby, and his own vehicle was too far away at the moment. Two other crime scenes, one where a stolen motorcycle was parked and another at a local motel, were also being combed over. The dead man's motel room was located after a key was discovered on the body.

Because the compound was considered a crime scene for the time being, the club had to be closed for the night. Thankfully, it was a Sunday and early enough in the evening when they alerted their members via a mass text, another one of Brody's ideas that came in handy occasionally. There hadn't been any members in the parking lot when the shot was fired, and the handful of staff and members already in the club never heard it over the music. Ian had called Mitch after they got the all-clear from Carter and told him to shut it down and send everyone home. The compound was now in lockdown with only the necessary personnel.

Devon had moved Kristen and Jenn, along with their

furry bodyguard, from his apartment to the rec room above the conference room because he needed them as close to him as he could get them. He'd been terrified when he and Boomer, only seconds after Carter's call, sprinted across the compound, up the stairs, and into his living room, only to find the women weren't there.

His heart started beating again when he found them in his walk-in closet with Beau in battle mode, a bunch of kitchen knives, and one of his 9mm handguns which Jenn knew how to shoot if necessary. Devon wouldn't admit it, but he'd almost cried with relief when he saw both women were safe and unharmed. And now, because the two had no federal security clearance to be with the team while they met with the investigators, upstairs was the closest comfortable place for them to be.

The conference room was now close to being filled to capacity with the six men of Trident, Carter, Dobrowski, Chan, Keon, and three FBI agents from the local office. The lead investigating agent had been brought up to speed, although Keon intentionally omitted some information after the incident on the bridge two nights earlier. Special Agent in Charge Frank Stonewall wasn't happy with Carter, who refused to say a word to him, including his name and who he worked for until the deputy director joined them. It didn't help when Ian, his team, and the two NCIS agents weren't forthcoming with much information, but at least they'd given him a few limited answers.

Stonewall had been firing questions at Carter every few minutes for the past two hours to no avail. The red-faced fed even threatened him with arrest, which only brought a bark of wry laughter and a shake of the undercover agent's head. After Jake heated the last three pieces of leftover pizza for him, their friend ate silently, then reclined back in his chair and closed his eyes. No one in the room was fooled, though —the spy was one hundred percent alert. Now, he was still relaxing in his chair, with his eyes open again and his feet resting on the table, mirroring Brody's own laid-back position. It drove Ian crazy when anybody put their feet up, but the boss let the infractions go for now.

Once the door was shut again, SAC Frank Stonewall glared at the man, who was still wearing his camos, and all but snarled, "Okay, Keon is here. Now start talking."

Carter didn't move, and his blank face never changed as he glanced at the two men with Stonewall and then at Keon. The latter understood what the operative never said. "Frank, why don't you have your agents here go check on the status of the scenes."

Stonewall was ready to blow his cork but conceded he was outranked and dismissed his equally pissed-off subordinates with a brief nod of his head. He was your typical fed from a bad movie—short, balding, overweight with a rumpled, ill-fitting suit and an arrogance you wanted to beat out of him. After the others left, he crossed his arms, lifted an eyebrow at the black-ops agent, and waited.

Slowly pulling his feet down, Carter leaned forward with a stern, don't-fuck-with-me expression, which most men feared, and rested his elbows on the table. Devon almost chuckled when Stonewall flinched. He would've missed it if he hadn't been looking directly at the SAC, but it was there nonetheless. The team knew what Carter would say since he'd filled them in before anyone else got there, but first, he would lay down some ground rules with the overconfident Stonewall.

Staring at the man, he addressed him in what his friends knew was his best Dom and super-spy voice. "The name's Carter . . . one word . . . and it's all you need to know about me. Don't write it down, and forget it after you leave this room. Don't ask who I work for because you won't get any answers you like. For this instance, you can say I report to Keon. Call it a temporary assignment or whatever you want. I don't give a crap. Don't ever threaten me with arrest or anything else again. I don't answer to you and can have your cocky ass demoted and working in some bum-fuck weighstation you've never even heard of before midnight. I have more federal security clearance than you could ever dream of, so sit your pompous ass down and stop acting like I'm one of your minions, or worse, a criminal, because that shit only pisses me off. And since someone is gunning for my friends here and almost succeeded in taking at least one of them out tonight, you don't want to piss me off any more than I already am."

A few mouths around the table twitched, and some bottom lips were bitten, but no one dared crack a smile. After a glance at Keon, who gave him a single nod, and then a pause to let them all know he still wasn't happy, a noticeably paler SAC Stonewall did what he was told and took a seat. He then indicated for Carter to continue with a polite flash of his upturned palm, although it probably almost killed him to do so. The fed was finally getting a little smarter.

Leaning back in his chair again, yet keeping his feet on the ground this time, Carter relaxed and related his information and the events leading up to when he killed the hired assassin. "Keon, as you know, I've been pounding the pavement, trying to find out why these guys have a bull's eye on their backs. Aside from a few vague and unsubstantiated rumors, no one's come forward with a who or a why. After the quote-unquote drunk driving accident, which totaled Brody's truck and sent everyone swimming the other night, I decided to head back here to keep a closer eye on things.

"I got back in the area around eighteen hundred hours and did a little scouting outside the line of detection of Egghead's security system to see if I could figure out who was targeting them. I knew the team was sequestered inside the compound, so it was a good bet the tango would be trying to find another way to get to them. The geek's system is one of the best I've ever come across, so—"

"Wait a minute. *One* of the best, my friend? Oh, no . . . it is *the* best." Brody always became indignant whenever his almost-unbeatable system was questioned. Everyone in the room who knew it groaned except Carter, who rolled his eyes.

"Or so you keep telling everyone. Anyway, I took a defensive position beyond that point and was scouting the area through my scope. It was damn lucky I spotted the guy when I did because he was preparing to take his shot." He gave his shoulders a dispassionate shrug. "I took mine before he took his. My shot was justified. I had no chance to warn the team or anyone else, and there was no opportunity to take him alive. After I eliminated the threat, I went over to see if I could figure out who he was. Unfortunately, his face is pretty much gone, and his fingerprints were removed a long time ago with acid."

His gaze shifted back to Keon. "That's all I got. Write it up, and, as usual, Larry, leave my name out of it and then shred it."

Even though it wasn't all Carter had to say, and the redacted report wouldn't actually get shredded, Keon acknowledged him with a single nod. He would get the rest of the info from the man after the local SAC was out of earshot.

CHAPTER TWENTY-FOUR

After Carter finished talking, he sat back and crossed his arms. SAC Stonewall eyed his superior with a stunned expression and began to turn red again. "That's it? That's all I get? What the fuck am I supposed to do with that? I've got three crime scenes and a dead John Doe out there, for fuck's sake."

Keon sighed with what felt like the world's weight on his shoulders. He took his glasses off and rubbed his eyes. Damn, he was exhausted, and at fifty-five, he was getting way too old for this crap. "You'll do exactly as the man said and forget you ever laid eyes on him. From this moment on, this entire incident is classified. I'll have some people in your office first thing in the morning. They'll take possession of everything—photos, SIM cards, evidence, reports . . . everything. If I find out there are copies of anything, or something accidentally gets left behind or lost, shit will come down on the head, which is you, Frank. Understand? There's already someone responding to pick up the body. Now, why don't you check on your agents? I have a few more things to discuss with these people."

The irate federal agent stood and stormed out of the room, not bothering to shut the door behind him. After one of the MPs in the hall did the honors, Brody performed his best James Bond impersonation, even though their spy friend didn't have a British accent. "'The name's Carter . . . one word . . . and it's all you need to know about me. Don't write it down, and forget it after you leave this room' . . . damn, I wish I could remember the rest." Smiles and snorts of laughter filled the room, while the man being teased only gave them a slight smirk and remained quiet. "Shit. I love you, man. Every time I see you, I almost peed my pants."

Boomer snickered harder. "I think Stonewall was close to it for a moment there and not 'cause he thought Carter was funny. You, dude, are the one person I never want to be on the wrong side of."

"Amen," Devon added when everyone else nodded in agreement.

Wanting to get the conversation back on track, so he could leave for his hotel and get some much-needed sleep, Keon glanced at Ian. "No luck on the Colombia files yet?" The last he'd heard, they got the coded message from their former lieutenant and narrowed down their search to one mission.

Ian shook his head with mild exasperation. "No. We almost finished reviewing the paperwork between waiting for you to arrive and Stonewall's questions. We'll finish up tomorrow. Then there's a ton of photos we took that we need to go through. Whatever Jeff found, or thought he found, has got to be in there somewhere. I'm not wrong about this."

The deputy director nodded. If Ian said the information they needed was there, then it was. "As I said, I'll deal with

Stonewall and get him off your backs. Do you need anything else for now?"

Ian scanned the faces of his team, and they all shook their heads. "No, we're good. Just need some downtime and a few hours of sleep."

Keon turned his head back toward the black-ops agent and sighed. "Okay, tell me the rest."

While remaining in his comfortable position, the man filled in the information gaps for everyone. "I recognized our corpse out there before I blew his head off. Name's Rueben Vega, mercenary for hire out of Colombia . . . the question still being, who hired him? Unfortunately, my contacts haven't been able to come up with any possible answers for me yet, but they're working on it. Vega had deep connections to Ernesto Diaz and his brother Emmanuel. He used to be one of the best, but rumor has it he's been hitting the booze too much over the past year and getting sloppy.

"I was a little surprised to find him here. It's been a while since I've heard he was associated with a job in the States, but that's not to say he didn't visit for other reasons. He didn't work exclusively for Diaz, but most of his jobs were contracted through their empire. His cell phone was a throw-away and had the history bleached . . . new technology to wipe it clean, and there's no way to recover it.

"You all know Emmanuel has been rebuilding what the U.S. of A. destroyed when they took out Ernesto. He's not at the point of operating on the scale his brother had been, but he's getting there. I thought the hit on the SEALs might be some payback for Ernesto, but according to my sources down there, it didn't come from the Diaz family. However, I firmly believe whoever hired him used the connection to do so. Whoever it is, he also has a connection somewhere within Uncle Sam because how else would they've known which men were on that mission? I've got a lot of ears to the ground, and hopefully, one of my contacts will come up with something soon, but for now, that's all I've got. Wish it was more."

Carter looked at Ian and raised an eyebrow. "Mind if I grab a shower and bed upstairs for a few hours?"

Ian jerked his chin up once. "*Mi casa es tu casa*. You know you can crash here anytime. And thanks again for having our sixes. As usual, we owe you."

The black-ops spy stood and smiled genuinely for the first time since he walked into the compound over three-and-a-half hours earlier. "Anytime, and by the way, this time . . . I wasn't just here for the food."

Thank God for that.

* * *

A few minutes later, the team stood out in the compound, checking in with the guards, ensuring the perimeter was secure, and seeing Keon, Chan, and Dobrowski off. After the feds finished at the scene outside the fence line, Ian arranged to have four snipers take a position beyond Brody's system's limitations as a precaution. It was doubtful whoever hired Vega would hear about the man's demise anytime tonight, but the team wasn't taking any chances.

As she climbed into the passenger seat of the rental car her partner was driving, Barbara Chan looked at them. "Let's try this again, gentlemen, shall we? This time without the gunfire. We'll see you at oh-eight-hundred with breakfast."

Devon and the others nodded at the woman, then he turned around, headed back inside, and took the stairs to the second floor. He found Jenn and Kristen sleeping on the two couches in the rec room. Tucking a blanket around his niece, he was careful not to wake her. She'd be fine there until morning with the rest of the team in the rooms down the hall and Beau sleeping on the floor next to her.

He gently woke Kristen, who, although a little heavy-eyed, willingly stood and let him lead her back to his apartment. He knew he was selfish by waking her, but he needed her in his bed with him. They'd survived another close brush with death, but thanks to Carter, the only person needing a rush order on a new coffin was the enemy. The team hadn't told the two women how close they'd come to a different conclusion of events since they'd been freaked out enough by the rifle shot.

By the time they walked up the stairs to his place, Kristen was once again wide awake, and Devon could see his desire mirrored in her eyes. The moment he shut his apartment door, he had her flattened against it, his hands delving into her hair and his hips grinding hers. He kissed her with an intensity he couldn't rein in, and she returned it to him in spades. The only sounds were their heavy breathing, moans, wet mouths, and tongues dueling.

He ripped her clothes from her body as fast as he could without hurting her, then removed his own. Grabbing her below her ass, he lifted her, so she could wrap her legs around his hips, and ground his steel erection into her mound. The change of position brought her breasts up, so he easily dipped his head to lick and suck them until she begged him for more. Her fingers were clutching his hair, her body writhing in his arms.

"Please fuck me," she panted as her head fell back against the door with a thud, and her eyes fluttered closed. Her moans of pleasure and desire were almost his undoing.

She shifted her hips, trying desperately to position his cock at her entrance, when he tightened his grip and lifted his head. "Easy, Pet. Slow down. I don't have a condom with me."

"Don't care."

Devon froze at her words, and she opened her eyes again. "I was tested after I found out my ex was cheating on me, and you're the only man I've been with since then. I've been on the pill for several years to regulate my periods. Please. I want to feel you—all of you."

Staring at her beautiful face, he knew he couldn't say no to her, nor did he want to. The thought of taking her with nothing between them thrilled him. "I'm tested every six months for the club and had my latest physical right before we met. I've never had sex without a condom. Baby, are you sure about this? This is a big step for us, and I need you to be certain."

A frustrated moan escaped her. "Yes, I'm positive. Please fuck me now."

When she again tried to impale herself on him, he wouldn't allow it. "My way," he growled as he lifted her away from the door. Shifting his hands to her ass, he carried her down the hall and into his bedroom.

Setting her on his bed, he ordered her to lie down in the center of it and put her head on the pillows. While she hurried to do as she was told, he worked his way around the bed, pulling out the leather straps he'd attached to the four posters earlier in the week. He'd kept them tucked under the mattress, waiting until he found the right opportunity to surprise her, and it appeared that now was the perfect time. At the end of the straps were wrist and ankle restraints. She was still bruised from the accident, and he was glad he'd chosen ones with a thick faux-fur lining.

At her wide-eyed expression, Devon smirked. "I've wanted to do this to you since the afternoon I shackled your wrists at the club. Stretch your arms up and out toward the corners and spread your legs wide. Do you trust me, Pet?"

There was no hesitation in her verbal and physical responses to his commands and question. "Yes, Sir."

He could see her pulse had increased by the rapid throbbing of the artery in her neck. The sight caused his own heart rate to surge. He grabbed her right arm and brought the leather restraint to her wrist. Before he attached it, he asked, "What's your safeword?"

"Red, Sir."

His cock jumped at her husky answer. He swiftly worked to restrain her wrists, taking a moment after each strap was secured to check he could place two fingers between the fur lining and her skin. He needed them tight enough so she couldn't get out of them yet loose enough that they didn't hinder her circulation or further bruise her tender skin.

When he was confident she was comfortable, yet at his mercy, he turned to his nightstand and took several items out of the drawer. An evil grin crossed his face when he heard her breath hitch at the sight of his chosen torture devices—a small leather flogger, a clit clamp, and the largest anal plug from the set of four he'd been using on her. He'd been increasing the size of the plugs he had her wear for several hours during the past week. This would be the last one he would need to prepare her for when he fucked her tight ass for the first time.

He placed the flogger and the jeweled clamp on the edge of the bed next to her, where she could see them from her confined position. Although he'd told her he wouldn't clamp her nipples due to her fear, tormenting her clit was on her soft limit list and, therefore, fair game. The other day, he'd picked out the green and amber stone-decorated clamp at the club store with her hard little nub in mind. Taking the plug and a tube of lubricant, he walked around to stand at the far end of the bed and studied her.

Damn, she was stunning. Her mouth was red and swollen from their make-out session in the other room, and her hair was messed up from him running his fingers through it. Her cheeks were flushed, and her nipples had stiffened, shamelessly begging for more attention. And her pussy . . . fuck, her pussy was drenched with her need for him. He wrapped a tight fist around his cock, dragging his hand up and down the shaft several times as he watched her tongue shoot out and moisten her dry lips. As much as he loved to fuck her sweet, hot mouth, he had other ideas for her body at the moment.

Dropping the plug and lube within reach, he climbed up on the bed between her wide-spread legs, ran his fingers through her wet folds, and brought them to his mouth. He couldn't resist taking a quick taste of her. She moaned at his actions, and he watched as more of her juices flowed from her core. After licking his fingers clean, he grasped the back of her knees and bent them upwards toward her chest. He then moved forward on his knees, spreading them out before resting the back of her thighs on the front of his.

The position she was now in was perfect for what he intended to do. Reaching back, he grabbed the tube and applied a generous amount of lubricant on her exposed asshole. Being gentle, he breached her entrance and eased one, then two fingers into her, working to get her ready for the larger object. Kristen was panting hard but concentrated on keeping her ass muscles and sphincter as relaxed as possible. "Oh God, Sir. It feels so good. Please . . . more, please."

How he loved to hear her beg—it was music to his Dom ears. He alternated between plunging his fingers in and out of her hole and scissoring them open to stretch her further.

"Oh, you'll be definitely getting more, Pet. Trust me, you'll be getting a lot more."

While he kept up the rhythm he'd established, he grabbed the anal plug with his other hand and covered it in more lube. When he was sure she was ready, he pulled his fingers from her tight cavity and replaced them with the plug. Her sphincter tightened for a moment as he worked the larger item into her, and suddenly, he was able to get past her body's natural defenses, and the plug slid home. Her rim closed around the notched end, greedily holding it in place. More liquid flowed from her pussy lips, and she groaned.

"Don't forget, Pet. You're not to come without permission."

"Y-yes, Sir. Oh, God!"

Her thighs quivered, and her hips jerked upward when he flicked her still-hidden clit. But that was about to change. He lowered her legs as he climbed back off the bed. Grabbing one ankle and then the other, he restrained them until she was spread wide open, her pussy exposed for what he planned for her next. Stepping into his bathroom, he hastily washed his hands before returning to her side and grabbing his next torture implement.

The flogger was made of soft black leather, with a knot tied at the end of each of the dozen strands extending from its handle. Starting at her right foot, he dragged the ends up to her shoulders, then back down again on her opposite side, her eyes tracking them every inch of the way. He repeated the entire process, once then twice, teasing her until her breathing was short and heavy, and her hips shifted impatiently. "Don't lose the plug, Pet."

His mouth turned up at the corners when he saw her clench the muscles in her butt, which in turn sent tiny shock waves through the nerves being affected by the foreign object. The sensations caused her to groan, and she begged him for relief once again. "Beg all you want, sweetheart, but I'll continue at my own pace. You won't get what you want until I'm good and ready to give it to you."

Returning to her right foot, he lifted the strands off her skin and let them fall back down softly. After another full rotation around her body, he would start over and make the contact a little harder each time. When the thudding increased to the point her skin began to turn a pale red, he concentrated on her thighs, hips, and breasts only. He'd near her crotch, but not close enough for the contact she didn't even know she was pleading for.

Finally, he flicked his wrist hard, and the knotted strands connected with her clit and pussy lips. She shrieked as the pleasure-pain shot through her, and her empty vagina clenched for something to hold on to. Devon repeated the strike again and again until she was alternating her screams between his name, curses, and pleas for mercy. Her wrists were straining against their leather and fur manacles to no avail. When he finally tossed the flogger to the floor, she was so close to her orgasm that it would've crashed over her if he struck her clit one more time, and he gave her a few moments to come back from the brink of ecstasy.

Grabbing the clamp, he positioned himself between her legs once more. Her little pearl was no longer hiding, and he could attach the clamp without further coaxing. Kristen was so far into all the different sensations running rampant through her body that he didn't think her brain even registered the clamp. A thin piece of fishing line attached the small weighted stones to the rubber-coated ends. It was designed so they would hang down, pulling on the little nub. For now, though, they would be in the way, so he rested them along the crease of her hip.

Reaching down, he undid the restraints around her ankles and, once again, bent her knees toward her chest. Kneeling at her sopping wet entrance, he lined up his uncovered cock and plunged into her with one smooth thrust, burying himself to the hilt without pause, despite the huge plug in her ass. Her walls cinched around him, and he saw stars. "Oh fuck, sweetheart. You feel so good, like silk."

She jerked her hips to get him to move, but he stilled her with his hands. "No, Pet. Give me a second, or it'll all be over too soon. Fuck, I've never felt anything like this before. You're my heaven and hell, all wrapped into one incredibly tight, hot package."

"Oh, please, Sir. Oh God, Sir, please . . . I need . . . I need . . ." Devon loved how the word "Sir" was so natural to her now. It flowed from her mouth without thought whenever he aroused her to the point of mindless pleading.

When he thought he could move without exploding, he dragged his dick from her passage only to stroke right back inside again. He punctuated his words in time with his tortuously short, slow thrusts. "I know exactly what you need, my love, and I'll give it to you right now."

He sped up and found a rhythm that had her hurtling toward the most powerful release she'd ever experienced. When she reached the edge, he abruptly released the clamp from her clit, allowing the blood to rush back in, and she screamed her throat raw as she plummeted into a vast chasm. Wave after wave of pleasure-pain crashed over her as she pulsated around him. Only two thrusts later, he followed her, shooting his seed deep into her womb and extending her orgasm, convinced he would never recover from the impact.

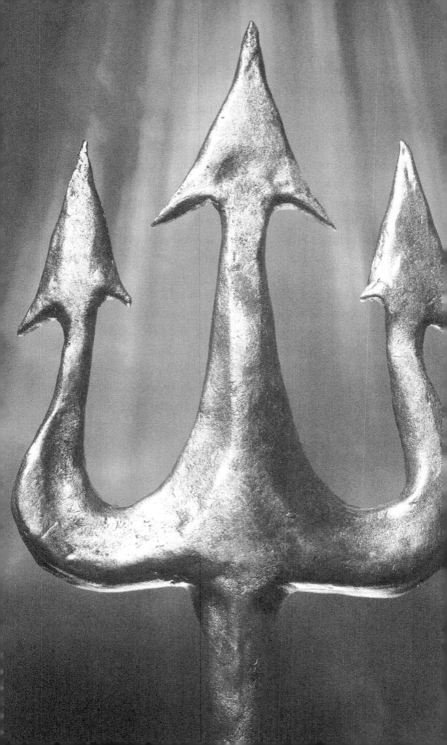

CHAPTER TWENTY-FIVE

After removing her wrist restraints, it'd taken Devon longer than ever to recuperate from their explosive lovemaking the night before. When he could get off the bed and stand without falling, he'd stumbled to the bathroom and retrieved a wet cloth to clean Kristen with. His sweet Ninja-girl had fallen asleep immediately after he removed her plug and settled her on her side, so he could spoon her from behind and hold her in his arms for the rest of the night.

Now, the sun was up, and it was seven forty-five. He had fifteen minutes before meeting everyone down at the conference room to find the name of the person who wanted some of them dead. He had showered, put on a comfortable pair of his tan military DSUs, otherwise known as tactical pants, a navy blue T-shirt, and his light-weight black combat boots, and was now sitting on the edge of the bed next to a still sleeping Kristen. She deserved the rest after he'd awakened her around three a.m. to take first her mouth and then her pussy once again. As much as he wanted to take her sweet ass, he'd refrained from doing so last night because they both would've been too exhausted for the bath she would need right afterward to prevent extreme soreness this morning.

With a light touch, he was playing with her hair and staring at her face when his eyes dropped to the simple black leather band still around her neck. It wasn't good enough for her, and in his mind, he began designing a permanent collar he wanted her to wear.

Permanent? Holy crap!

Yeah, it was pretty much official. Devon Sawyer's confirmed bachelor days were over . . . permanently. He'd found his true love, his perfect submissive, and yet his equal. She was the woman he'd never known existed and now wanted to spend the rest of his life with. First, he would collar her in a ceremony at the club, and then, when she was ready, he would also put a ring on her finger.

In all honesty, while the ring would make their union legal, the collar would mean the most to Devon. It would symbolize Kristen's ultimate trust in her Dom to cherish her in every possible way—mind, body, and soul. To keep her safe from harm, to pamper her silly, and most of all, to love her every day of their, hopefully, very long lives.

But for now, his team needed to find the person responsible for the murders of four members of Team Four's family, and as soon as possible, before anyone else was hurt or, God forbid, killed. After kissing her forehead, he left her sleeping and headed to the office.

As promised, the NCIS agents brought bagels and egg sandwiches for everyone. As they ate their handheld breakfasts and coffee, they dove back into the daunting task. Thankfully, Paula was heeding the orders and advice Ian had given her in private on Friday and was back to being an efficient office manager with minimum interruptions.

A few minutes after ten a.m., Devon was reviewing a

stack of over a hundred 8" x 10" photos he'd taken the night of the gala in Rio de Janeiro when he was keeping an eye on Ernesto Diaz. There'd been approximately 500 people in attendance at the biggest hotel in the city, so Devon had tried to get a photo of everyone Diaz had made contact with. At one point, the drug lord had disappeared into a small sitting room down the hall from the main ballroom. Devon had waited a few moments before following, pretending he was looking for his lost date for the evening.

He'd barely gotten three quick yet hazy photographs of Diaz in the room using a hidden camera in a pair of false eyeglasses—a little James Bond-like but quite effective. The pictures he took were from the hallway, looking past the partially open door into the room before Diaz's bodyguards interfered and ordered him to return to the ballroom or risk bodily harm. With no other choice, he'd been escorted back down the hallway and was pissed he couldn't get pictures of the person or persons Diaz was meeting without jeopardizing his cover. And it was unlikely their spy friend would know who Diaz met since the Colombian hadn't been Carter's target while he'd been there.

Devon finished inspecting the clearest picture out of the three and was about to move on to another photo when he realized there was a reflection in a medium-sized mirror on the wall behind Diaz. "Hey, Egghead, can you do something with this?"

He held up the photo, pointing to the mirror for Brody to see. The geek squinted at what his teammate was referring to, then jumped out of his chair and headed for the door. "Yeah, I should be able to enlarge it and clean it up some. Let me grab my scanner from the war-room."

The war-room was the extra-large office Brody used, which housed his many computers, multiple HD screens, servers, and assorted gadgets. The team was convinced if he needed to, Egghead could launch a space shuttle from the room. It was also one of the places in the office which Paula didn't have access to, and the man took great pleasure in knowing it drove the office manager crazy with curiosity.

A few minutes later, Brody had the picture scanned into his laptop, and the photo appeared on the big screen on the conference room wall. He was playing around with an image-enhancing program, and the person in the mirror became larger and clearer, yet he still seemed a little fuzzy to everyone . . . well, everyone except for Brody. "Son of a fucking bitch! You've got to be kidding me!"

Everyone stared at the stunned and irate man as if he had two heads. Ian asked, "You know who it is?"

The geek stared back at everyone. "You don't?"

When they all shook their heads, Brody opened his mouth to say something but quickly shut it again and took the photo off the big screen before looking at Ian with obvious worry in his eyes. Having trained and worked with him for a long time, his boss understood the man's hesitation.

Ian turned to the two NCIS agents. "I know you have a certain level of security clearance, but I get the feeling we've stumbled across something which could possibly jeopardize your careers or lives and those of your families if it becomes known you have this information. You have two options—take the risk or step outside for a moment. I swear to you, no evidence will be removed or erased from this room."

The two agents eyeballed each other, and it was apparent, after a moment, they'd made their decision. As they stood, Barbara Chan said to her partner, "I think I left my cell phone in the car—do you mind helping me look for it?"

Dobrowski nodded and moved toward the conference room door. "Sure, it'll probably take five minutes to find it."

When the door shut behind them, Brody returned the image to the large monitor and began typing away at his computer again. The screen split in two, and a photo, courtesy of CNN, appeared to the right of the enhanced photo Devon had taken. The rest of the team stared at the two images in utter disbelief. The man was a little younger and leaner in the five-year-old photo and had a trim mustache and goatee, but without a doubt, he was the same man in the news photo—Senator Luis Beltram from Brody's hometown of Dallas, Texas. And if the rumors were true, the next Democratic candidate for President of the United States.

Holy fucking shit!

Hailed as the first-ever Hispanic-American candidate for the Oval Office, Beltram had been elected to the Senate seat for his state a little over two years ago and fast-tracked through the Democratic Party. The lawyer turned politician had been born and raised in Texas, lost his working-class single mother to cancer as a teenager, and somehow managed to finish high school and put himself first through college and then business law school.

He'd carefully chosen his battles and political platforms and was well-liked by his constituents, fellow democrats, and even a few republicans. The press expected an announcement of his candidacy within the next week or so, but the evidence currently in the Trident Security conference room would end the man's political career faster than a jackrabbit on amphetamines.

The knowledge of the senator having a private meeting with a Colombian drug lord, who ran not only one of the largest drug cartels in South America but was also involved in human trafficking and arms dealing, would not go over well with the American public. The fact Diaz also supplied weapons to terrorists, who were determined to undermine the American way of life, would be the final nail in Beltram's coffin. The team was sitting on political dynamite.

Using the room's speaker phone, Ian contacted Keon to give the man one of the biggest shocks of his life. "We've got him, and it's not good."

There was a short pause on the other end of the line. "I'll be there in fifteen minutes."

* * *

When Keon walked into the room eighteen minutes later, the two agents had returned, and the large monitor was once again blank. No one said the senator's name in front of the agents because for the rest of the investigation, the less they knew, the better off they were. Brody hacked into numerous systems and managed to locate the tenuous connection between Beltram and Diaz, who'd also been born in Texas before his family moved back to Colombia when he was six. Beltram's illegitimate father had been a cousin of Ernesto Diaz's mother, making the two men second cousins. Luciano Esperanza had been a longtime associate of the Diaz cartel and was a name the team had recognized. He'd died of cancer about seven months after his cousin.

When the future lawyer was in college, Beltram had the paternal information on his birth certificate, which was on file with the Texas State Department of Health, changed from his sperm donor's name to "no information available." Unfortunately for the senator, he didn't know or forgot the original copy stayed on file with the new certificate, which is how Brody located the information.

Keon sat down and sighed. "Tell me."

Ian nodded at Dobrowski and Chan, who once again left the room. This time, with the Deputy Director of the FBI present to keep an eye on the boxes of classified information, there was no need for subterfuge. Ian then glanced at Brody, who hit a button on his laptop, bringing up the two photos again.

Usually a passive man, the team had never seen Keon pale in plain disbelief before, but it's exactly what they saw. However, it only took him a few seconds to recover from his shock. "Holy shit," he mumbled before clearing his throat. "Is Carter still here?"

Ian shook his head. "No, he was gone when everyone got up this morning. One of the guards said he pulled out around oh-five hundred."

* * *

Three nights later, the man known by one name picked the lock to the back door of the comfortable bi-level home on the outskirts of Dallas. He was inside within twenty seconds and, with his gloved hands, pulled out his weapon. The two men from the target's private protective detail had been eliminated by a drug-induced slumber and were hidden behind some shrubbery on the four-acre property. The burglar alarm and backup systems had been interrupted with a quick flick of a Swiss army knife, rendering it useless. The target's wife and college-age children were not at home, and it was amazing how easy it was to get close to someone who thought he was invincible.

Having thought he was safely ensconced inside his house with the alarm set, Senator Luis Beltram was relaxing in his home office, sipping a glass of amber liquid from an eight-hundred-dollar bottle of Macallan scotch. His gray suit jacket and tie were laid over the back of one of the two guest chairs opposite the desk where he sat. His white shirt sleeves were rolled up to his elbows. This was the last night he'd be alone before the Secret Service took over his protective detail when his presidential nomination was announced tomorrow afternoon. The press would then start camping out at the end of his driveway.

He smiled to himself, enjoying the silence which permeated the five-bedroom ranch. At least he did until the door to his office swung open without a sound, and he found himself staring down the barrel of a SIG Sauer P226, complete with a silencer. Beltram froze at the sight before putting his drink down and easing his hand toward his desk drawer.

"Come on, now. I know you don't have any morals, but you're not exactly stupid. After all, you've come this close to being the next American president." Carter took three careful steps into the room, knowing full well the senator had a handgun in the drawer he was reaching for. The spy wasn't worried because the arrogant bastard would be dead before his fingers ever touched the brass pull handle.

Without any abrupt movements, Beltram lifted his empty hand and placed it next to his other one on the wood surface of his desk in full view of his unwelcome visitor. Sweat was forming on his brow and upper lip, and his skin was paler than it had been a few minutes ago, yet those were the only signs of the man's fear. His eyes barely blinked. "Who are you, and what do you want?"

Carter's mouth ticked up into a smirk. "Who I am is not important. What I want, however, is something altogether different. I want to save this great nation I live in from having a traitorous scumbag like you as its president. I want to avenge the deaths of three Navy SEALs and one very nice lady who didn't deserve to die when and how they did. But first, I'm curious. Why were they killed in the first place? Payback for killing Ernesto Diaz? How did you find out Team Four was responsible for your cousin's death?"

If the man was shocked to hear Carter knew of his

familial connection to the Colombian drug lord, he didn't show it. In fact, the smug fucker snorted, picked up his glass of scotch again, and eased back into his black leather chair. In the process, he pressed his knee to the inside panel of his desk and hit the silent panic button there. The movement didn't go unnoticed by the man with the gun. He now had less than ten minutes to finish the job and escape without being discovered at the scene of an assassination. The senator was crazy if he thought he had a way out of this.

"Please. Whoever fired the shot into Ernesto's heart did me a favor. I was going to have to have him eliminated at some point anyway. If someone found out about my relationship to him, my career would have been over."

His weapon still aimed at Beltram's head, Carter took several more steps forward, stopping between the two guest chairs on his side of the large desk. "Then why? What did Jeff Mullins have on you?"

Before answering, the senator took a sip of his expensive scotch, savoring the taste on his tongue and the burn down his throat. The man was cockier than a rooster in a hen house. "I was at a political function for one of my constituents in Virginia and was introduced to Mullins by Admiral Richardson. I didn't know who Mullins was, but I got the feeling he knew me and wasn't happy about it. I had a friend do a little discreet checking and found out Mullins was a retired SEAL, specifically one who had been on a fact-finding mission in Colombia and Rio de Janeiro looking into Ernesto. I remembered meeting my cousin in Rio at some big shindig down there at the time and put two and two together. Mullins must've recognized me from there, and if he made the connection, there was a good chance the rest of his team would too. It was a risk I couldn't take."

He shrugged as if ordering the deaths of seven highly-decorated SEALs was no big deal.

"Did you always know Diaz was related to you, or is it something that came as a surprise?"

"After my mother passed away, God rest her poor soul. I found a copy of my birth certificate and decided to find my bastard father. The search led me to family I didn't know I had. Ernesto and I became . . . associates, I guess you can call it. He funded my education and lifestyle, and I, in return, became a valuable asset in Dallas for him."

He paused. The backup guards for his missing protective detail should be here at any moment, so he just had to keep talking. It didn't matter what he said since the intruder wouldn't be alive in a half hour. "Now, I've answered your questions, so how much will it cost me to get you to walk out of here and leave me alive?"

Carter fired one barely audible bullet into Senator Luis Beltram's head and another into his chest then turned around and strode out the door before the dead man's forehead hit the desk.

"Not a damn penny."

EPILOGUE

Ten Weeks Later...

Devon peered at Kristen sitting next to him in their first-class seats on their flight to Nepal. He normally didn't flaunt his money with expensive purchases, but he flew first class whenever possible, especially if they were spending sixteen hours in the air. She was staring out the window, and he could tell she was nervous by how she fingered the diamond and platinum collar around her neck. It was stunning on her, yet simple enough to wear it daily. When she got dressed up, a large blue sapphire pendant could be added with a small hidden latch and hook. The sapphire was her birthstone, and he loved how the color complimented her ivory skin. She said she loved it because it matched his eyes.

He'd removed her black leather collar and replaced it with the one he and a jeweler with BDSM experience had designed for her during a surprise collaring ceremony at the club seven weeks ago. What she didn't know was he had also purchased a matching engagement ring for her at the same time. The ring sat safely in its little blue box in his carry-on luggage. He planned on them being an engaged couple before they returned to the States in two weeks, in time for Christmas.

They were on their way to meet with his parents at a medical clinic about an hour from the airport, where they'd be landing soon. It was the first time she would meet his folks, and although he tried to assure her Chuck and Marie Sawyer were down to earth and would love her at once, she was still anxious to get the introductions over with.

He'd met her parents and step-parents at Thanksgiving. Her stepmother had invited her mother and Ed to join them for the holiday after Kristen told them she was bringing someone special home. Devon had liked her parents almost immediately, and he'd won them over by the end of their first day together. Before they left for Tampa again two days later, he'd taken Kristen's dad aside to ask permission to one day put a ring on his daughter's hand, and Bill Anders had granted it along with a handshake and back slap. Her father had told Devon Kristen's limp-dicked ex had never asked for his blessing, and if he had, Bill would've told him no. He thought the guy wasn't good enough for his daughter, but at the time, she'd seemed happy, and he hadn't wanted to disappoint her by voicing his disapproval.

A lot had happened over the past ten weeks. After they'd returned from Pennsylvania, Kristen had moved in with him permanently. It wasn't as if she didn't spend every night and almost every day there anyway, but she wanted her parents to meet Devon before making the final step. She'd been packing her things since he'd first asked her to move in with him several weeks earlier, so the actual process of moving her things had been easy a few days after Thanksgiving. With the help of the team and a few of the club's employees, they'd made fast work of the job, and within one afternoon, they were officially living together. He loved how Kristen's personal items were now mixed in with his, and whatever furniture didn't make the move into Devon's place had been donated to a local women's shelter.

Nina DeAngelis succumbed to her cancer five weeks ago. Marco and his sister's friend, Harper, were both devastated by their mutual loss. The team had been pleased to see a large turnout of Trident associates and club members at the funeral. It'd been a beautiful yet tearful moment when about twenty-five of Nina's former students stood at the front of the church and sang "Amazing Grace" in honor of their beloved teacher.

Brody had bought a three-bedroom house, which was closer to the compound than his one-bedroom apartment had been, and would be closing on it after the first of the year. He'd told Devon that although he didn't need all the extra space, the property was a good investment and a write-off on his taxes, which he needed. He'd also replaced his totaled truck with a brand-new model, thanks to his insurance money.

Jake had confided in Devon when he'd broken up with the guy he'd been seeing shortly after the whole drama of being the target of a hired assassin. His now ex-boyfriend was a cop in nearby Clearwater and had been pretty pissed because Jake never told him about the attempts on his life. He'd found out about them a few days later, after coming across a newspaper picture. It'd been taken after the accident on the bridge and showed a soaking-wet Jake and Devon standing watch over Jenn and Kristen while they were being tended to by the EMTs. Jake said he didn't tell the guy because he didn't want to worry him, but Devon thought there was more to it.

Jenn was almost done with her first semester but was

having a hard time with the coming holidays. This would be her first Christmas without her parents, and they were all doing what they could to make it a little less depressing for her. At least they'd been able to tell her that, although the person responsible for killing her parents would never serve a day in jail, justice had been served. As for Carter, no one at Trident had seen him since the night he'd saved their lives with one bullet.

Kristen was also an official full-time member of the club now, along with her friends Kayla and Roxy London. The wife and wife couple had brought Will Anders as their guest for Devon and Kristen's ceremony, and Will was considering the lifestyle after meeting Shelby and Matthew, the submissive who worked the front desk at the club. Will had clicked with the other two and became fast friends with them. The subs had been answering a lot of Will's questions about the lifestyle, and although Will hadn't submitted a membership request yet, Devon expected one soon. There was a Dom who Will was interested in, and his curiosity about BDSM appeared to grow as each week passed.

Devon glanced back down at the folded copy of the Tampa Tribune sitting on the tray in front of him. The article it was turned to was a follow-up story on the assassination of Senator Luis Beltram two and a half months ago, on the eve of his anticipated Democratic presidential nomination. Yesterday in a press release, the Deputy Director of the FBI, Larry Keon, reported how the man who'd murdered Beltram in his home was, in turn, killed by US Navy SEALs in an attempt to capture him in the jungles of Colombia where he'd fled. It was still unclear why Rueben Vega killed the senator, and the investigation was at a standstill. The Trident Security team knew a motive would never be found, and it wouldn't be long before Beltram was old and forgotten news.

Devon didn't realize Kristen had said something until she took his hand in one of hers and used her other one to touch his chin and turn his head toward her. "I'm sorry, honey. What did you say?"

She smiled because she'd caught him daydreaming. "The pilot said we're getting ready to land. You need to put your seat and tray up."

He was surprised he hadn't heard the pilot's announcement.

"What were you thinking about just now?" she asked as they prepared for the descent.

With a seductive grin, he leaned forward and put his mouth against her ear. "I was thinking that I can't wait for you to read me the last chapter you wrote a few hours ago. While you were typing away, your breathing and heart rate sped up a few times, and I know I'm going to like it."

He turned her hand in his so he could put his fingers on the pulse at her wrist and was pleased to feel it accelerate again as her face turned pink. He loved how he could still make her blush so easily and knew if he put his hand between her legs, he could get her off before they landed. However, the stern-faced stewardess sitting in her jump seat less than ten feet in front of them would have a fit.

Over the course of writing her book, he had Kristen read many of the steamy passages to him, and the sex they had afterward was always off the charts. Several nights ago, he had her play with herself while she read aloud, and he'd forced himself to sit across the living room from her while her fingers delved in and out of her drenched pussy. He'd ended up flipping her over the end of the couch and fucking her into oblivion before she even finished the chapter.

"I know you will since yesterday morning was my inspiration," she whispered.

His face lit up, and his dick hardened as he remembered interrupting their morning coffee to bend her over the kitchen island and spread her ass cheeks. Before he'd rammed his cock in her tight hole, he'd first knelt behind her and tongued her rimmed opening, driving her higher and higher until she begged him to fuck her hard and fast, which he was more than happy to do after he made her come twice.

Thankfully, he'd made sure there was a tube of lubricant in every room of their apartment and in both of their vehicles because it turned out his little pet loved to have her ass fucked whenever he wanted. But although he loved taking her ass and mouth, he would never get enough of her hot, wet pussy. And it's where he planned to shove his cock the first chance he had after they got off the stifling plane. He shifted his hips to give his hard-on a little breathing room.

"Are you sure they're going to like me?"

It took him a second to follow her change of subject. "Sweetheart, they're going to love you. Even Ian and Jenn told you they would before we left. I can guarantee my mom will be spoiling you rotten before the day ends. She's been bugging Ian and me to settle down for the past ten years. I'm just glad I'm no longer on her nag list."

She giggled at him. "At least until she wants grandchildren."

Devon's thumb, which had been rubbing her wrist, abruptly stopped, and his brain seized. "Um, wow. We . . . uh . . . we never discussed kids, did we?"

Her pretty eyes filled with worry. "You don't want children?"

He thought about it for a moment. How could he have ever thought of being a father when he hadn't been able to imagine being a husband before meeting Kristen? There was no doubt he could be a good one, having been raised by one of the best.

An image of a little girl or boy with soft brown hair and striking hazel eyes came to mind, and he knew what to say. "As long as they take after the most beautiful woman in the world, I want as many as we can possibly have." He brought her hand to his mouth and kissed her knuckles. "I love you, Ninja-girl."

"I love you, too, Master Devil Dog."

Ready for the next installment of the Trident Security series? Check out *His Angel* now!

Come hang out in my Facebook Reader Group - the Sexy Six-Pack's Sirens!

Also by

***Denotes titles/series that are available on select digital sites only. Paperbacks and audiobooks are available on most book sites.

THE TRIDENT SECURITY SERIES

Leather & Lace

His Angel

Waiting For Him

Not Negotiable: A Novella

Topping The Alpha

Watching From the Shadows

Whiskey Tribute: A Novella

Tickle His Fancy

No Way in Hell: A Steel Corp/Trident Security Crossover (co-authored with J.B. Havens)

Absolving His Sins

Option Number Three: A Novella

Salvaging His Soul

Trident Security Field Manual

Torn In Half: A Novella

***HEELS, RHYMES, & NURSERY CRIMES SERIES
(WITH 13 OTHER AUTHORS)

Jack Be Nimble: A Trident Security-Related Short Story

***THE DEIMOS SERIES

Handling Haven: Special Forces: Operation Alpha
Cheating the Devil: Special Forces: Operation Alpha

THE TRIDENT SECURITY OMEGA TEAM SERIES

Mountain of Evil
A Dead Man's Pulse
Forty Days & One Knight

THE DOMS OF THE COVENANT SERIES

Double Down & Dirty
Entertaining Distraction
Knot a Chance

THE BLACKHAWK SECURITY SERIES

Tuff Enough
Blood Bound

MASTER KEY SERIES

Master Key Resort
Master Cordell

HAZARD FALLS SERIES

Don't Fight It
Don't Shoot the Messenger

THE MALONE BROTHERS SERIES
Take the Money and Run
The Devil's Spare Change

LARGO RIDGE SERIES
Cold Feet

ANTELOPE ROCK SERIES
(CO-AUTHORED WITH J.B. HAVENS)
Wannabe in Wyoming
Wistful in Wyoming

AWARD-WINNING STANDALONE BOOKS
The Road to Solace
Scattered Moments in Time: A Collection of Short Stories & More

***THE BID ON LOVE SERIES
(WITH 7 OTHER AUTHORS!)
Going , Going, Gone: Book 2

***THE COLLECTIVE: SEASON TWO
(WITH 7 OTHER AUTHORS!)
Angst: Book 7

SPECIAL COLLECTIONS
Trident Security Series: Volume I
Trident Security Series: Volume II
Trident Security Series: Volume III
Trident Security Series: Volume IV
Trident Security Series: Volume V

Trident Security Series: Volume VI

About Samantha Cole

USA Today Bestselling Author and Award-Winning Author Samantha Cole is a retired policewoman and former paramedic. Using her life experiences and training, she strives to find the perfect mix of suspense and romance for her readers to enjoy.

Awards:

Wannabe in Wyoming (co-authored by J.B. Havens) won the bronze medal in the 2021 Readers' Favorite Awards in the General Romance category.

Scattered Moments in Time, won the gold medal in the 2020 Readers' Favorite Awards in the Fiction Anthology category.

The Road to Solace (formerly *The Friar*), won the silver medal in the 2017 Readers' Favorite Awards in the Contemporary Romance category.

Samantha has over thirty-five books published throughout several different series as well as a few standalone novels. A full list can be found on her website.

>Sexy Six-Pack's Sirens Group on Facebook
>Website: www.samanthacoleauthor.com
>Newsletter: www.geni.us/SCNews

- facebook.com/SamanthaColeAuthor
- instagram.com/samanthacoleauthor
- bookbub.com/profile/samantha-a-cole
- goodreads.com/SamanthaCole
- tiktok.com/@samanthacoleauthor

Made in the USA
Coppell, TX
05 October 2023